All This Time

J.Clark

Contents

Dedication   V

Introduction   VI

Prologue   VII

1. The Painter and the Writer   1

2. Mind Games   13

3. The Preacher's Daughter   23

4. The Criminal's Son   47

5. Halloween   58

6. Another Spring Semester   83

7. Dueling Swords   100

8. The Head and the Heart   108

9. Homecoming   118

10. Her Knight   131

11. Breaking Up   143

12. The Cost of Love   158

13. Coffee and Kicking Back   170

14. Movie Madness   181

15. Brotherly Reunion   197

16. A Time at the Gala   208

17. Playful Passion   228

18. Dinner with the Parents   243

19. Detangling Issues   256

20. Loose Ends   268

21. Square Up   277

22. Semester's End   288

Acknowledgements   316

Meet the Author   318

Summer Semester   320

Dedication

This book is for the lovers.
The ones that are young and fruitful.
The ones that are mature and steady.
The ones that are looking towards eternity together.
The ones that left their other half far too early before the
end of their story.
Dedicated to the lovers,
especially my late husband
who was once my own.

Introduction

All This Time is a romance mostly written in English (US) although there are sections of French, Spanish, and Japanese that are written throughout the text.

Translations of uncommon words and phrases will be written next to their original counterparts, in italicized parentheses *(show up as this in the text.)*

Example: "Je suis une femme." *(I am a woman.)*

Prologue

TWO HOUSES, ALIKE IN DIGNITY...

I ronic that Shakespeare could encompass the life of a Southern teenage girl as fear anchored deep in her heart as the sun reflected off the barrel of her father's gun.

"Dad, don't!" The other end was pointed at her short haired friend trembling in front of her. Michelle was sure that Osirion's life was flashing in front of his terrified brown eyes.

"Boy..." Her father's thick Southern drawl surfaced. His hand was steady as his finger ghosted over the trigger.

Michelle saw someone charge out the corner of her eye as the blur tackled her sturdy Dad to the ground. The gun flew out of his hand with a bang causing Michelle to scream.

Osirion flinched, not moving a muscle. Time stopped for everyone. Her father stopped wrestling with the shorter Asian man that had charged him like a bull. Michelle slowly moved towards her friend as her eyes darted along his lanky body.

"You're okay?" Michelle whispered.

"I'm okay." He stumbled slowly until he collapsed into her arms. "I wasn't hit..."

"Well..." She motioned to his cheek. "You don't have a hole in your face."

A crack and a scream caught the two teenagers' attention as the men continued their battle on the ground.

The Painter and the Writer

ADALA UNIVERSITY

Osirion closed the door to his room and fell on his bed. Figure drawing class was finally over leaving him with the rest of the day free. He ruffled his growing locks and gazed at the calendar. Today's date was circled in bright red ink and a smile crossed his face.

The package should have been delivered by now. Kanojo ni denwa shi nakya. (I should give her a call.)

It was a very special day after all. He fished his computer from his bag and waited for the hardware to boot up. The silence of the room made him realize that he was the only one home for the moment. He ran a hand down his face, jolting as his hand caught the slight texture on his right.

My life has become steady but rather dull without Michelle being around.

The two longtime friends had to split after high school to go their separate ways, but he missed her day by day. At least with technology they could still keep in touch from miles away.

"Happy Birthday Michelle!" He laughed as her face popped up on his screen. Camera chats were always the best.

"O-si-ri-on, you remembered!" She dragged out the syllables in his name, her hair cut into a small Afro with the brightest smile on her face. She held up a medium sized box so it came on screen. "I did just today. I'm glad you called so I can open my present."

"Go ahead!" He relaxed on the bed as she opened the package. The first thing she pulled out was a small bag of oil paints and new brushes. A large smile graced her features, warming up his heart.

"Oil paints!" She jumped with glee. Even as a grown woman she held some childish qualities but that was a part of her charm. "I wanted some so I could experiment. Let's see what else you sent me . . ."

"Keep going." He sighed in relief as she ranted on how much she loved her new paints.

"You are just the worst." She couldn't keep the humor out of her voice as she pulled out a silky purple bra and panty set. "Who buys their friend lingerie for her birthday?"

"Someone has to do it." He laughed as she shook her head. "Your dates have no taste and you'll wear boxers until the end of time. At least now you have something frilly."

"You don't hold any punches, do you?" She smirked. "I can only hope that you are as in tune with your ladies as you are with me."

He tried not to flinch on camera and if she caught it she didn't react. "*I*'m a very attentive man to those I care about."

"This is very true." She gave him a wide smile. "You even got the correct size and everything. I will make sure to tell you how it fits when I try it on."

Watashi no tame ni sore wa chaku te. (You should wear it for me instead.) He couldn't stop the thought that popped in his head.

He waited patiently as she dug through the box again. The last present was the one he was most unsure of unveiling. He hoped that it landed right with her sense of humor.

"This is very interesting." She pulled out a pocket planner. "Are you helping me get more organized?"

"It would help but you need to look through it first."

He knew she saw his nervous face as she flipped through the pages. Her eyebrows raised on the camera as she looked through the pictures.

"This is a custom planner I see." She chuckled while flipping through the pages "I like how it starts off sweet and gets . . . more interesting."

He smiled as she got to the last page, as she laughed a light and nervous tinkle in the air.

"What is this supposed to be?" She turned the page to the camera for him to see the detail.

"I am going to college for art." He gave her his sweetest grin. "Do you like it? It's the final in a series I titled 'Putting

You in Your Place.' You can always see the others if you would like."

"This is what happens when the fainting little boy gets out of high school?" She stared at it, face turning red in real time as she licked her lips.

Osirion dedicated hours into the small details of the picture before deciding to give it as a gift. The way her eyes conveyed surprise at the slight stretching of her illustration's throat and the way her kinks looked being gripped in between his fingers was something he' seen in his mind for years. He was dedicated to the craft if anything.

"Well I would draw things like that in high school at times. I just never let you see them because . . . well how would you have reacted to a picture of you choking on my dick?"

He could see that her cheeks finally turned a darker shade on her chocolate skin as she smirked. "Oh really? You sure you're packing enough to choke me? Tic-tac size doesn't count, you know."

"You've seen pictures before but if you would like a live view I'm more than happy to demonstrate how it will be done." A spike of triumph surged through his body when he saw her eyes dilate.

"You're an ass sometimes." She started laughing. He knew her sense of humor well enough to not get cussed out. "I do lots of photo editing so pictures can easily lie with a little skill. Are the other pictures so detailed?"

"Down to the cute blush and your little overexcited stutter of course!"

"Oh my. Don't turn your dark fantasies into a comic series?" She fanned herself over the screen. "You might have a future career as a hentai artist if you keep this up."

"Well, I didn't think about making them into a convent manga, but since you brought the idea to me I could." A slow smile spread as he started to work all the ways this new project could bring a surprise to her day. "Just with a little formatting and a cover I could ship it over to you in a matter of weeks."

"The devil stays busy trying to stroke my libido." She laughed. "You are exceptionally naughty today."

"Who says I was just trying?" He arched an eyebrow, not able to stop himself. "Trying implies that I have failed at the task. You have a cute little flush on your face if I am correct. Did I do all that work for no effect?"

Her eyes turned to the picture and she coughed into her hand. "I wouldn't say that you failed."

"Then what would you say dear?" His voice dropped a note.

"That it's going to be hard to explain where I ordered this planner to other people." Both let out giggles at her statement. "This might be your new business though, making erotic planners and calendars on the side."

"If they are paying customers, I would be glad to do so. You are the only person that gets the free personal experience from the artist himself."

"I'm the only one huh? Does that include your current girlfriend as well?" He picked up on the notes of jealousy in her voice and smiled. It made his heart flutter.

I'm not the only one that gets jealous, I see Miss Winder-son.

He tilted his head to the side before answering. "Well, anyone I am dating does get more than pictures so it evens out."

"Well, that is the benefit of dating an artist I guess." She gave him a soft smile. "I have to prepare for my meeting soon. Thanks for all the presents, you never disappoint!"

"Tell them I said hello." He chuckled.

She rolled her eyes. "They still don't really like you silly. Talk to you later!"

"Talk to you soon." He sighed and disconnected the call.

I wish you were here so I could give you a proper birthday present.

He indulged for a moment, letting a devious smile grace his lips.

*An earnest smile disarms
  better than a fist.
  A quiet one's words
  will knock you on your face.
  A poet's pen
  will lay your life to waste.
  A writer's soul
  will scatter you across time and space.*

One woman
can march a thousand men to their fate.
Keep mind these strategies
when warring love in a game of hate.

Queens Technical University

A set of sepia-brown hands stopped on the keyboard as she looked at the time. Michelle groaned as she turned off her laptop and got out of her seat. She opened her planner and penned her word count in the pages.

This is a useful gift ironically. Even if the pages are…interesting.

Her eyes trailed over the lines of the drawings on the opposite page as her face started to warm up again.

I'll have to leave this one deep in my bag where someone can't find it.

Michelle closed her writing planner and placed it in her bag.

That's such an explicit gift to give a friend. I can just imagine the two of us together in those positions…stop! Osirion's already taken—most of the time. Be a good girl and not a horny little slut right now.

Michelle let out an annoyed grunt as she walked out the door.

Michelle sighed as she put out the snacks for the meeting. The Black Student Alliance at Tech was small, with only ten members, but the group got involved with community projects and general hang out nights. Her button up stuck to her dark, melanated skin as she stirred the tea.

Summer's not even here yet Georgia is always so warm and humid this time of year.

The large house was pretty quiet despite just having ten minutes before starting.

Perhaps I should invite Osi and his girlfriend to the campus party? It would be nice to see him in person instead over the screen. It would be a three-hour ride for him though.

She sighed at the way her spirits lifted at just the thought of seeing him again. She was a fool in love with her best friend. Her best friend with girlfriend, no matter how much they switched from on to off again.

At least I'll have Tyrone there as well if Osirion does decide to show up. Maybe they will become friends and we can double date!

Tyrone shared the same Monday-Wednesday-Friday evening class as her and after three months of persistent asking Michelle finally agreed to a date last week. She had to admit he was an attractive man at six-foot-one. Built like a linebacker with long dreads, he had this deep voice that reminded her of melted chocolate.

She walked into the kitchen to start a pot of coffee for addicts like herself. She took out the three different varieties of creamer along with a small bowl of sugar and half and half. Michelle was humming as her mind worked, tuning out the world around her.

"Hey Michelle!" Lisa came in with pixie cut hair. The color was an electric red paired with caramel colored skin and a youthful face. "Need any help?"

Michelle jumped as her heart rate spiked. "You startled me, Lisa! Is it time for the meeting to start already?"

"They are coming in." Lisa smiled as she helped put out the last of the salty pretzels. "How has your day been?"

"It was pretty good. This heat is killing my love of button ups though." Michelle pointed to her sticking shirt. Lisa wore a long orange maxi dress to beat the oppressive heat.

"You know what to wear around here." Lisa wagged her finger at Michelle. "Button ups and baggy clothes don't fly in this humidity! You have options!"

Michelle groaned. "I have to change out. Let me run to the car and get my bag real quick."

"You won't miss anything in the first ten minutes." Lisa waved her off. "I'll hold it down for you."

Michelle stepped outside of the air-conditioned building and faced the full brunt of the heat head on. It was over ninety degrees and the high humidity made her feel like she was cooking in a soup.

You're a woman, aren't you? If you started dressing like one maybe you wouldn't be single.

She couldn't ignore her father's voice in her head as she popped her trunk. She grabbed the black workout bag before heading towards the restroom.

You would look so pretty if you dressed more like Linda. A nice dress. Some heels. A touch of makeup but you don't need it. You're such a pretty young woman . . . if you let it shine through.

Michelle stripped down her sweaty clothes in the stall with a grimace. She didn't smell **too** bad but she cleaned up with a few wet wipes before applying another layer of deodorant.

Dad, you want me to dress like your twenty-year-old girlfriend to attract other fifty-year-old men?

Michelle chuckled as she relived the conversation. She had shut her father up for at least a week with that one.

After changing, she wore a pair of jean shorts and a tank top with sneakers. Definitely looking more feminine now, Michelle walked back inside to see everyone waiting for her.

The planning was tedious but rewarding and it took over an hour to organize a date and to-do list. A buzz went off in her pocket, causing her to check her phone.

> *Negus: a title of a sovereign of Ethiopia, a king*
>
> *—-Ty*

Tyrone was keen on texting her various bits of African knowledge. It was a small gesture but Michelle did smile.

She had let slip that she liked intelligent men and men with a creative streak.

He might have some hotep qualities but he's not full blown in it yet. Hopefully he doesn't get there.

"Michelle, are you going to invite your Asian friend to our event?" Lisa crossed her arms. "I want to be prepared for another discussion on the greatest artists of the 20th century."

"I was thinking about it, but not quite sure yet." She bristled as the red head chuckled. "I have to invite both him and his girlfriend. I don't want to be troublesome in another's relationship."

"Oh! He has a girlfriend again?" Lisa smirked. "Is it the same one or someone different? Must be rough to be the 'best friend' all the time."

Why she gotta bring up stuff like that?

"It's not like that." Michelle narrowed her eyes. "He's just my attractive best friend."

"He sent you a lace underwear set for your birthday." Lisa deadpanned. "I've also seen your little planner as well. Any of those drawings based on reality?"

Michelle coughed in embarrassment. "That's just his overactive imagination. We've always been platonic."

There was this one time on the phone...don't think about it. I'm not in my private room. Stop thinking about it. It was just a moment of pent up tension...

"Hello? Are you there?" Lisa snapped her fingers. "**Anyway**, did you finally go on a date with Tyrone?"

"Yeah, and I had fun bowling with him." Michelle smiled. "I gave him my number. He doesn't seem like a bad guy."

Lisa nodded her head in approval. "So are you going to give Tyrone a chance and leave Osirion alone?"

"My love life is shaping up just fine." Michelle huffed with a small smile. "Does Lisa approve of Tyrone?"

"He's very attractive." Lisa listed with her fingers. "Masculine. Single. Tall with big feet. His grandmother goes to your father's church. The universe just gave you the man lotto and you're asking me?"

"You do make a good point." Michelle rubbed her scalp, fingers entangling with her short curls. "Many women accept much less in love."

"Well you don't want to miss your good thing because you were pining over a man who's already taken." Lisa shrugged and popped some ginger candy in her mouth. "I'm sure that Osirion would want you to be happy, so he'll understand."

He is my best friend! Of course he'll be reasonable about me dating someone. I really do think too much sometimes.

Michelle took a ginger candy as her reply.

He was hot and sweltering yet this moment was worth every rolling drop. Skin as smooth as cooling chocolate and as rich as wine was held constrained by contrasting pale rope. She was burning from both the heat and the drumming passion through her veins. He walked over to the table and filled a ceramic cup with sake for his pleasure. Her brown eyes bored into him, following the liquid as it traveled down his throat. He savored this sweet victory.

"You've finally decided to stop resisting." His voice was so thick he barely recognized it.

The rope pulled as she tried to adjust her position to keep her face from going into the sheets. Her hands were trussed behind her in a very intricate pattern. "I'm even more impressed that you would be into trying some *kinbaku* style bindings."

The spaces in between the rope created a beautiful and restricting trapezoid pattern that both accentuated her skin and trapped her arms. The final result heavily out-weighed the time it took to safely proceed. He grabbed a bottle of water and a straw as she struggled to speak. Beads of sweat were rolling off her form and being absorbed by the natural fibers. He gently held the bottle as she took several sips of the refreshment.

"It's so hot in here." She huffed as she flexed her arms. "May I please sit up on my knees?"

"Please what?"

"Please *Shujin*." Both his ego and his erection swelled at the sound of her voice. She was needy as he granted her request. Sitting her up the intricate pattern traveled around her neck, split around her chest and united at her stomach before branching off and disappearing between her legs. He checked the strands to make sure he didn't overdo it on the pressure.

"Is that a bit better?" He parted her knees as they found the best way to balance her on the bed.

"How much practice have you had?" Michelle pulled against the binds to make sure she's comfortable. "It's firm but not too tight. My limbs aren't tingling."

"I've had a good deal of practice on myself...and a few others." He lifted the ceramic cup to her lips and she took a small sip. He noticed her eyes narrowed at his comment.

"What will you do now, Shujin?" She raised her head to look into his eyes. He could see the wave of curiosity, the sparks of nervousness, and the burning flecks of re-belliousness in her eyes as she stared at him down. All of her emotions were on full display. It made his pants tighten with anticipation.

"Now I finally have you after all these years." He cupped her cheek. "As I told you before, I am going to **dominate** you for our enjoyment at last."

He took her braids in his hand and appreciated the intricate pattern as the ends dangle against her chest. He knew better than to tug her hair while in box braids; instead, he tied the strands in a high ponytail.

"This would be a good position to do so." She let out a light laugh. "I am at your mercy, **Master.** " The emphasis on the last word made him preen like a peacock.

"I'm glad you realize it." His hand went to his pants, and he slowly removed the fabric from his body. Why make her wait for her eventual surrender? Her eyes conveyed her shyness and he reassured her with a kiss on her lips.

"You're finally all exposed." She stared him up and down now that he was finally nude in front of her. Her eyes shimmered as she took him in below his navel, traveling down the dark little hairs and settled down on the prize of debate for a good number of years. "I guess those pictures were telling the truth."

His response was to lift her from the bed by her unbound legs and wrap them around his waist. Her mouth parted in shock as he let her feel everything against her bare flesh. "Didn't think I could pick you up hmm?"

"I forget how strong you are sometimes."

"Despite what you think dear I am *very* capable of handling you." He smirked at her arched eyebrow. Even trussed up and restrained she gave him a disbelieving look. Her skepticism didn't last long as he impaled her slowly with a groan.

"Such a greedy little woman..." He pushed the last of eight inches inside of her as her walls tightened in response. "Can you talk now?"

Her expression was something he would remember forever. Her mouth was slack as a small sound escaped her parted lips. Her eyes were so big and wide as she stared past him, lost in another plane. Her muscles fluttered around his shaft as her eyes turned to him. "I'm...full..."

He chuckled. "Kanpeki." *(Perfection.)*

Her astounded gasps rung next to his ear as her head lulled on his shoulder. To have this much pull over her body made his blood boil as he started his slow piercing pace. She shook in his arms as he kissed her mouth sweetly with a beautiful tenderness. She was completely bound and dependent on him to balance and hold her body while thrusting, all standing on his two feet.

I couldn't do this if I skipped my workouts.

She was a petite woman but the strength needed was taxing. She was moaning and biting his shoulder as he increased his pace with a dark chuckle near her ear.

"Has your opinion of me changed yet?" The question was like holding a loaded gun as he laughed. He flopped her on the bed, her arms pinned down from her body. "After all you always love to talk about *my* submissiveness but you are not putting up much of a fight."

His fingers gripped her sweaty skin as he snapped his hips into hers, spreading her legs wide. Her body tensed under each stroke, her legs moved with a deep twitch she couldn't control.

"Oh y-y-yes sir." Her voice was stuttering between the squish of her wetness and her own lewd noises. "I **like** this."

He opened her legs wider with a feral smile, bottoming out inside of her as he leaned forward. Long, wet hair tickled her face while he gave her a passionate kiss. "You're beautiful."

"Oh Osirion." Her eyes were filled with love. "Fuck me before my arms go numb."

He kissed up her legs while leaning forward on the bed. He thrust as deep as he could and she bit her lip from it all. His hair enveloped her in a dark curtain. "**My** bratty little one feels so good gripping around me."

Her breath hitched at his words and her walls squeezed him tighter. "Y-y-y-you're so vulgar."

"Me, vulgar?" He stopped kissing her with a look of fake surprise. "I want to flood your pussy while I cum—-now that is being vulgar dear."

His thrusts came harder against her skin filling the room with the loud smacking of their joined bodies. He had good control but each thrust was bringing him closer and closer. "Give into me, Zaria."

He whispered her first name in her ear and she clenched around him in response. They both felt the end nearing. She shook her head in denial not trusting her voice and his mercy for her disappeared. His grip on her tightened as his fingers dug into her hips. His thrusts turned relentless and he bit down on her shoulder as he let go.

"I give! Please!" He made her yell as his ears caught her staggering breath and the muscles in her leg tensed against his hand. He leaned down to bite her shoulder with his guttural moan.

The bow broke as he gave one last snap of the hips and poured into her body. Muscles twitched and spasmed around him as she hit her climax with a long, drawn out moan.

He slowly unfurled her from her compact position, stretching her legs so they dangled over the bed. His hair was hiding a flushed face and dilated eyes as he gazed upon her still quaking body. "I finally got you."

Her smile was sweet and her teeth dazzled his senses. "I would hope so. This is a good way to start off our honeymoon but my arms are starting to ache."

"Let me get the box cutter and some water." He kissed her lips before leaving to retrieve the items so she can be freed. "This is a good start to the week."

His eyes snapped open as he looked around the dark room. He could hear the blood rushing through his body and see the tented sheet in front of his eyes. His eyes looked over to see the back of a blond head; the heavy argument slowly came back to mind.

"You may command my body in the bedroom but it's too bad you're so timid outside of it." Beth laughed before he struck her rear, turning her left cheek a shade of violet.

"What does that mean?" He closed his eyes, breathing through his nose. In and out.

"You know what I mean." Her blond hair swished as she turned to look at him. "The fact you think I'm stupid is an insult."

"Go on and tell me." His voice was hard. "Since you know so much."

"I'm not the woman you want." She laughed at his shocked expression. "You're not the man I want either, but for now we have each other."

Disappointment filled his heart as he slowly rose from the bed.

All of that was just a dream. A wonderful, horrible dream.

He groaned, throwing the sheets off to get up. His room was quiet save for Beth's breathing and the pounding of his heart. A buzz from his phone caught his attention.

Dare ga denwa shi teru no ka shinji ra re nai. (I can't believe who was calling.)

Osirion grabbed his phone and closed the door behind him. On the screen was Michelle's name with a jazzy tune as her ringtone. He plopped on the living room couch, using a blanket to cover his erection. "Hello?"

"Hi there." Her voice was low and soft, like she was waking up from slumber. "It's not too late, is it?"

He swallowed. "N-no."

"You okay Osi?" He heard the stretch in her voice. Instantly the image of her splayed out on her bed came into his mind, toned legs spread as she wiggled her toes. "I wanted to see if you watched Iron Man? It came out two months ago but I can send you a DVD and we can have a watch party over the phone."

"Of course." He laid back on the couch, hand going down his stomach and into his boxers. He pulled down his clothes, exposing his swollen head dribbling warm, clear fluid. "I haven't seen it yet."

I love her voice. I can hear her now, screaming my name...

His strokes were easy between his sweaty palm and slick dick, using his foreskin to envelop him in warmth.

"Are you alright over there?" Michelle had stopped talking about her day with a chuckle. "Did I wake you up?"

"No." He closed his mouth but a lone moan slipped from his lips.

"Then what are you doing?" She teased him over the speaker. "Being a naughty boy Osi?"

His hand pumped faster and a moan slipped from his parted lips. "What...do you think...I'm doing?"

"Oh..." She gasped, surprise coloring her voice. "Were you thinking about little ole me? Why would you do that?"

"Ah...shut up." He snapped at her as sweat beaded on his forehead. "You talk too much." His grunts and moans filled the quiet air as he screwed his eyes shut.

"Stop." Her voice was breathy yet steady. His hand followed her command without thinking.

"What?" His grip shook but he didn't resume.

"Naughty boy." She chuckled. "I didn't say you could masturbate when I'm on the phone, did I?"

"You called me!" He almost yelled at her but kept his voice low.

"I know." She moaned right in his ear. "I was being a good friend. *You* were being naughty."

He heard a steady buzz over her end along with a chorus of pants and groans. "...you're getting off, aren't you?"

"Of course I am. I'm a good girl." She let out a breathy moan. "This feels so good...too bad you're not here."

His shaft swelled in his hand as he pumped his hand harder. A flash of anger heated his body at her audacity. "You're such a brat."

"Me?"

"Me?" He mocked her voice with a high tone. "Yes, you! What I wouldn't give to punish you right now."

"Don't make me sit on you." She gasped loudly. "Actually, that's more of a reward than a punishment for your mouth."

The coil of pleasure tightened as he heard her on the other end. His voice was ragged with pleasure as he screwed his eyes shut. "Sono manco kara noma se te." *(Let me drink from that pussy.)*

She moaned over the line as he released into the soft, warm blanket. He knew she had no idea what he said but to have her reach climax after saying something so filthy...

Naze kanojo wa watashi wa kurushimeru no? (Why does she torture me?)

The two were silent afterwards. Osirion didn't know how to break the tension now that his head was cleared from his lustful haze.

"I'm calling you in the daytime from now on." Michelle laughed. "...I forgot what else I wanted to tell you now."

"Seriously?" He swallowed hard. He was tired and sweaty and longed for sleep.

"Yes." She caught her breath. "I'll go and let you clean up, since I know you made a mess."

He looked down to his sticky shirt and soaked blanket. "I'll talk to you another time."

"Good night." She chuckled before hanging up the phone.

Michelle belonged to the Winderson family, and that came with some responsibilities. One of her responsibilities had her stuck in church on a Tuesday night as Mother Ruth held her captive by teaching New Adult Bible study.

I need to talk to Dad about my plans for the next year. Mom said that their divorce would affect how my schooling went...

"Michelle." Mother Ruth stopped her lesson. "Are you listening?"

"Of course." She was the only person in class today. There wasn't anyone else for Michelle to look at. "I was just thinking, Mother Ruth."

"About my handsome grandson?" The elder winked at Michelle. "Tyrone was so happy after he came home from your recent date."

"Oh, I'm glad." Michelle smiled at her. "I was thinking about the divorce though."

"Baby, I'm still reeling." Mother Ruth sat down to alleviate her aching joints. "I can't believe the Pastor and First Lady split last year. I can't imagine how you children must feel."

Stressed. Michelle was worried about where her Mom would stay. Her material family was back in Louisiana and her Mom had cut ties with them to marry her Dad.

Sad. They weren't always a great couple. Logically she knew they must have loved each other with a passion although she couldn't remember seeing them display affection towards one another. They shared three children together so she assumed they must have a passionate side somewhere.

Curious. Michelle wondered what was going to happen now. Would her Mom still come to this church? Will she go back home? How will the holidays go?

"It's a lot to take in." Michelle shrugged. "Might be for the best in the end."

"Bless your heart." Ruth spoke with a thick Southern accent. "You're a sweet girl. That's why I knew you would be perfect for Tyrone. He needs someone from a good family instead of the floozies out here."

Oh boy. Michelle groaned low in her throat. *This is going to be a long Bible study.*

Tyrone had big, warm hands that held her face gently as he kissed her. It was a cradle rather than a tilted hold on her head. His lips were full and warm. She never initiated kissing with him but he didn't seem to mind. She guessed he liked positioning her the exact way he would want.

Kinda like a living doll.

The comparison made her outwardly cringe but his lips were still moving on top of hers. The tendrils of shame curled around her slowly as she mentally fought against the feeling.

Whore. Does this feel good to you? Kissing someone who's not your husband.

Despite the church's belief, Michelle wasn't a blushing virgin. Prom night would correct that assumption but that was a secret she wouldn't tell a soul. She needed to keep a few things to herself.

Stupid strict upbringing.

Seated under the gazebo as the wind blew away the last of Spring classes at Tech she knew the insistent pressure under her rear was his erection. That was expected as their kisses turned hot and their hands were wandering all over the place.

What she didn't expect was what bulged down his pants leg as she sat. Her pooled excitement turned into worry.

"Could you stand up?" Michelle eased off his lap. "I just wanted to see something."

"I know, baby." Tyrone stood with a cocky smile. "Hard to believe you got so lucky."

He dropped his pants and she gaped. She cleaned her glasses off to make sure her struggling eyes were seeing things correctly. Tyrone was big. Big, thick, and an **immediate** health risk. Her excitement turned into genuine concern. "How is this going to work?'

"You never had sex before?" He was confused. "Nobody told you about how to make babies?"

"Not that part." She rolled her eyes. "You have a weapon between your legs. I know you aren't experienced at warming a woman up."

"Why should I do that?" He shrugged. "When you're this blessed you don't have to do all those extra steps."

The statement froze the blood in her body. She stared at him in disbelief. "Extra steps? You will perforate someone's uterus without those steps!"

"I just moved it once!" He groaned. "She was alright once she got discharged. I even sent her one of those fruit flower arrangements."

Michelle couldn't leave his presence fast enough. *This is a conversation for another day. I will not be the second to fall for this foolishness.*

The Summer brought hot weather to couple with the humidity that Georgia was known for as the temperatures soared. One of the best times to barbecue and throw down some games. Faithview Baptist Church was hosting a neighborhood cookout on a sizzling hot Saturday.

"Make way for the King!" Michah was balancing a plate of meats as he walked over to the grill. The smell of charcoal and wood filled the church compound as everyone was enjoying themselves. Children ran in the playground. The men stood near the fire or were seated in chairs, talking loudly. The women were split between the kitchen inside prepping the quantities of food to be cooked, watching the children on the playground, or mingling in small pockets around the church.

"Michelle." Tyrone flagged her down from her seat on a tree branch. "Can you get me a drink?"

"The kitchen is less than a three minute walk." She stopped writing in her small notebook.

"I don't want to get up." He motioned to the men around him. "We're having a good conversation!"

"I was writing something." She balked at him. "If you can't wait ten minutes you can walk and get it yourself."

A chorus of "get that drink for your man," "don't be so mean," and "it'll only take you five minutes" answered back at her. Tyrone didn't have to say a word as she closed her notebook in irritation. They wouldn't stop until Michelle got him a drink; she'd seen this happen to other young women enough times to know.

"I'll come with you, Sis." An older man rose from his seat. "My sugar's dropping and the first plate of food hasn't been cooked yet. Forgot we were on BP time today."

"Hi Deacon Thomas." Michelle jumped down from her seat and waited for him.

His gait was slower than most but his eyes were kind as he walked with his cane. "How you doin girl? Everything alright?"

"It's okay." She struggled to match his pace but succeeded.

"Don't mind us old heads." He waved to his group. "We just like it when a pretty lady does something nice for us."

"Tyrone is from my generation." Michelle sighed. "You had your shots this morning?"

"Yeah. Brenda takes good care of me." Thomas lit up at the mention of his wife. "Ty isn't old but he was raised around old souls. He don't mean no real harm by it."

"I'm sure he doesn't." Michelle held the door open so they could walk inside. The kitchen was busy with a few women moving back and forth while the rest sat down at the tables to get out of the way.

"Thomas!" A curvy woman called his name, hair as silver as her jewelry. "Your sugar getting low again?"

"You know these folks take forever to grill!" He laughed. Michelle smiled at the older couple as Brenda handed him a banana and some flavored water. "I'll die before I get a plate."

"Don't say that!" Brenda laughed, swatting his shoulder. "Hey Michelle. You need something too?"

"I would but I was sent to get water." She sighed.

"You go ahead and get something to eat." Brenda placed a few waters in a bag. "I'll get them squared away outside. Tyrone and them, right?"

Michelle grabbed an apple and joined Brenda's husband at a table. The older woman swept through like a force of nature carrying the scent of cocoa butter and sweet cream outside with her.

"Brenda has always liked you." Thomas ate half his banana in one bite. "This tastes so good. Hits the spot, you know."

"I like her too. Both of you." Michelle bit into her apple. It was crunchy and sweet like a perfect apple should be.

"You always been family." He patted her hand. "Tyrone treating you right? I know y'all just getting to know each other but I have to ask. I heard some things."

"What things?" Worry flowed through her body.

"Nothing too bad. He's not crazy or likes to hit women." Thomas finished off his food. "I heard he's just...dense. Like if you want romance you'll have to spell it out for him."

"Oh." She relaxed. "I've told him the dates that I like. Nice restaurants, amusement parks, food festivals..."

"That's wonderful." Thomas leaned in. "When he tries to put it down, for the love of God make sure he takes his time! Go slow! Not full force sweetie."

"You know about...that?" Michelle leaned in. "What happened to her? Like Tyrone said he sent a fruit arrangement but never told me what went down."

"It was my granddaughter." Thomas's somber tone made her gasp. "Sure he sent an arrangement but now she has a 30% chance of having children. She had to get surgery to undo what he did. What good did cut up fruit do for her?"

"A 30% chance?" Michelle felt the blood leave her face. She was too dark to be 'pale' but her warm undertone was washed out.

"Something like that." He frowned. "Cut the chance by more than half. Just be careful if you're going to be with Tyrone. I'm not saying he did it maliciously to her but..."

"Intentionally or not she has to live with the consequences." Michelle gave his hand a squeeze. "Thanks for telling me. I'll be more careful now."

"She's forgiven Tyrone. He's not a bad guy. It's just..." Thomas pulled out a bag. "She gave him a chance after months and **that** happened. I don't want that to happen to you either."

Michelle reassured Thomas as he took his blood sugar. She appreciated the older man and his words, even if they only increased her sense of unease.

I guess that means sex is off the table for Tyrone.

Michelle knew that she had a problem. At first, it started out small like most problems have a habit of doing. Before dating Tyrone she had a fantasy...well more like a hormone-laced dream. It was a simple one: face down getting pounded from behind, sweat dripping off the small of her back. It was a nice, heavy dream enough to rouse her from her slumber with a wonderful damp spot through her panties and a sheen of sweat on her body. The only problem was *who* was ramming her through the bed, and God help her it was Osirion.

Over four years of high school friendship plus their adult years and **this** is how her body betrayed her? He had grown into a handsome young man, but their paths had separated and she was at peace going to Queens Tech. She should have felt shame envisioning her best friend in such a lewd light but the forbidden nature of it all just made her want even more.

Why couldn't she dream about Tyrone: he was six-foot-one, built like a linebacker, long dreads, and this deep voice that reminded her of melted chocolate?

So why am I fantasizing about my best friend instead of the fine piece of man that I'm too afraid to call to help me with my desires?

Michelle knew she would be up for the reminder of the night, which was only two hours before her alarm would go off. She booted up her computer, opened a document, and gave it a header.

One.

She closed her eyes before typing, working to catch every detail she could from the dream realm. Putting it down would make her feel better, and the sooner she got her hormones out of her system the quicker her heart and mind could forget about her personal temptation.

Osirion would never need to know. Especially since he was over three hours away at the Adala University.

Out of sight, out of mind.

Despite the danger, Michelle felt that Tyrone deserved a chance to win her heart. With proper precautions she could have a meaningful relationship with the endowed man. He wasn't a bad person, she could say with certainty. He was kind and a bit set in his old fashioned ways. She saw his grandmother's influence, especially when he talked about women and finding a wife. Mother Ruth worked in the home with her seven children and the older woman was a sticker for traditional roles.

Michelle enjoyed her dates with Tyrone but after a few months she felt the ache of unfulfilled desire. She had her tools to get the job done when the urge became too much but she wanted **more**.

Desire had always been her vice. Desire for an education. Desire for a career. Desire to live however she pleased. Michelle wanted things like any young adult trying to find their way.

Sometimes Dad would say that I wanted too much, too fast. That's why I had to go to Purity Camp.

Memories of a summer spent in church discussing why her teenage horniness was something sent straight from Hell flooded her with anxiety. The aftermath had left a deep scar in her inner self. She couldn't bring herself to initiate kisses, touches, or anything sexual with Tyrone that would bring them closer.

He was starting to try harder and harder to turn her on. He would rub himself against her back, hoping to plant almost a ruler's length of flesh inside of her body. Combined with Brother Thomas's warning and Mother Ruth grilling her throughout the summer weeks, Michelle realized that having sex with Tyrone would be an endeavor she would have to prepare to take on.

Everything has to be complicated.

Once again she was up in the middle of the night, mind whirling like her old laptop as it booted up. She stared at the screen, eyes almost burning from its dull glow. She had a problem that was growing stronger and stronger.

If anyone can help me it's Yvette. She would know what to do in a time like this.

She turned over in her bed to look at the time. It was almost four in the morning. Michelle knew Yvette was a morning type of person but even this felt too early.

If you ever need anything don't hesitate to call day or night. If it's morning I'll definitely be up.

Michelle grabbed her phone and dialed the number before she could talk herself out of it. Her older sister always said she could talk whenever, right?

"Good morning little sis!" Yvette's voice reminded Michelle of toasted vanilla cupcakes: sweet, fragrant, and good for your soul. "You calling this early in the summer? What's going on?"

"I..." Michelle paused, struggling to speak. "I don't know what's wrong with me."

"Oh, sweetie." Yvette dragged out a chair to sit in. "Just start from the beginning."

Michelle just stared at her computer screen, black text taunting her in the night. Her idea wasn't working and she needed outside help. "I keep having erotic dreams."

Yvette wanted to laugh but held it in. "Is that a problem? Tyrone is a handsome man so I can see why you would."

"I'm not dreaming about Tyrone." Michelle admitted. "I haven't done more than be kissed by that man. I keep dreaming about Osi."

"Oh!" Yvette made a noise. "That is a problem! You and Tyrone have been dating since mid-Spring right? You don't find him attractive?"

"He's very attractive. It's a problem since...well..." Michelle didn't know how to spell out the man's reputation.

"Tyrone has a sword in his pants." Yvette chuckled. "I was worried since he put that poor girl in the hospital..."

"Does everyone know about that?"

"Not everyone but enough." Yvette sighed. "How are you handling not being intimate?"

"You know how I'm handling it as always. Tyrone is getting snippy every time we cuddle and kiss since he knows it's not going any further." Michelle sighed.

"Damn camp." Yvette clicked her tongue. "He probably isn't used to waiting so long for a woman. I knew this would be a problem sooner or later."

"Yeah." Michelle trailed off. "Tyrone will be a problem by himself but why am I dreaming of Osirion like this?"

Yvette let out a deep sigh. "Desire is a fickle thing. Maybe you could solve both problems by biting the bullet at last?"

"Excuse me?" Michelle squeaked.

"Safely, of course. I think your mind is making up dreams because you are longing to experience intimacy. Osirion was the one that got away, in a sense. I feel if you and Tyrone elevated your relationship, then you would stop thinking about your male friend and start thinking about your boyfriend."

That actually makes some sense.

"You might be right." Michelle clicked her tongue. "It's worth a try at least."

"There you go! Please make that man arouse you first before he dips inside you. Your only other sexual experience I know of is that Phantom at prom night. You were white girl wasted when I picked you up." Yvette laughed.

"I wasn't that drunk! The punch was spiked!" Michelle groaned. "I...don't judge me Sis. It was a masquerade-themed night."

"I'm just glad nobody came out and told on you. Some teenage boy got to deflower the Tomboy Princess and probably didn't even remember it. You are very lucky!"

"Tell me about it." Michelle felt her face flush as she thought of the patchy memory. "My glowing fairy costume was awesome though."

"Just think about my suggestion." Yvette laughed. "I have to cook breakfast for Brian and Raphael. You good?"

"Yeah. I'll give it a shot." Michelle smiled. "Talk to you later Yvette."

To Michelle's credit she tried going down on Tyrone later that week. She figured it was a good first step towards a healthy sexual relationship with him. He was excited as she whispered in his ear in the backseat of his car, hands pulling at the waist of his pants.

Here goes nothing, right?

It was an absolute disaster. He was already big and clumsy, wielding his penis more like a spear than a tool of enjoyment. She almost got halfway down, slowly and steadily, before he shoved her down the remainder. When she tried to get off, he held her by the hair and made use of the cavern she called her throat. She tapped his thighs but he only pulled her up to gain friction around his shaft.

I should bite him.

Michelle restrained herself at the last moment and sent a strong punch into his stomach. He instantly stopped and she pulled herself off to cough outside the car.

"You asshole!" Her throat ached from the rough treatment. "You choked me!"

He did seem remorseful as she cursed him out but she could tell he enjoyed the experience from the salty taste lingering in her mouth.

"If you just take it a couple of times full force you can loosen up!" He shuffled through his dashboard, holding up a small spray bottle. "Maybe some numbing spray for your throat?"

The words made her stomach roll. If he was that rough with her throat, she didn't want to imagine any other part of her body being vulnerable to him.

"Numbing spray?" She felt her sanity slip away like shifting sand in a desert. Her urge for violence was astronomically strong yet she tempered her wraith.

I can't tell if it's intentional cruelty or if he just can't wrap his head around the situation.

"I'm sorry." Tyrone held his hands up. "I got **too** excited, you felt so good. It's a compliment if you think about it."

Michelle grabbed her purse from the passenger seat and walked back to her car.

It's better to go home than to stab my keys through his throat. See how he would like numbing spray for that.

Time marched on as the sweltering humidity of Summer gave away to the windy crispness of Fall. Fall semester meant classes were back in session and Michelle had four to keep her busy. She had signed up for the last one of her Japanese language classes, along with the other three of her common core requirements.

This will be my last semester at Tech. I know Dad's upset about paying for my transfer to Adela University this coming Spring but I'm glad Mom is making him do it as part of their divorce settlement.

Tyrone groveled at her feet for forgiveness following the choking incident. She dragged out her anger, not in a hurry to forgive the aggravating man. The congregation called her petty after three weeks, not knowing why she was upset in the first place.

Well that idea was a bust. It's been a few months but I can't stop thinking about that phone call I caught him on the line.

Michelle didn't mean to catch her longtime friend masturbating on the end of the line. She knew he had evening classes from email and she called at a time when he would be free. She didn't expect to hear the bite in his voice as he was trying not to pant on the other side.

He doesn't know yet either. Oh, when he finds out I know a bit of Japanese he's going to pass out.

She knew exactly what he said that made her soak her soft satin sheets. His voice was thick like honey as his tongue twisted the words from his parted lips. Michelle had wondered about dirty talk in another language and he didn't disappoint.

He sounded so good over the phone. Damn it, why couldn't Tyrone make me forget about him? This is ridiculous...he's my best friend right?

Michelle threw herself into church life to distract from her persistent desire. She helped out with the music ministry as much as she could between her studies to tire her mind out. For the most part it worked until her mind would wander in the dead of night.

This was one such night. The slight breeze from her cracked window was cool but it couldn't calm down the volts traveling down her body. She screwed her eyes shut as one hand was stuffed in between her wet thighs.

Sono manco kara noma se te. (Let me drink from that pussy.)

Michelle didn't know she needed to hear that come out his mouth until after he said it. Her eyes fluttered as pure pleasure warmed her nude body underneath the sheets.

Slut. Whore. Night-walker. A shame to your family and community.

The voices of scathing church women echoed in her head, breaking though the pleasurable waves she was experiencing. Lessons on proper womanhood conflicted with her desires causing her to stop and open her eyes. The house was quiet save the occasional movement down-stairs from the family huskies, David and Baba.

Think of a story. A man cradling a woman's face. Kissing her. Whispering in her ear. Giving her praise and adoration. A tall man with smooth skin and muscles gleaming in the moonlight—

Michelle tried to bring back her thoughts to Tyrone over and over. His smooth skin, muscled body, and the rest of his persona should have been enough to set her blood on fire. It chilled her body instead.

At least I know what to think about to stop myself from lusting. Damn.

Michelle could confidently state that this was a first. She was sitting in the pew, of all places, listening to her Dad go on about the Biblical tenets of love. Tyrone had his arms crossed, taking the words to heart. She knew he wasn't too happy being rejected for some intimate fun, but he didn't have much of a case to stand on.

It was bad enough to think about Osi on a normal day but daydreaming about him at church was something else. She didn't have an erotic vision while trying to concentrate on the sermon, thankfully, but rather she saw his face filled with concern as she relived the memory.

"Is this Tyrone treating you right?" She saw the long-haired man frown over her computer screen.

"Yeah. He's a pain sometimes but he's a good guy." She didn't have too many complaints about the other man. He was kind to her and could be decent company to be around. Her father loved him. He came from a good, churchgoing family. He was a good catch on paper.

"Good." Osirion crossed his arms. "You know I would come over and teach him a lesson if I had to, right?"

"I know." Her heart swelled. "Beth wouldn't like you getting hurt on my account though. He is 6'1 to your 5'9..."

"...being taller doesn't mean better." He huffed. "Anyway, Beth wouldn't care at the moment."

"You two are off again?"

"Yes." He glared. "And no judging me, thank you."

"I wasn't!" She held her hands up in defense. "It's your relationship! You two will be back together within a month."

"Maybe." He sighed.

"You sound tired." She stated the truth. He closed his eyes for a moment, exhaling a deep breath. "Is everything okay over there?"

He smiled at her concern. "Hai, just you know. Conflict of personalities."

"Wish I could get some love about now." Tyrone's whisper broke her trance. "Who knew the Pastor's daughter was a cross-dressing prude."

She bristled at his remarks, hands smoothing over her nice navy-blue suit. She wasn't supposed to hear him but he couldn't whisper low enough for her not to catch it.

He can also be passive aggressive, mean, and a bit vindictive when he doesn't get his way. Reminds me of a mean toddler, just a lot bigger and stronger.

She chose to ignore him for the time being, concentrating on the bigger issue at hand. She desired more than a physical relationship, frowning as her heart sped up at the mere thought of her longtime friend. His gentle smile. His face was full of concern as they talked over video chat. The years of gentle friendship, since she first met him in ninth grade.

This wasn't an erotic fantasy like the others, but that made it count even more. She had fallen in love with Osirion, and that was worse than anything her hormone-flooded mind could have come up with.

"Princess." Michelle was in the last minutes of band practice at the church when her Dad sat down on one of the pews. Usually he didn't stop by on a Wednesday night practice with the musicians and choir. She was cleaning her flute with her cloth as they wrapped up for the evening.

"Hey Dad." She waved him over as she started to disassemble her instrument. She carefully took it apart, wiped it clean of her warm spittle and fingerprints, and placed it in her softly lined case. The process didn't take long but she liked to be as thorough for the next time.

"How's everything?" Her father was dressed in casual clothing suited for the cooling weather. As he sat down her eye caught the vertical scar on the side of his face. A constant reminder of a scarier time.

At least it healed over nicely.

"It's going good." She smiled. "Classes are good. I'm excited about transferring next semester."

"That's what I wanted to talk about." He looked nervous.

"What's wrong?" Michelle tried not to let her worries show but she knew she failed. "I'm still going to Adala right?"

"Yeah, yeah!" He gave her a reassuring smile. "Everything is paid for between your scholarships and whatnot. I can't let my precious daughter worry about finances when she's getting her education!"

"What's up then?" She turned to give her Dad her full attention.

"I was just thinking about how young girls go wild when they leave home for the first time." He cleared his throat. He seemed uncomfortable but continued. "Drinking, partying, sex...those types of things. I'm just glad I won't have to worry about that with you."

Is he talking about...

"Um, okay?" She gave him a look. "Why are you being weird?"

"I'm just glad you went through Purity Camp back in high school." He gave her a friendly smile. "Honestly I was worried as you went through puberty with your tastes in..."

"Dad, don't." A chill went through her body at the mention of "Purity Camp." It was an invention of her Dad's design, backed up by a few local pastors in the area as well.

A collaboration in the importance of remaining sexually pure to keep your body sanctified until you become someone's wife.

"I know I leave these things to your Mother but I'm your father." He protested. "I knew you used to write those sex stories with the whips and blood and other questionable things. You really didn't like me for a long time after camp, but it showed you that intimacy and sex isn't something for any man you date."

"Dad, that place messed me up." Michelle closed her eyes. It was the feeling of being seventeen again spending her entire summer being taught how to be a proper woman twenty hours a week.

"It set you straight." He frowned. "I know you haven't kissed Tyrone yet or even tried to have intercourse with him."

"How do you know that?" She balked at him.

"Him and I talk on the phone." Tony blinked. "I like him. He's a bit pent up but any man his age would be with a beautiful girlfriend. Perhaps this will motivate him to put a ring on your finger?"

"Dad, you're disgusting." Michelle blurted out the first thought in her mind. "Besides, Tyrone is a health hazard."

"You still haven't kissed him." The older man looked at his daughter. "Intimacy is a sacred part of a relationship. He's kissed you a few times, but you haven't made a move to initiate with him."

Tyrone is telling my Dad our relationship secrets?! I don't want to have this conversation but he's not going to let up.

"I...I can't." She turned away as shame started to burrow in her chest. "When I think about it, I feel..."

Scared. Ashamed. Angry. Embarrassed.

"Good about yourself." Tony finished her sentence. "I know he's going to pressure you especially leaving home but I know you'll do the right thing and make him wait. Tyrone will come around like men do and do the right thing."

"Is that all you think intimacy is for, a man?" She wanted the floor to swallow her whole but stood her ground. "What if **I** want it? I'm not made of stone."

To be held gently. To be kissed with adoration. To be cradled with passion.

"You have worldly desires like anyone else." He coughed. "Those desires are to bring you closer...to your **husband**. Not to be indulged in like some common prostitute. Those things feel good to get you to procreate. It's a small token to make up for the immense pain and suffering of childbirth."

And he wondered why I have trouble keeping female friends in school.

"I'm not talking about babies with you." Michelle groaned. Her head was starting to hurt, and her patience was running thin. "It's creepy that you know my romantic business. I hated Purity Camp and everything it left on me. It's not a sweet memory like it is for you."

"Well living the right way usually isn't sweet. It's hard and sometimes a burden but it's not worth tainting your soul over temporary pleasures." Tony reiterated his point with his hands. "Plus, you need to stay pure hearted for your gifts to flourish."

"I'm not sure that's biblical." Michelle sighed. "Besides, I wouldn't mind **not** seeing colors around people at odd times."

"Those are the spirits around their bodies, not just colors." Tony admonished her. "If you meditated more and read your Bible your gift would manifest itself more like mine."

"So, I can see even more than I do now?" Michelle frowned. "No thanks."

"That's your choice, but God cannot be denied." Tony sighed as the conversation was coming to a close. "I just wanted to remind you of that before you left home. I'll see you later tonight at the house."

I can't wait to leave fast enough.

Am I really a coward? Why couldn't I just tell her how I feel? As he walked towards his classes his mind wandered to his conversation with his 'best friend' a few weeks ago.

"Hey Osirion!" Darius walked up towards him. The brown skinned man stood at six-foot-three, and he dwarfed everyone around him. "How have you been?"

"I'm doing alright." He shrugged as his long hair wafted in the wind. "Classes aren't too bad at the moment. How are you?"

"Same." The two walked alongside each other. "How's your lady? Things are getting serious or are you two still playing around?"

"Um..." Osi stalled for a moment. "Beth?"

"Yeah." Darius smirked. "Unless you want to talk about your 'best friend' Michelle?"

"First off Beth and I are keeping it light and casual." He rolled his eyes. "Second, Michelle is my best friend. You don't have to put quotes around that."

"I heard you on the phone a few weeks ago." Darius let out a billowing laugh. "That was just a 'friendly conversation', right?"

"'Naughty boy." She chuckled. "I didn't say you could masturbate when I'm on the phone, did I?" Her voice replayed in his head as realization dawned on him.

Osi stopped walking to stare at his friend. "Are you serious?"

"I am." He arched his brow. "I saw you on that couch on that phone. Beth was right there in your room, and you were talking the nasty with your 'best friend'? You're not fooling anyone."

Shit. I should stay in my room next time.

"That was...a conversation." Osi hurried into a large building. "I have Figure Drawing in ten minutes. I'll see you around!"

"You have to be a better role model for him!" The angered voice of his mother roused a small Osirion out of his slum-

ber to stand in the doorway of his home. "You're his father Makoto."

"Are you saying I'm a bad role model?" His father balked as he paced back and forth. "He's not that bad…"

"He broke that kid's nose for not giving over his lunch money!" His mother crossed her arms. "Where did he get that from?"

"So Osirion is a bit…aggressive." His father withered under his mother's glare.

"This is the third fight he's gotten into this week!" She lowered her head. "He's just nine years old. If we can't change his behavior now, just imagine him as a teenager. Plus, Toshiro looks up to you and his older brother."

"I— His father turned his head to see Osirion listening in on their conversation. The boy didn't dare move as his parents regarded him with a knowing look.

"Did I do something wrong?" Fear caused his voice to come out in a small whisper.

"Come here and let us talk." His father waved him over with a hand.

The studio was quiet in the evening save for the light scratching of his brush against the canvas. Repetitive as he brushed layers of color over the light sketching his pencil left behind. The overall vision was in his mind's eye as he started the process of the piece.

Things have been quiet lately. Classes. Homework. Projects. Nothing out of the ordinary.

He rinsed off his brush before dipping it in the bright yellow paint. Osirion paused for just a moment to admire the vibrancy of the hue.

It's too bright for me but I know someone who would look great in yellow...

He swiped his brush along the canvas and deposited the color on the material. Rinse. Blot. Another color. Repeat.

Beth was busy with a group project right now. Darius went to class. Toshiro was running around on the other side of the world.

I wonder what Michelle is doing right now.

He looked towards the window to see the sun beginning to set over the horizon. The colors in the sky were beautiful but paled in comparison to the woman that made his heart race.

I need to get a grip. She's my best friend. I just need to get my mind off of her.

He pulled out his phone and sent a quick message to his occasional girlfriend.

Osi applied a few more layers of paint before his phone buzzed.

Busy in the library.

Distract yourself.

Or text your ACTUAL girlfriend? She must be busy with her man.

He flipped his phone over after sending a glare to the screen. Beth was wonderful in the bedroom but a nuisance anywhere else.

She tells me the truth, no matter if I want to hear it or not.

Osirion put down his palate with a frustrated groan. He thought about calling Michelle but stopped himself before he could press her name on the screen.

She must be busy with her man.

Of course, he knew about Tyrone. Her persistent pain that actually ended up going on a date with her, of all people. He's tall, dark, and handsome to a woman. As an artist he could see why Michelle agreed to date Tyrone, besides going to the same school as well. As a man, he hated every second they were together.

We were best friends all throughout high school! I should have...

Osi stopped himself from spiraling down with his thoughts with a shake of his head. They couldn't be together. He knew better. She knew better. His fingers ghosted over the raised white line against his skin spanning from cheek to ear. His heart picked up involuntarily.

A few centimeters over and her father would have killed me. At fifteen, just for having a crush on her!

Every detail from that day was etched into his memory. The light bouncing off the barrel of the gun. The way she screamed as the shot fired off. The way his heart stopped, and searing pain bloomed on his face and everything became quiet except for his harsh breathing.

Osi couldn't fully see the expression on his father's face as he tore at the shocked pastor still standing on his front porch. The two men went at it blow for blow until a cool cloth was placed on his face.

"You're okay." Michelle was standing in front of him, hands quivering against his cheek. "It grazed you. There isn't a hole anywhere."

"...oh." Osi couldn't manage any more than that from his lips. His eyes cut down to the grass. There wasn't any blood dripping down so that was a good sign.

"Hold still." She fumbled with a small pouch but managed to pull out a colorful band-aid and open it after a few tries. His eyes closed as she applied the bandage against his wound.

"Musuko." His father's harsh bark grabbed Osirion's attention. The older man had blood running from his face, as well as his hands were stained. Osirion never saw that expression on his father's face before but suddenly all of his cruel stories made perfect sense.

The older man marched up to Osirion and investigated his body. He saw Michelle scramble backwards to avoid any residual wrath his father might be holding inside.

"She helped me." Osirion forced himself to speak.

Osirion never saw Michelle as scared as she was in that moment. Her eyes cut behind the duo, probably to her own father somewhere in the background. She looked like she wanted to run but just couldn't manage to do so.

"Thank you." His father's voice made both teenagers jump out of their skin. Osi couldn't hear any resentment towards the young girl. "Go to your father."

"O-o-of course." She ran off after managing to speak.

"Iko u." Osirion turned at the command and wobbled back to their house. That was the last time he stepped onto the Winderson property.

"Sore wa takaie sou da ne." Toshiro arched a brow over the computer screen. His younger brother was walking back and forth on the screen in his bathroom brushing his hair. "Sono neckless ni ikura tsukak ta no?" *(That sounds expensive. How much did you shell out for that necklace?)*

"Honno suu en." Osirion worked the smooth metal over his fingertips. He felt the light indentions of the scales as the moved along the gold serpent. "Tokuni nani mo..." *(Just a few yen. Nothing too much...)*

"Ikura?" Toshiro smiled. "Suu sen hito?" *(How much? A few thousand?)*

Osirion turned over the serpent's head in his fingers. The small gems caught the light and reflected a light blue in his eyes. "Yaku 468,000 en zengo desu." *(Like 468,000 yen give or take.)*

Toshiro stopped brushing his hair mid-stroke. "That much! Onichan, honki na no?" *(Big brother, are you serious?)*

"Kanojo wa aishi te i masu. Suu en wa nani demo ari mase n." Osirion wiped down the golden snake before putting it back in the gift box. *(I love her. A few yen is nothing.)*

"Wow." Toshiro gaped. "Omae wa crazy da." *(You're crazy.)*

"Shitsu te i masu." Osirion sighed. "Watashi wa sore wa katazuke masu." *(I know. I'll just put it away.)*

"Ii yoi. Yatsu te mi te." Toshiro let out a manic laugh. "Kanojo wa anata wa aishi te iru yoi." *(No. Go for it. She loves you.)*

"Un?" Osirion joined Toshiro with a small chuckle. "Ore ni nani ka okashii to omotsu te nai?" *(Yeah? You don't think something is wrong with me?)*

"Omae, nani ka okashii zo." Toshiro clarified. "Dakar? Kanojo wa kimiyo wa aishi teru. Kimiyo mo kanojo wa aishi teru. Saya, yatsu cha i na yoi." *(Something is wrong with you. So? She loves you. You love her. Just do it.)*

"Maji de?" Osirion placed his gift away in his top drawer. "Kore de ii no?" *(Seriously? You're okay with this?)*

"Un." Toshiro placed down his brush. "Umaku itsu tara oshie te ne, ii? Ika nakya. Ganbatsu te ne." *(Yep. Tell me if it works out, alright? I have to go. Good luck.)*

"Mata ne." Osirion waved as he hung up the call. *(Later.)*

Thick streaks of crimson caught his eye as he stared in the mirror. A youthful face of a scared boy, pupils dilated wide shook him at his core. Bits of torn flesh caused his heart to stop in its chest. One blink, and all the gore was gone. No more trails of clotted blood and seared skin. His face was now crafted by puberty to show an angular jawline among his soft features. Against his golden skin a pale scar spanned from his cheek to almost touching his left ear.

Iki. (Breathe.)

Osirion lathered the bottom half of his face, taking caution of his left side. The scared area didn't grow facial hair, but the untouched portion had no issue. He twisted his face taut on the right and dragged the razor in one clean swipe. He rinsed off the cream and cut hairs before repeating once more.

Sore wa hontouni ... hidoi. *(It's so...nasty.)*

Against his better judgement, his warm brown eyes caught his scar once again. It was so blatantly obvious being on his face. Forever branded by his past mistake.

Koi ni ochiru. *(Falling in love.)*

"I did nothing wrong." A deep frown reflected in the mirror as he finished his right side. Tiny bits of cream on his left remained. He muttered into the silence. "That man was psychopath."

I should be grateful I didn't lose my eye.

The upward tilt of the textured skin made his skin prickle. Just an inch higher...

Bandages. Patches. Gauze. Globs of cream to starve off infection. Mother's shaking hands as she cleaned and redressed the wound.

He rinsed off the last of the shaving cream and wiped a warm cloth over his face. Smooth enough not to go over again. He cleaned the sink before leaving the bathroom.

Screams filled his ear as he collapsed to the ground. Searing pain filled his head as tears burned into his flesh. Terror and agony filled his pores. Michelle dropped to the ground as she sobbed. Her hands shook as she reached out to comfort, to hold him. It all hurt too much to bear.

"Hey Osi!" Michelle's chipper voice came through the phone speaker as Osirion laid back on his bed. The sun was just setting on the horizon, and he was finished with all of his classes for the day. Homework, on the other hand...

"Good evening, Michelle." He smiled at his friend. "How are your classes going?"

"They're good." She laughed. "Math is a bit challenging but it's not unbearable. I'm sailing through my general Lit class though."

"I'm sure you'll figure it out." He chuckled at her. "You always do."

"Thanks for the vote of confidence." Her voice seemed distant through the speaker. "How about you?"

"Going well. Just finishing a few of my core classes." He paused. "Anything on your mind?"

"Why you ask that?" Her voice has a higher tilt than normal.

"Your voice." He settled into his pillows. "You sound tense. Unsure. What's going on?"

"I didn't call to dump on you, Osi." Michelle sighed. A moment of silence passed before she opened up again. "It's Tyrone."

The mere mention of **his** name made Osi grip his phone tighter. "Oh? What did he do now?"

"Don't say it like that." Michelle grumbled. "He's been in a mood for a few days."

"Why?"

"He's frustrated." Michelle let out a quiet chuckle. "I don't think you wanna go into this with me, hon."

Halloween. At Faithview Baptist, it was the Devil's Birthday. Don't go outside, don't pick up any candy, and surely don't dress up to go Trick-or-Treating. There was a Trunk or Treat that was held in the church parking lot the day before, and usually after the age of thirteen people would make weird comments if someone still dressed up for the candy. Halloween was a big no-no at both Michelle's church and home lives.

October 31 was also her favorite holiday. While her Dad went on yearly tangents about the evils of the season, her Mom Tisha snuck her children out for a night of getting some candy from all the neighbors in the suburb. Michelle came to realize that her Mom was Southern but not the Georgia-Alabama-Florida variety.

Now as a grown woman Michelle still loved the costume part of Halloween. She was a bit too old for the candy part but that's why adults have Halloween parties.

She checked her vest, zipping up the brown leather attire. Underneath she wore a white long sleeve paired with brown leather pants and brown boots with a gold metal accent on the heel. She looked very Southern Gothic as she pinned her hat with a gold hat pin. Rich brown leather with gold undertones was the theme for Michelle's night.

"You look creepy." Michah poked his head into the bathroom. He was a melaninated vampire complete with silver contacts and gold fang inserts. He looked very Victorian in his own right. "It's a long ride to the hookup."

"I'm coming." She grabbed her metal bracelet and furry brown ears and stuffed them in her backpack. Michah was right—the drive to Adala was over three hours going one-way. It would be so late that the siblings got rooms at the B&B right on the cusp of the campus.

"I know you're excited for next semester." He started the car as she got in. "A bit of freedom from everyone."

"I can't wait." Michelle sighed. "Dad doesn't like it but he'll live."

"Yeah. He paid for my degree from there with no problem." Michah frowned. "I guess he regrets that now though..."

"Don't say that." Michelle shook her head. "He's always tough on you but he's proud. You have a salary career at the church. You're young and single. You have no kids. You have your pick of all the women near Atlanta. You have the world in your hands, bro."

"He still gripes because I didn't study theology but you're right." He shrugged as he pulled onto the highway. The sun was just setting as they were caught in rush hour traffic.

Michelle knew they would be stationary for a while as everyone trudged along slower than a snail. "You didn't forget your present in that bag?"

"Of course not." She smiled. "Osi will be happy to see me face to face."

"I know he will." Michah wiggled his eyebrows . "Especially on his birthday.You two have always been soft for each other, right?."

Michelle coughed to hide her flustered face. "That's what best friends are for. I really think he'll like his present this year."

"Sis, be real for one second." He gave her a brotherly look. "You still like Osirion don't ya?"

Am I really that transparent?

"No!" Michelle tried to sound normal, but her voice rose an octave. "Not anymore than a regular friend?"

"Don't bullshit me, Sis." Michah laughed. "Y'all known each other too long for nothing to be there. You two never even entertained the idea?"

"You know why we couldn't!" Michelle crossed her arms. "Dad shot him in the face. Be serious for a minute."

"True." Michah cringed as they inched along bumper to bumper on the highway. "Yet that didn't stop either one of you in high school or—

"Or what?" She glared at him. "Finish your thoughts."

"I mean my room is right next to yours at home. The walls are really thin, Sis." He coughed. "I heard an interesting phone conversation a few weeks ago through the wall. Something about a 'naughty boy' ring a bell?"

She stared at him for a moment before realization had her gaping at him. "Are you.... shut up!"

"Oh, I heard enough." Michah clasped his hand and performed a jerking action. "So nice to help your friend through such a **hard** time."

Oh my God. This can't be happening.

"Did anyone else hear in the house?" She didn't want to ask but needed to know.

"Nah, Dad was knocked out in his study." Michah arched a brow at her. "You can't convince me you two are just friends."

"Fine. I want him. Satisfied?" She pressed her palms against her eyes. "We both have significant others. I'm just going to his party as a friend.

"Oh real?" Michah weaved in and out of traffic as things started to loosen up. "Reach in my bag and take you some protection. Gotta look out for the young folks."

"What is wrong with you?" Despite her protests Michelle reached in and swiped four foil covered condoms and stuffed them in her bag.

"Four? Are y'all planning a marathon?" He couldn't help but to tease his embarrassed sibling. "How long has it been since you've seen each other in person?"

"Three years." She stared out the window to avoid his eyes. "We're sophomores now. Next Spring starts our junior years."

"Gonna join any sororities?" Michah pipped up. "Or maybe some new clubs? You'll have so many more options when you get there."

"Fall is pledge season so I'll have time to think about it." Michelle felt a thrill rush through her body. "I can't believe it's been three years already."

"Time goes fast." Her brother mused. "Too fast to live with regrets or not go for what you want. Or who."

"Is that why you're not going to rat me out to Tyone?" She paused as if to consider the third party in her relationship. "Bro code?"

"I feel for him but technically Tyrone is in the way of this romance drama and I want to see how it plays out." He let out a dry laugh. "Dad is so uptight with us. He wants to plan out who we marry, when we have kids, when we're going to take over the ministries...look at how he tries to interfere with Yvette's life. She's got a husband and he's still not satisfied."

"She's got a boyfriend and a husband." Michelle clarified. "I'm not sure if it's a polycule or a throuple type of relationship?"

"Either way Pops is salty cause she hasn't popped out babies yet." He shook his head.

"He's a successful mega pastor so nobody can't tell him nothing but if you can make him wake up, there's hope for me."

"Michah, you got this." She was the youngest sibling but suddenly she felt the weight he carried on his shoulders. "Just go and live your life."

"I can't do that yet. I'm the first son."

"You're the only son." She corrected him.

"Exactly." He frowned as the sunset colored the sky in its beautiful hues. "Who will follow in his footsteps if not me?"

Michelle went silent, not sure how to respond to his inquiry.

He patted her hand with a resigned smile. "Well, I'll give you a room key when we get close to campus. You're in 101 and I'm in 102. As long as I don't hear anything bad coming from your room I'll leave you be for the night."

"Gotta pick up some ladies from your alma mater?" Michelle tried to lighten the mood in the car.

"I mean." He shrugged. "I have today and tomorrow off of work. I'm going to enjoy myself, that's all I'm saying."

The music vibrated the building inside. The siblings opened the door easily as someone tumbled onto the porch. The smell of alcohol overpowered the cheap scent of air spray.

"At least he's drunk and won't feel that knot until the morning." Michelle stepped over the passed out man. She followed Michah into the kitchen, grabbing a bottle of water from the refrigerator.

"Be safe Sis." Michah sipped something from a red cup once hidden from her view. "If you need me, come and find me. Go downstairs where the real party is at.

"Thanks Bro." She kissed him on the cheek before she went into the crowd Michelle didn't tell Osirion that she would be coming in person so it would be a surprise.

She passed the varieties of cheap vampires and slutty varieties of costumes. Downstairs the lighting was much darker and people were pressed up close to another. A tall, burly man stood at the door blocking her entry.

"What are you supposed to be?" His deep voice reverberated in her bones. "A Victorian aristocrat?"

Michelle was going for a Gothic werewolf kind of character with clawed nail rings on her hands and furry ears. "A cultured werewolf, sort of based on the old were-man archetype. Move please, you're in the way."

"This is a private party." He leaned down before laughing. "Is your name Michelle?"

"How do you know my name?" Michelle cocked her head to the side. "Have we met before?"

"Cause your boy keeps on talking about you." He pulled out his phone and showed her a picture. There he was standing with a few other guys with Osirion at the front. "He didn't say you were coming here."

"He doesn't know." Michelle placed a finger over her lips. "I wanted to surprise him for his birthday."

"Ah! I see now." He put out a large hand for her to shake. "I'm his roommate Darius. He's inside."

"Thanks Darius." Michelle gave him a shake and a smile. "Nice to meet you."

The music turned slow and sensual as the dancing couples moved against each other. A few other people were sitting down on the sofa or the bean bags sprinkled around the area. Her eyes adjusted as she walked towards a well lit patch in the room.

Now where would the birthday boy be hiding?

"Zaria?" She caught the eye of a...mere-man or some sea creature. Michelle turned at the voice.

"Happy Birthday, Mr. Najimi." She looked over his costume. His makeup was done by his own hand, shimmering scales placed around his eyes, neck, and chest. His teeth were shark-like in his mouth. Gills were painted in astounding detail leading down to a thick gold necklace in the shape of a snake around his neck. The light caught a matching bracelet and ring on his left side. In short, he looked **amazing**.

"Isn't this a surprise." Osirion grabbed her in a hug as he lifted her from the ground. "Why didn't you tell me you were coming?"

"It's part of your birthday gift." She laughed at his joyous outburst. "I have your present as well!"

Michelle couldn't help the spreading warmth as he gave her a full smile. Her eyes caught the detail of his costume as well as his bare chest all out in the open.

He just has his chest all out in October? Look at how he's changed over the years...

Her heart drummed in her chest, wild and frantic, as she let out a calming breath. She pulled out a box from her bag and put it in his hands.

I really hope he loves his gift.

"Thank you." The box was wrapped in colorful paper and tied off with a bright red ribbon. He opened the gift and gaped at her.

"I know you would love it." She beamed at him. "At least I think so. Am I wrong?"

He whispered at her with reverence. "You shouldn't have...but thank you."

It was an autographed New York Yankees baseball complete with an autographed jersey in Osi's size. He looked at her for a moment before motioning with his head. "I have something for you too."

Now I'm curious.

Osi let her through the small crowd in the basement and upstairs towards the common area. He pointed to a man sleeping near the entryway with a chuckle. "Our RA finally passed out. He better stay shut if he wants to keep his job and room."

"I'm sure he'll be quiet." Michelle laughed.

The two walked to the end of the hall and walked up a flight of stairs. Away from the music they walked a few doors down before stopping at a singular metal door. The place was tidy on the inside, with basic amenities save for the large television in the living area.

"This must be your dorm." Michelle looked around the living area.

"Yeah. My private room is on the right." Osi walked into his room and stashed his present away. He walked back with a small black box and handed it to her. "This is for you."

"Who gives gifts on their birthday?" Michelle laughed but accepted the box. She opened it and paused. Inside was a beautiful long golden snake in the box. It wasn't as bulky as his own necklace and longer, probably to wrap around her neck at least twice.

It's a matching necklace.

"I don't think I can accept this." She turned it over in her fingers. The metal was solid instead of hollow like she expected. "This looks really expensive."

"You can accept it." He stood behind her. The cool metal wrapped around her neck twice before the serpent head and tail rested on her collarbone. "The gold matches your costume as well."

"I don't know what to say." She walked into the bathroom to see her reflection. It complemented her beautifully. Dainty enough to go with a dress but thick enough to go with a large tee and pants. It fit both sides of her equally and her face warmed. "How much did this cost?"

He shrugged with a smile. "Ki ni shi nai yoi. *(It doesn't matter.)* You don't need to worry about it tarnishing or getting it wet in the shower. Now, let's go back and celebrate."

He switched back to his mother tongue. I'll get it appraised later to really see but it feels extravagant.

Michelle nodded as the two walked back to the lively party. She had accepted his gift but knew it wasn't a simple article of jewelry just from examination. It was too well made to be something he picked up on a whim. The very act flustered her enough to grab an empty cup and fill it a quarter way with jungle juice. She could smell the alcohol coming off of the punch bowl and took her drink outside on the porch. She leaned on the banister and took a sip of the sweet alcoholic mix.

Oh, what do I do? Giving it back would be offensive, and he did insist for me to keep it. It should be okay to accept such a lavish gift just this once.

"So, you're the other woman." The banister creaked under the weight of another. Michelle looked over and almost jumped. "Or perhaps I'm the 'other woman' here. It's hard to tell."

"Beth." Michelle acknowledged the other woman. She's seen her from photos but forgot that she would be present at her boyfriend's birthday party. "Nice to see you in person."

The blonde woman brushed some strands of hair away from her face. She was dressed in a matching mermaid costume, as beautifully decorated as her male counter-part. "Nice to see you too."

Michelle gave her a nod. "Matching couples cos-tumes. You look good."

It was an honest compliment. Her dress showed off a generous bosom almost spilling out the top hugging a small waist and a modest rear end. While Michelle was pear shaped Beth was an apple. "Thanks. You look good too. I see he gave you a matching necklace."

Oh hell.

"Um..." Michelle was caught off guard. "This?"

Beth took a large gulp out of her cup. "Gold fits your skin tone. I'm more of a silver girl myself."

"That doesn't piss you off?"

Beth looked Michelle up and down for a moment. "We've come to an understanding about **you**."

"What kind of understanding?" Michelle glared through her gold frames. "I don't do street fights over men."

*No matter who they are, I'm not **that** desperate.*

"Nothing like that." Beth waved her off. "I have more interesting things to do than to fight over a love struck man...I see your brother is here."

"Michah came with me." Michelle wasn't surprised that people knew them with their father's reputation.

Perks of being the children of a well-known preacher.

"He has his own room tonight?" Beth arched an eyebrow. "Since it's getting late to drive back."

"He does." Michelle smirked. "Are you going to keep him company for the night?"

"Maybe." She laughed. "He's very attractive. Perhaps I can get Osirion for a threesome if I'm really lucky."

"I didn't know you two had such an open relationship." Michelle knew they were always breaking up and getting back together but he wouldn't directly tell her why.

Just how much has he changed in our time apart?

"I just know the rules of this one." Beth finished off her drink. "It's complicated. See you inside."

She's unnaturally nice to me. I better keep an eye on her while I'm here.

Michelle looked out at the full moon illuminating the clear night sky. A group played hacky sack on the front lawn, away from a couple that were moon gazing. The banister creaked again as more weight was placed on it.

"I see you and Beth had a talk." Osi rubbed the back of his head. "Sorry. I know she noticed what you were wearing."

"She wasn't angry, at least as far as I could tell." Michelle finished off her drink. "You might get lucky tonight, but you'll have to see my brother naked."

"Excuse me?" Osi shook his head. "Your brother?"

"Beth's going to put the moves on him as we speak." Michelle saw him look back before taking a sip out of his cup. "If you're into guys my brother is a good catch...for my **brother**. She'll have a great time though."

"That's not funny." He narrowed his eyes before turning to the moon. "She can have him all to herself."

"You're not the jealous type?" Michelle questioned.

He glared at her. "I am. I'm just not jealous about Beth."

"But you're sleeping with her." Michelle chuckled. "And now she's trying to sleep with my brother...I need a diagram for this."

"Are you, of all people, slut shaming?" Osi laughed. "I'm appalled!"

"I'm not! I think it is liberating actually." She rolled her eyes. "If we were dating, I would only get the most handsome men to come back to our love nest. I can't be out embarrassing you, now can I?"

"You would only be sleeping with me." He took a long sip.

"Why do you say that?" A smile graced her features. She saw his jaw tense up as he stared her down.

Man, look at that body language. He's so pissed!

He opened his mouth to reply but took a big gulp instead. "You would be my good girl, that's why."

She stared at him, mouth gaped open. She didn't miss the way his voice dropped an octave as he looked at her in the pits of her eyes. She felt her ears burn as the blood rushed to her face. "E-excuse me? What was that?"

He smirked as he leaned closer, almost daring her to look away. "My good girl. I can take you back to my room if you would like."

Michelle felt her mind just cut off. No random thoughts, no commentary, not even a smart remark entered her head. She slowly turned her head back towards the moon.

God, I'm trying to be a good friend. Why now? He's over here smelling good, whispering with that sexy voice, calling me a good girl...

"Did I break you?" He poked her shoulder. "Sorry! I didn't think you could get so flustered."

"Um...uh..." She cleared her throat. She felt like she was rebooting like her old computer. "I'm fine! You just took me by surprise, that's all."

I'm trying not to jump in your lap sir!

"That's good." He let out a breath. "I was prepared to catch you if you fainted."

"I appreciate it." She fanned her heated face. "If I pass out from overheating, the least you can do is take care of me."

Osi was about to respond but Michah came through the door with three women clinging to his costume. "Happy Birthday O!"

"Thank you." Osi smiled at the older man.

"Three?" Michelle was flabbergasted. "Where are you going?"

"To enjoy myself, Sis." Michah managed to get down the stairs. "I'm retiring for the night. Call me if you need me."

"Have a good night." She waved her brother off with a chuckle. "Someone is going to have fun."

"He's not the only one." Osi pointed out a familiar blonde head in the trio of women.

"Damn, on your birthday too." Michelle winced. "Beth wasn't lying but ouch. Good thing you don't get jealous then."

"Nan da yoi?" *(What the fuck?)* He groaned.

Same Osi, same.

"Come on, birthday boy." Michelle grabbed his hand. "Let's turn that frown upside down."

Two hours of video games does have a habit of cheering someone up. Even the birthday boy whose friends with benefits went off with her older brother to get her back blown out could be cheered up with some games, a few snacks, and a few good jokes.

It's not hard to be a good friend. Good job, Michelle.

"Years later and you still suck at fighting games." Michelle laughed at his defeat once again.

"Why don't we play another shooter?" He stuck his tongue out at her.

"So, I can let you shoot me another hundred times?" She smiled. "Go ahead. It's your birthday, why not? Everyone gets a wish on their birthday."

"You're giving me a birthday wish?" His grin was wicked. "How many?"

"One." She stared him down. "Don't try to be funny either or I will leave you here."

"On my birthday?" He sent her a look of mock hurt. "I can't catch a break today."

"Ha, ha." She rolled her eyes. "What's your birthday wish?"

"I'm saving it for later." He loaded up the game and laid back on a hill of soft pillows. His living room was quiet, and comfortable, with the distant bass of the party still going on in the lower levels. "I do have an intrusive question though."

"What do you want to know?" She had shed her leather vest and boots to get comfortable next to him. "We're best friends. You can ask me."

I didn't say I would answer though.

"Are you satisfied..." He paused. "...with your life so far?"

"Yes." She eyed him. "I have a great family, great friends, a decent lover, and I'm busy with my studies. I'm satisfied so far."

"Decent lover?" Osi snickered. "*Only* decent?"

"Oh, like you can talk." She shot back at him. "Decent. We get to learn from each other with time and patience."

"How bad is he?" Osi killed her on screen yet again. "From a 1-10 scale."

"You just assume the worst. I'm sure when I do have sex with him it will be worth it." She laughed. "Like you could do better."

The screen suddenly paused. Sure, Michelle was once again getting killed but she didn't expect the whole thing to stop. She gave him a curious look.

Did I say the wrong thing this time?

His lips touched the top of her head. The kiss was warm, sweet, and chaste—a stark contrast to their current conversation. Osi next kissed her nose with the same sweetness, as well as her left and right cheeks. His eyes were lidded as he leaned in towards her lips.

I should turn him away...but I don't want to. What's the harm that one birthday kiss can do?

Michelle expected the same pure hearted pecks to meet her expectant mouth. He pressed against her lips with a smile before parting hers as his tongue slipped into her mouth. She gasped in surprise. A flood of feelings filled her heart, and at least this time desire pinned down her impending shame. Their bodies heated up as their hands traced each other's face, neck, legs, hips with timid, fleeting touches. Her hands pushed against his shoulders until he laid on his back.

He pulled back first for air. "I know what I want for my birthday."

"Hmm. You want to fuck me?" She stared into his dark eyes; the soft cinnamon color has turned onyx black.

"Tempting, but no." He shook his head. "I want you to stop fighting yourself."

She gave him a confused look. "What do you mean?"

"I can see it." He leaned in with a kiss to her ear. "That push and pull you do when you think for too long. The way you fight your desires constantly. You're doing it right now."

Am I that easy to read?

"Everyone has a vice they struggle to fight." She tilted her head.

"Yes, and yours is desire." He nuzzled her nose. "For years you have fought against your own desires. You try to be a good person by denying what you really want."

She felt the fringes of annoyance and comfort intertwine with one another. Comfort because Osi knew her well and the thought made her feel pleasure inside. Annoyance because he knew her well despite years of keeping herself in check, as best as she could, with both fear and discipline.

"How is it working for you?" His mocking tone caught her ear. He was below her, long hair splayed out in a dark halo around his head. Her eyes traced his arms to his hands that were massaging into her leather clad thighs. His skin was glistening as the warm lamps bounced the light off. His smirk was infuriating.

He's the one under me but he's in the driver seat.

Michelle resisted the urge to wrap her hands around his throat. She would study the way he got under her skin if it wouldn't leave her a flustered mess all the time. Her hands traveled down his chest, brushing over his erect brown nipples in the process. "You love to talk."

"Especially to you." His hands wandered along her legs and backside. "Am I wrong about you?"

"No." She placed her frames on an end table with a sigh. "The question is can you keep a secret?"

"Of course." His expression grew soft. "If I need to I will."

"That's good." She leaned down and kissed him on the lips. The kiss was brief and sweet yet filled with a nervousness behind her lips. She braced her hands on his shoulders and rolled her lower half.

So, this is how it feels to kiss someone first.

His hands tightened on her hips immediately. He gasped as she rolled her hips into his groin again and again. There was a certain satisfaction that spread across her face at his reactions.

"W-what's w-wrong?" She rubbed the seam of her pants against his firm erection. Her leg muscles twitched under his fingers. He was too busy panting to notice the stutter or her pauses as the pleasure started to tighten below. "You wanted me to stop fighting myself, right?"

He grabbed her hips with a look and thrust upwards to meet her movements. "Finally. This will be our little secret...just for tonight."

Their gasps and pants filled the living space as only one goal entered both of their minds. Michelle leaned down to lick and bite at his neck, teeth just above his golden necklace. She was close to her end, but he was much closer as she held him down. She saw him throw his head back as his body tensed underneath her, a deep lascivious moan escaping his mouth.

She's warm all around her thighs, her entrance, her soaked through curls...she felt him throb and pulse as he soaked her tight, leather pants all the way to her skin. His hands went slack as he released her, face turning a bright shade of red as he caught his breath.

"Good thing I have a change of clothes back in my room." She laughed. "But you were **so pretty** when you came. I'll never forget your expression."

How long has he been holding that in? Months? Years?

His gaze was unfocused as he caught his breath. He licked his lips as his body calmed back down. "I didn't tell you my birthday wish yet."

"You're done." Her laughter was haughty and cruel. "You should go to sleep, Birthday Boy."

A low growl from his throat was her only warning before he flipped her on her back. He pinned her hands together and stared down at her face. "Let me help you since I ruined your pants."

He stood up and pulled downwards as she squeaked. The crotch of her pants was cold now and he saw why as he pulled them down her legs. "You didn't wear anything under these?"

"They were **too** tight." She shivered; his hand traced the inside of her leg.

She caught the expression on his face, and it took her breath away. His eyes were blown wide, lips parted as he took shuddering breaths. She felt his gaze rake over her small curves as his hands worked off the rest of her clothing. His impassioned voice took her by surprise as she felt his fingers breach her entrance. "You're beautiful and tonight you are mine."

"Oh." She moaned out, his fingers stretched and twisted inside. "To the right..."

"Like that?" He pushed a little to the right, following her direction.

Squishing sounds filled the room as her legs parted further. "Up a little."

He curled his fingers inside of her, making her jump as pleasure shot through her body. "Ii kanji?" *(Feel good?)*

"God yes." Her back arched as he smiled. He rolled and pushed the small nub under the pad of his thumb and her muscles fluttered around his fingers.

"Did you answer me?" He whispered to her. He was sweating as a drop ran down from his chin and splashed onto her chest.

Uh oh. She didn't want to come clean this early. "Don't...be silly."

He twisted his fingers, brushing against her walls. "Are you sure?"

"I'm sure!" His fingers pumped faster as she arched against the scratchy carpet. Spurts of wetness leaked out of her and soaked into the floor below them.

He laughed at her as she writhed on the floor, hips moving against his hand. "Look at my good girl. Move those hips on me."

"I'm...so close." She sped up her hips. "Don't slow down, don't speed up. Just...right there."

"Oh Love...take your pleasure." His voice washed over her like the waves on the beach. His voice was smooth and deep in her ear as her hands ripped the carpet out as her climax crashed into her.

"Ugh...oh wow." Her body went slack as all the energy drained out of her. She looked to see him sucking his wet fingers with a deep groan.

"Wow indeed." Osi laughed at her as he sighed. "Let me clean you off and get us something to drink."

"Are we done for the night?" Michelle panted as she laid on the floor.

"No, not unless you are." He laughed. "We have all the time in the world, just for tonight."

One night. All we need is just one night, right?

He thought that his birthday night would add some relaxation to his mind. The party was great. Darius made sure everyone didn't get too out of hand. Seeing Michelle in person was the big surprise of the evening. He assumed that her gifts would be coming in the mail in the coming days but to see her right before his eyes...that was it.

Her costume was creative. The furry tail, the ears, and the metal claws reminded him of a half furry creature, which was close to a werewolf type woman. It was cute. It was creative. It was compelling him to rip her clothes off in the privacy of his own room. Instead, her gift made him smile: an autographed baseball and jersey for the Yankees. He knew that was a hard gift to come by and the fact that she was able to get it overwhelmed him.

Giving her that serpent necklace was a happy accident. He bought it on a whim and stashed it away permanently. There the box sat in his drawer, a constant reminder of his true intentions towards her and a symbol of his own hesitation. The cool gold metal would look right at home on her neck if he could take it out and put it in her hands. He remembered the look on her face as he put it in her hands and insisted that she take it.

The smile on her face as she put it on...it was worth it.

Osirion didn't regret finally taking the leap of faith with Michelle. It was a long time coming. The sounds he pulled from her lips would fill his dreams for months. He took her all in trying to commit every single detail to memory.

Her expressions. Her body in the light. Her desires playing out all over her face, unburdened by the expectations of others.

Having Michelle coming apart by his touch definitely stroked his ego. She wore many hats in her life: best friend, pastor's daughter, church girl, the little writer...and now to add his lover to her list made both his heart and head swell up.

For once he persuaded her to let go and do what she wanted after all these years. The image of her wearing nothing but her golden gift writhing on his floor would never leave his mind. Yet...

"Stay with me." He whispered into her sweaty shoulder as the couple finally wore themselves out. "Be my...."

She eyed him as his voice broke away. "Be your what? Girlfriend? Lover? Secret fling?"

He struggled to say what he really wanted and used a substitution instead. "Just be mine. For more than one night."

"I love you, Osirion." He leaned into her touch with open eyes. At least as she rejected him, he would see her own

inner battle in her eyes. "We can't be...you know why. I can't do that to you."

Her thumb ghosted over his scar intentionally. The warring. The drama. The hostility. He received her message clearly without another word being said.

"Then I hope that one night will be enough." He planted a hard kiss on her lips, and he felt her hands thread through his hair as an answer.

Since he couldn't have her, he was going to take everything he could from her. Make her crave him as badly as he craved her after tonight. If he couldn't get any reprieve, he'll make sure she won't have any either.

He pulled himself off the floor and placed himself between her damp thighs. Sparks fired off where his bare skin touched hers as he stared her down. Tight coils clenched around his heart, but it wasn't love or lust that he wanted to convey through his eyes...it was possession. "Mine."

If Osirion was a good person, he would climb off of her and go to sleep for the night. He knew her weak spots. He knew she tried to be considered 'good and holy' since he's known her. He also saw the burden of those expectations on her shoulders the times her masked features would unconsciously slip. He saw the people pleaser in her as others bossed her around. He saw her annoyance as others would say scathing remarks with such a casual ease to her face. He saw the cracks along the surface of her image as she buried her feelings and desires so far down, he assumed she would never want to feel them again.

"Love." He cooed at her. His head brushed against her opening and ripped a gasp from her mouth. "I know what I want. The question is "Can I have you?"

He saw her eyes go wide; her breath caught in her chest. Her hand reached out and touched his bare chest right over his heart. "If I could afford to, I would but...I can't."

*He took a deep breath through his nose and exhaled from his mouth. His hands tightened around her thighs, but he didn't dare go against her wishes. He felt her hand trail over his flat stomach, and she cleared her throat. "Can I help you in my own way, sweet**heart**?"*

The way she drew out the last word in her Southern accent made him chuckle. His muscles tensed under her touch as he gave her a smile. "Touch me, Love. Please."

Her hand wrapped around him and everything else was a pleasurable blur behind his eyelids.

"Hey Osi!" Michelle ran up and gave her friend a tight hug. "We finally transferred to Adala! "

"Michelle!" She saw him jump in the air before he returned her embrace. "How are you paying for this place?"

"I got a creative writing grant, a few scholarships, and my Dad was ordered to pick up the rest!" Her light laughter filled him with happiness. "I have someone I want you to meet!"

"Is this Tyrone?" He let himself get dragged by her. "He transferred with you?"

She laughed. "He's not much into the arts but this place has a great Africana studies program." She presented her current beau to her bestie. He had muscular arms, legs, and large hands. He was several shades darker than her and *skin was smooth and moisturized. He flashed the shorter Asian man a smirk.*

"Tyrone! This is Osirion!" She introduced her boyfriend to her friend. "We have been friends since high school!"

"O'riley it's nice to meet you." Tyrone stood over Osirion looking satisfied.

"Don't be so rude!" She chastised him. "His name is **Osirion** *not O'riley! That wasn't even a close attempt!"*

"It's alright Michelle, I'm sure that Timmy didn't mean anything." The two men glared at each other while she shook her head...

They still don't get along...

She tapped her finger to the music through her earphones, whispering to herself. Michelle thought that one night would make her fantasies go away but instead they got worse.

The constant dreams...his touch still lingering on my skin months later.

Tyrone has to be suspicious, especially after she came back with this gold necklace—but he hasn't called her out yet. Either he doesn't care, or his free time is being spent with someone else. Either way she knew they would have this conformation sooner or later.

"Yo Michelle!" Instead of red the woman's hair was now blonde styled like the famous Queen of R&B. "You going to the BSA meeting?"

"Hey, Lisa! I'm going there right now." The two women walked together. "You set up the food and drinks for this evening?"

"Of course. I got some snack foods for today." Lisa nodded. "This place is much bigger than Tech."

"Definitely." Michelle opened the door to a large building. The two women walked through a set of wooden doors. The room was a small area with various bean chairs and a table lined with the chips and soda of the evening. It wasn't a full course meal, but it was better than nothing. Some fellow members were currently getting their fill.

Michelle grabbed a small plate of snacks. "Tyrone said this meeting was super important. I would have skipped out, but he seemed determined."

"I can't blame you. The homework here is insane." Lisa piled her own plate. "Essay here. Test there. Projects all the time. Adela University doesn't play around."

"It's known for a reason." Michelle took her seat. "The programs here are taught by some of the best in the South but that means the work is brutal."

"That's true. At least Tyrone found his place here really quick." Lisa sipped her drink. "Less than a month in the semester and he's already running BSA. What do you think this meeting is about?"

"Not even sure." Michelle sighed. "He's got a chip on his shoulder about the increase in interracial dating discussions around the school."

"Really?" Lisa arched a shaped eyebrow. "You know it was on the unofficial forum app but gossip, trash, and controversy is always on that thing."

An open, unmoderated forum of students. That sounds about right for ATalk.

"For real?" Their conversation caught a few of the members that were in the room. "I'm not a sellout like some other chicks."

"We are loyal to our Black men in this room." Lisa poked her in the side. "...except for Michelle over here! She's already dated a white boy!"

Michelle groaned as they snickered. *Oh, here they go again.*

"It was in high school and what's the big deal?" She adjusted her headband over her kinky Afro. "I don't have a racial preference when it comes to dating."

"That white boy is nothing! What about that Asian dude she's always around? Laughing at his jokes!" Some of the members sent her disapproving glances. "She has a man and still can't help herself."

Michelle glared at the people around her. "People don't understand that men and women can just be friends do you? We've been friends since ninth grade."

Very sexy friends that do some not-so-friendly activities but friends all the same!

"We know you find him attractive!" Lisa added her thoughts in the discussion. "He's not bad looking but *nothing* compared to Tyrone. He's shorter, looks weaker, and I'm pretty sure he's not as 'well equipped' as Tyrone either."

*Does **everyone** know how large Tyrone is down there? He does keep bragging about that poor woman that he sent to the hospital.*

"Why are you comparing the two like one is better than the other?" She blushed and adjusted her glasses. "Different strokes for different folks. Anyway, what woman doesn't like eye candy? Looking isn't a crime."

"Hey baby!" Speaking of the devil Tyrone came strutting in the room. Every woman turned their head at the attractive man. His hair was shaped up and low cut, telling of a recent barber trip. His clothes were fitted, making his tall figure even more imposing. Broad shoulders and a dazzling smile just added to his good looks. He gave her a kiss on the lips as he walked to the front.

He has every straight woman in here about to faint and he knows it. Even Lisa, as her friend, couldn't help but to fan herself like she was in heat.

"Now I know everyone is busy, but I wanted to call this meeting. One of our building blocks includes celebrating Black love in the heterosexual form. The Student Government Association is passing a bill allowing more visibility of LGBT+ in campus spaces." Tyrone paused to drink some water. "I have nothing against that community but here in BSA we are about rebuilding and celebrating structured Black people. As president of the club I have opted BSA out of the inclusion bill. This just means that we will not be recognized as a LGBT+ visibility space on campus. Any questions?"

"Why would you do that?" Several eyes turned to a teal-haired woman with a light complexion. Her frown was deep as she stood before everyone. "Why **can't** we be a visibility space?"

"Angel, the executive board and I didn't think that this is of importance to BSA." He shrugged. "We are a student organization focused on highlighting and improving Black economic and social issues on campus. This bill has nothing to do with us."

"Are there not Black LGBT+ members in this club?" Angel looked around. "I know for a fact that everyone here isn't a straight-laced bore. Why can't a few of us go in for that much needed rep?"

"Sister, I'm not arguing with you on representation." He folded his hands. His face was tight, displaying his irritation to everyone. "You're represented here as an Afro-Latina right? All you have to do is go outside for your lesbian representation. Just because we are not participating doesn't mean that the Pride Alliance isn't."

"You know most of the LGBT+ representation depicts non-Black individuals." Angel held her own with an impressive glare. "The amount of Black LGBT+ rep is much smaller overall than non-Black LGBT+. I was hoping that we were going to spearhead a more diverse campaign on campus."

"Sorry sister but BSA will not help with that charge." He turned away from Angel, dismissing her. "Here are the other items on our agenda we need to decide on before the end of the month."

Michelle watched the tension in the room as the meeting went on. She actually voted to include the SGA bill in the group but as the only supportive executive member the idea didn't stand a chance of taking shape. The silence told her everything.

I wish the older executive members stayed on instead of handing it over to us, but I understand why they dropped with the course load. *Shouldn't Black rep also include the full diversity of the Black experience?*

Michelle was uncomfortable but didn't have a leg to stand on. She saw Angel withdraw in frustration as everyone else deemed it a non-issue.

"...I think we are done for today! The next meeting will be at our normal time next Wednesday here at 5:30!" Tyrone dismissed everyone from the room. The students shuffled along, grabbing the last bits of free food before leaving. Michelle walked towards Angel, but the blue haired woman swiftly ducked out before Michelle could stop her.

I hope she's okay. I'll catch her back in our dorm.

Michelle turned to Tyrone as the two started to walk out. "That was tense." He looped a hand over her shoulder and pulled her close. "She was not happy."

"I wonder why." She deadpanned. "You basically told her she doesn't matter enough for BSA to help make her more visible."

"Angel is always visible with that blue hair." He countered. "Plus, she's loud all on her own. Can't miss her."

"You know what I mean." Michelle frowned. "What's wrong with having a few members from BSA show up to the Government meetings now and then?"

"Why? She chose to be lesbian, and the Pride Alliance is the club for that kind of thing." He frowned. "I'm surprised you voted in favor since you're a straight preacher's kid."

"I can't be an ally?" She pushed his arm off of her shoulder. "And you think me being attracted to men is a choice? Sexuality is a natural thing."

"You're saying it's natural to be a lesbian?" He spat out with a frown. "Pastor Tony's daughter from Faithview Baptist Church saying that homosexuality is natural? Your Daddy would have a fit!"

He had to use the WHOLE church title to call me out.

"Yes." Michelle glared at him. "I don't think about why I like men but rather I just **do**. I'm sure that Angel feels the same way towards women. Even more so because most women are prettier than most men."

"Women are pretty **for** men." He rolled his eyes. "BSA is about building and establishing black people. We don't deal with issues of sexuality or sexual expression or whatever else that you weren't absolutely born with."

"That's our issue. We don't include non-hetero people, non-binary people, or even anyone who chooses to express their gender in a different way!" She motioned to herself, drawing attention to her rolled up shirt, dark jeans, and black suspenders. "You do realize if I'm queer then you're in a queer relationship, right?"

"Baby you're just a tomboy!" He tried to pull her close but she blocked him. "Yeah you look cute in boy clothing but that's not what a man wants his woman to wear! You look much better in feminine clothes because you **are** a woman. Plus, you have a woman's body. You're not queer because you're an occasional cross dresser."

"Not every woman who wears men's clothing is in the 'tomboy phase.'" She started to walk into the art building. "And it's offensive to even suggest it. Say that to the wrong person and get snapped at."

"Your home church calls you the 'Tomboy Princess.'" He blurted out. "I'm a straight man. You date men. The sex part is coming but you haven't slept with a woman in your life. You're as straight as me. How are you queer again?"

Michelle didn't have an answer for him. Besides her flash of anger, he wasn't wrong about her, but she never felt 'normal' in the traditional sense. She huffed. "I'm going to paint for a minute. Don't wait up."

"I'll come by in an hour to walk you back to your dorm baby." He walked off before she could decline his 'polite' offer.

Michelle groaned in annoyance before starting her walk to the canvas room. It was later in the evening, so Michelle cocked her head at the light coming from the studio.

"Well, this is a nice surprise." A husky male voice caught her as she crossed the room's threshold. He had turned towards her, holding his brush in mid-stroke. The gentle breeze from the cracked window tousled his long, inky hair, exposing a slender scar on his left cheek.

Michelle smiled. "No ponytail this evening? Just flowing locks everywhere?"

"A pleasure to see you, Love." Osirion gave her a wide smile. "Why not? It does tickle my shoulder. A change of pace is nice."

"Yeah." She grabbed a canvas and easel to set up. "As you see I did the Big Chop before transferring over here. Being natural is different but I just love these kinky tight curls."

"It definitely fits your features. I love it." His brown eyes stared at the canvas as he laid out his choice strokes in vivid green paint. His face was calm yet focused on his task. "Is your insecure lover in the building?"

"You both just keep going at each other huh? He'll swing by much later." She dabbed some blue on her brush. "I needed some alone time from him."

"Hope you don't mind my company." He locked eyes with her. Her heart pounded in her chest, almost making her pant.

Girl, get a grip on yourself! He's working on a canvas, not you! It's just a Paint and Hang.

"I never mind your company." She gave him a bright smile. "We need to catch up anyways, and the crack of dawn morning classes don't count."

"Ah." He laughed. "Do you mind if I decide to paint you then?"

"You want to paint your subject, painting another subject?" She cocked her eyebrow. "I'm not that interesting but go right ahead, Sweetie."

"Every artist needs a muse dear. You just happen to be mine." A small blush started to creep up on his face. "You already know that."

"What did I do to get such an honor?" She flashed him a cheeky smile as the two worked. The air was comfortable as they made small talk but Michelle did have something to address with Osirion.

"You know I have to ask." She leaned away from the canvas to see him. "Why don't you and Tyrone get along better, besides him being an ass?"

"Because he is an ass." Osi arched an eyebrow. "He's rude, condescending, and sounds like a stupid boyfriend from the issues you two had had in the past."

Osi was my vent buddy when Tyrone got on my last nerves.

She couldn't argue with him. To Osirion, Tyrone was extremely rude. "I-I know."

"Kare wa fuyukai na ningen desu." *(He's an unpleasant human.)* He whispered under his breath. Michelle tried not to react as she translated his harsh criticism from his native tongue.

Didn't even have to curse him out. Ouch.

He washed out his brushes. "Ever since our first meeting he has messed up my name even **after** being corrected. He always looked pissed off at my mere presence. I can't see how you can stand his presence honestly."

Always fun when the man you want starts to question your choices. I saw this coming from a mile away.

"Why do you like him so?" He turned a critical eye on her. "He's always mouthing off on what he doesn't like in a woman yet still you two are still together."

She paused. It wasn't because she was at loss for words but rather, she needed a moment to process his cold tone. "He challenges my thoughts and forces me to see things from a new perspective."

"Challenges you." He gave her a lofty nod. "Or is he reprogramming you? It must be tiring to argue about the same things all the time with his grating voice. Is spiritual masochism a Christian trait or is that exclusive to you?"

Damn. She flinched. *When he takes a shot, he really doesn't miss.*

"What would you know about masochism?" She retorted. "I have my reasons for dating someone like Tyrone, just like **you** have reasons for going back to Beth again and again."

"That's different." He snapped back. "Her and I have a mutual understanding."

"Boring fuck buddies? That sounds really fulfilling." She went back to her painting, noting his frustration. "Does my answer really frustrate you so?"

"He's not special." He rolled his eyes. "Dating someone so opposed to your authentic self is torture at best. I rather get sex from someone who respects me instead of a man that is actively trying to change who I am."

She floored him with a glare. *I've had enough of this, especially since you're the reason I'm dating Tyrone in the first place.*

"Well, I'm not dating you, am I?" She grew weary of his attitude. "Any other 'valid' criticisms?"

He placed his palate down with a sigh. From the way he stood up Michelle expected him to walk out on her. "How long have we known each other?"

That question surprised her. "Counting six...no, seven years since ninth grade. Why?"

Osi rolled his neck with a moan. "I **know** he's not your type so why do you torture yourself?"

She placed her tools down, avoiding eye contact. "How would you know what my type looks like?"

"You did stick your tongue down my throat so I can assume I would be your type." He smirked.

She closed her eyes. One hand lifted her glasses off her nose while the other massaged the bridge where they were resting. "You want to do this now? We were seventeen. I was ovulating. Two years before that you almost got killed for telling my Dad that you wanted to 'fuck his daughter for the rest of your life'."

He looked out the window. She saw that his cheeks were burning red as he crossed his arms. "I was fifteen and I **wanted** to say 'I want to make her happy in our short lives'. My intrusive thought came out before the logical one."

"Good thing your Dad was fast enough to save you." Michelle snorted. "We both fumbled but we made it out alive! You're with Beth and I'm with Tyrone. Any other points you want to make?"

He stared her down, eyes traveling down her frame. Michelle shivered under his gaze feeling overly exposed. She knew he could find every small detail in her body posture, expressions, clothing choices...his eye for detail was well trained. She looked everywhere in the room to alleviate being examined so heavily.

Why does he look good when he's all worked up like this? Lord, why did you make the lanky, awkward boy grow up to be a fine-as-wine man with a naughty streak? My literal weakness in the flesh.

"How long has it been since you were squirming on my living room floor?" She felt his words cut right to her heart.

"Three months? Has Tyrone even come close to making you feel that way?"

All the air left her lungs immediately. She silently sat down her brush and palate on the small table nearby before taking three deep body breaths. Behind closed eyes she saw him leaned over, pleasure written on his features as they gave in to each other again and again throughout the night. Her body flushed in response to the memories that were occupying her mind.

He really went there huh? Just cut me to the core after saying it was a secret? Oh, I got his ass.

"You really went there right now." A manic chuckle erupted from her lips as she looked directly in his eyes. "If I wasn't so nice I would—

"You would what?" He raked his eyes over her body. "Come closer and say it. I dare you."

He wants to get into some trouble. Look at his eyes. He wants me to come over there.

"Careful." She cleared her throat, choosing to retreat for the moment. "You don't want Tyrone to catch you eying his **girlfriend** do you?"

His brown eyes darkened under the studio lights. "He can sit down and watch for all I care."

Oh God, he looks like he wants to eat me! This is not the time to freeze like a deer on the side of the road.

"I can sit down and watch what, **Lee**?" Tyrone's voice interrupted the couple. Of course, the building wasn't locked so students could come and go as they wished.

"My name starts with an 'O'." Osi cut his eyes at the other man. "I can't believe they admitted you in college."

"Okay and?" Tyrone smirked but the light didn't reach his eyes. "I just came by to walk you home in the dark **baby**."

"I was going to walk her back when she was ready. You weren't really needed but that's really sweet that you came by." Osirion smiled.

They're about to get into it right here, aren't they?

"I don't trust you alone with **my** woman Shan." Tyrone grabbed her bag from the floor. "I'll tote this sweetie."

"Gentlemen." Michelle broke the tension. "Behave before you two start to break something way too expensive to replace. I need to get back to my room anyway."

"I'll see you tomorrow for our walk to class?" Osi smiled at her, eyes soft and tender.

"You know it." She gave her friend a quick hug and walked out with her man. Those two going at each other wasn't anything new.

This obviously isn't going to get any better. Either I need some sort of ingenious plan for them to see eye to eye...or I'll have to choose one over the other.

"I think your relationship with him is inappropriate." Tyrone broke through her thoughts. "I saw the way he was looking at you."

Michelle wanted to feel guilty because Tyrone had a point. She should break it off with Osirion immediately, but she felt flattered. She tried to use a guilt-ridden voice with him. "We're friends. Sure, there was some tension in the past but we grew out of it."

Yeah...like the recent past but still in the past technically. Does thirty seconds count as far enough in the past? My love life is in shambles...

Tyrone wasn't convinced naturally. "In the past? Do you think I'm as blind as you are without glasses?"

He didn't have to say it like that.

"It's still there but I didn't go over and throw myself at him." She let out a deep breath. "I've gotten better at setting boundaries."

*Good girl. Be a good girl. You **are** the good girl. You're **his** good girl...stop thinking like that!*

"Why didn't you two just fuck in high school?" He glared. "Like seriously? Sure, you were with that white dude but you had four years together?"

"It was never the right time." She looked at his disbelief. "Usually, one of us would be dating someone else. Besides, our families have some outstanding beef with each other. Things just never went our way in high school."

"Tell him to keep it pushing now." He took a gulp of soda. "You know the one thing that he wants. You're just a Black woman fetish with a nice face for him."

The comment always managed to take the breath from her lungs. It was a harsh, cold way of saying she wasn't worth any romantic effort from Osirion's point of view. Not the first time she'd heard it but it made Michelle frown. "Thanks a lot. **That** makes me feel special."

Tyrone groaned. "I didn't mean it like that. I'm just sayin'...you understand."

"What are you sayin'?" Michelle stopped in front of her building. "I want you to tell me."

Tyrone looked around, avoiding eye contact. "I don't like him, and I never will."

"I can see that." She crossed her arms. "I'm heading in. I'll see you tomorrow."

"Good night." Tyrone leaned in for a good night kiss but she stepped back. "Are you still offended by what I said?"

"Good night Tyrone." Michelle walked inside, closing the door behind her.

"**O**sirion!" Tyrone flagged the shorter man standing in front of the building. He was holding two hot cups of steaming hot coffee. It was a quarter past seven and Tyrone knew he had another fifteen minutes before Michelle would be joining. "We need to have a small chat."

"So you can pronounce my name." The shorter man bristled with a deep frown. His shoulder length hair was tied back in a low ponytail, while his fingernails were painted black. Tyrone's stomach rolled in a combination of anger and disgust. "Why are **you** here so early?"

"I'll get straight to the point then. Stop bringing my girl coffee in the mornings." Tyrone made a mental note to thank Lisa for her invasive snooping. Tyrone knew about his morning coffee walks with Michelle but didn't know which days they would do so together.

"Why should I?" Osirion smirked right in his face. "We both have morning classes three times a week. I get her coffee before we walk to campus together. You should know your girlfriend can be cranky without a coffee boost this early."

"Oh, I know but my problem is why do you keep doing it?" Tyrone glared. "Something like **this** is her boyfriend's job."

"Yet you're not clocked in and ready to go," he admonished. "Do you even know how much cream and sugar she likes? What's her favorite blend? Type of coffee drink?"

Tyrone glared. The questions should have been simple, but he was honestly clueless. "I don't pay attention to small stuff like that."

"I'm sure coffee isn't the only thing you don't pay attention to." Osirion's words cleaved into Tyrone's pride.

"I have something **much** more effective than coffee." He had to regain some of his ego at the shorter man's expense. "An all-natural supplement that can wake her up without all the effects of caffeine. Maybe I should sleep over more often so she can get that energy boost..."

"I don't want to hear how you manage to get her to touch you." Osirion looked like he was about to throw up. "Are you done?"

Can't compare with the bigger man, can you?

Love was a battlefield for Tyrone, and he was going to use every advantage he had.

"Stay away from my woman." Ty locked eyes with him. "You lusting after her is embarrassing. Have some pride."

"Lust?" Osi took a sip of his own drink. "I guess that's the only emotion you can identify in your sad life."

Ty resisted the urge to connect his fist with the man's nose. "You just have a black woman fetish so go after another and leave mine alone."

"A fetish?" The look he sent Tyrone was filled with hostility. "It's really convenient for you to say that my desire for her is some perverse longing due to her skin tone?"

"You're Asian." Tyrone pointed out. "A man like you can't build a kingdom with a beautiful, Black queen."

"Why settle for a measly kingdom when she can have an empire?" Osirion didn't back down. "We've known each other for years. We've fought, laughed, and cried with each other longer than our other friends. I've stepped back *every single time* she wanted to go and find love and even supported her through the heartbreak."

Tyrone cut in. "So, you are stuck in the 'friend zone'. Stop bitching about it. Simping gets you nowhere."

"Let me finish moron!" He took another sip. "I support my friend because it's the right thing to do. I see her as a human that can make her own choices. I don't have to agree with them but I'm not going to leave her if **she** wants me to be close."

"Don't actions speak louder than words?" Tyrone stepped closer, using his height against the shorter man. "She has a king to care for her now. She doesn't need a jester anymore."

"...you are no king, emperor, or pharaoh." Osirion stared upwards. "You are just a man-child that is insecure as hell because I *can* make her forget you even existed."

"You talk big for someone with such a little dick." When in doubt, Tyrone could always go with this old, tired stereotype. Even more so because he was an outlier below the waist.

He flashed Tyrone an evil sweet smile. "Ask your girlfriend about the size and stop telling her what to do. She's the only reason why I can even tolerate your presence."

What the hell does that mean? I drop my pants, and she runs away. There is no way they...

Tyrone pushed down the jolt of shock with a straight face. "Michelle wouldn't be happy if I beat you into the ground."

"Wouldn't be the first time since I'm the one she calls when you eventually do something stupid." Osi stared. "In the short amount of time you've been with her she's been angry and horribly stressed out. You two are not meant to be together, and it's only a matter of time before it all ends."

Tyrone felt a pang of fear hit his chest. "Why don't I grab you by the hair and beat you senseless?"

"It is too early for this shit you two." Both men jumped. Michelle was tapping her foot irritated. The yoga pants and short top hugged her body just right as Tyrone swallowed. In masculine clothing he could resist eying what she had going on but in feminine clothes that didn't work. A small case was attached to her hip as she rolled her eyes.

"Coffee." Osi handed her a cup.

"Thank you Osi." Her eyes lit up in gratitude and she took a sip of the warm caffeine.

Tyrone hated the smile that graced her face. "Hey baby."

"Tyrone." Her voice was flat. No sadness. No anger. No annoyance. It was filled with nothing of substance.

It's only a matter of time. Osirion's words bounced about in Tyrone's head. She didn't care for him honestly. Tyrone wasn't stupid by any means. The suspicious gold necklace she now wore around her neck. The way her face lit up when her 'friend' was around. The excuses she gave here and there to persuade herself instead of accepting the truth in front of her eyes.

I'm not giving up the future mayor's daughter to this dude. She can open doors and take years off of my professional life. I'll just make her fall in love with me again, that's all.

Michelle and Osirion turned away to head towards their respective classes. Tyrone touched her elbow. "I'm sorry baby. What I said was out of pocket. I didn't mean to hurt your feelings."

"Thanks." Her face was straight, but he heard a bit of gratitude. "I'll see you later."

Tyrone looked as she walked away. Her gait held a gentle bounce as she conversed with the other man. Tyrone didn't even cross her mind anymore.

This is going to be harder than I thought.

"Oh, this feels so good." Tyrone grunted, burying an impressive ten and a half inches into Lisa's willing body. The woman yelped in pain but forced herself still to adjust.

"Go slowly." Lisa grunted, breathing deeply. "You're so big."

"I just need this." He grabbed her tense thighs and snapped his hips. There was nowhere for Lisa to run as he started a steady tempo. "You women don't understand men need sex. Michelle doesn't understand...but you do, don't you Lisa?"

She grunted deeply, concentrating on the sensations.

He went faster as the sound of slapping skin filled his dorm room. His grip on her thighs was tight as his fingers left imprints in her flesh. He closed his eyes and visualized his stubborn girlfriend. Black hair sprawled out on the pillow; eyes screwed shut as he took his pleasure.

"Ah!" Lisa yelled, a mixture of pain and pleasure.

He saw her eyes. Michelle's eyes full of surprise and shock in his mind. It's the same expression she had when he tried to have sex with her the first time in their relationship. Tyrone knew he was blessed in that department but what woman doesn't want a large man to satisfy her sexual needs?

The tightness wrapped around his shaft was too much. The wet heat was too much. He stared at Lisa and could see that same expression on Michelle's face in an instant, and it was too much. He came in strong spurts as he filled her to the hilt, holding her body flush against him.

Tyrone withdrew as he softened up with a grimace. It was a messy sight. Spurts of white coming out of her body, fluids tinged with streaks of red as Lisa wrapped her arms around herself. The red became stronger as her groaning became louder.

"Ow..." Lisa bared her teeth. She reached down to touch tender areas, seeing more blood than anything else. "I think something is wrong."

"What do you mean?" He wiped her down with a towel, starting to panic. Tyrone started to get Deja vu all over again.

Lisa tried to get up but crumpled in pain. Tyrone was able to catch her before she hit the floor. "I need to go to the hospital."

"Oh shit." Waves of guilt washed over his body. He cheated on Michelle but getting sex elsewhere made their sexless relationship bearable until she was comfortable enough to take on her full womanly duties. He only felt a little guilty about that, but Lisa really didn't look well. "Okay. Let's grab a dress and I'll drive you to the ER."

He truly hoped that Lisa wasn't permanently injured as she hobbled along, seeing a rivet of blood run down her leg.

I have to send another gift card and edible fruit arrangement to her hospital room. This is getting ridiculous. Are these women just too small for me?

EIGHT

The Head and the Heart

Twack! Twack! Twack!

Small, gauze wrapped fists hit against the worn canvas punching bag over and over. The rhythmic hitting should have calmed her mind but instead it allowed her to grow angrier.

Was I really this blind all this time? Or did I not care enough to see it?

Michelle and Tyrone immediately went to visit Lisa once they heard the bad news. She expected Lisa to welcome her with open arms but instead she burst out in tears once Lisa saw Michelle. It was so bad that Michelle excused herself from the room, leaving Tyrone with her distraught friend.

"Why is she here?" Lisa's voice carried through the crack in her room.

"She doesn't know." Tyrone hushed her. "It's cool, just calm down."

"What is this?" Lisa moved around in the bed. "A fruit bouquet?"

"A way of saying sorry." Tyrone lowered his shoulders. "For all of...this. I didn't mean to hurt you the other night..."

Michelle didn't mean to eavesdrop through the door but she was easily able to put everything together. Realizing that a man that doesn't get sex in his relationship might go out and cheat with another woman wasn't jarring, but the fact that it was her friend.

That's low. He could've picked anyone else but Lisa.

Another set of blows to the bag happened in quick succession as her anger rose. It wasn't enough to not arouse her or to even try to learn what she liked, but now he goes and has sex with her best friend behind her back as well?

Especially after I turned Osirion down on his birthday from fucking me straight through his floor?

The blow to her pride made everything even worse. She withdrew her fists and spun around to plant a solid roundhouse onto her target. The grating of the chain coupled with the swaying bag made her feel a tad bit better but not by much.

At least I can let out my anger at the gym.

"That was solid." A tall and rather pale figure walked towards her. "That kick. You do kickboxing pr anything like that?"

"I've taken a few years." She fixed him with a dismissive stare. "Self-defense classes growing up. I just needed to work out some stress."

"Nice." He didn't pick up on the hostility. "I'm Dante, president of the MMA club here on campus. You are?"

"Michelle." She shook his hand. "I'm not really looking to join right now. I just transferred over from Tech and I'm still sorting out my classes."

"What year are you supposed to be?" He ran a hand through his uneven red hair.

"I'm supposed to be a junior but three of my sophomore level classes didn't transfer." Michelle griped. "Had to retake two and substitute one here for the other credit to count. So, I'm a sophomore-junior this semester."

"That throws you off of graduation by a semester or so." He winced. "I know that feeling. I transferred out of state to go here."

"Ouch. I guess I could make it up in the summer or take an extra class in the Fall." Michelle walked over to her water bottle. "Which one is better?"

"Summer." He smiled. "One class does suck but it's better than to pile it on in the Fall. All the clubs and Greeks recruit in the Fall semester. You don't want to miss that fun."

"Thanks Dante." She slipped him a warm smile. "Do you have to join your club to use your equipment?"

"It helps but nah." He shook his head. "Free to all students, especially a cute one like you."

Michelle chuckled. "Flattery will get you nowhere, but thanks."

"Will it get me a spar?" He flexed his arms. "Just a small one? You look like you know what you're doing."

"You would spar with a woman?" She didn't hide her surprise. "That's a new one."

"Women can fight as well." Dante started to wipe down the equipment. "One small match. I like to find new opponents to stay fresh."

Interesting. Looks like his hands are rated 'E' for everyone.

"Sure." She shrugged. "Not right now but one day, why not?"

"Alright then Michelle." He pointed to a paper hanging near the entrance. "Just drop by during our hours and I'll probably be here. See you around."

"See ya, Dante." She waved him off as she left the building.

Break every chain...break—

Michelle fished her ringing phone from her purse. "Hey Mom!"

"Hey honey!" Tisha's voice came through loud on the other end. "I meant to call you sooner and see how you were adjusting to university. I'm sorry I got caught up with my move and everything."

"That's alright." Michelle sat down at a table. "You did have to move in such a short time. I'm just glad you found a good apartment on short notice."

"Thanks sweetie. How are you doing with everything?"

Michelle let out a long sigh. "Classes aren't giving me too much trouble. Sucks that I have to retake some of them but I'm only behind by a semester or so."

"Okay. How's living away from the family?"

"I like the freedom." Michelle cracked a smile. "Sure, I share a room with Angel but she's cool. We get along well so far."

"Sounds like everything is smooth sailing." Tisha chuckled. "I guess you don't need some sagely mother advice right now."

"I mean..." Michelle paused but pushed on. "I need some dating advice but that's so stereotypical."

So stereotypical it hurts. Men, men, men...ugh.

"Hey, that's what I'm here for!" Tisha tutted. "Give me your best shot and I'll try to help."

"Well, my boyfriend cheated on me with my best friend and put her in the hospital." Michelle opened up strong. "We went to visit, and I overheard some of their conversation."

"Oh hon, I'm so sorry!" Tisha groaned. "I told Tony that boy wasn't good enough for you! Your father never listens to me!"

"I'm madder at my friend betraying me than him stepping out and dipping in other ponds." Michelle sighed. "I really want someone else, but I shouldn't."

"Is it because he's a bad boy?" Tisha whispered over the line. "I know those types seem exciting but it's not worth it, I speak from experience. Get the humble type instead."

"It's Osirion. You know, from high school."

"Oh right, Akiko's oldest boy!" She let out a happy laugh before gasping. "Oh. Yeah, your father shot him in the face. How is he, by the way? I know you both took that leap year before enrolling in college."

"Oh, he's fine." Michelle coughed. "He's grown up rather well. Not that I'm looking but—

"Ah." Tisha let out a sagely noise. "Do you still love him?"

"Mom, he's my friend." Michelle whispered even though nobody outside was paying attention to her conversation.

"Fille, you know what I mean!" Tisha clicked her tongue. "Do you want to lick his lollipop or not?"

Oh my God, that's so out of pocket!

Michelle took the receiver away from her ear and just paused for a moment. She could hear her mother's loud cackle through her phone's speaker. "Mom, what is wrong with you? That's out of pocket!"

"You're finally an adult!" Tisha still was cracking up. "I can finally talk to you woman-to-woman. You still didn't answer though."

"Mom..." Michelle felt her hot cheeks with her fingers. "He's better at licking than I am."

"What?" She heard her mother almost stumble over a few noisy items. "He's...did you two finally have sex? It's about time—

"No!" Michelle yelled. "We...didn't go all the way...this is embarrassing."

"Alright, I think I see the issue." Tisha calmed down. "Can I tell you a story?"

"I already know how you and Dad met." Michelle yawned. "He was stationed at Jackson Barracks and you swooned over a man in uniform and eventually settled down."

"That's all true." Tisha chuckled. "But I never told you about the man before your Father. My real first love."

Michelle perked up. "Your real first love? Hold up."

"Yeah, we have been friends since grade school." Tisha let out a sigh. "My first boyfriend, my first kiss, my first sexual experience...very intense first love type things. For the longest he was it."

"Oh, then what happened?" Michelle didn't want to pry too much but curiosity caught her. "Did he break up with you?"

"I ran." Michelle could hear notes of shame in her mother's tone. "I got heavy into the Bible and saw my more...spiritual family as evil so I ran. Your father was my ticket out of my old life."

Silence stretched on as Michelle slowly digested every word that was said. "Oh. That's why we didn't see Gran growing up?"

"Yes." Tisha sighed. "By the time Yvette came along I reconnected with my family and friends, but it wasn't the same. Your grandmother forgave me, but our relationship has never been as close as the 'before times.'"

"What happened to your first love?"

"He moved on." Tisha sighed. "He got married, had children, lost his wife. He's a widower now. Ironically, we've been emailing back and forth and he's updating me on everything that's happened back home."

"That's kinda of a happy ending?" Michelle saw the lesson but wanted to remain optimistic.

"Is it?" Her mother's tone told a different story. "We talk about what could have been. He doesn't hate me anymore, but he's still hurt after all this time. Even in our mid-fifties we still love each other. Knowing he moved on and had a happy life with another woman tears me up on the inside. Plus...you three don't even have an idea about my culture."

"I mean..." Michelle couldn't argue. "We picked up on some French?"

"In secret! Your father wouldn't let me fully teach you three about my home. I relented to keep the peace, but I should have insisted. I literally broke generations of strong spirituality in my bloodline because I saw hoodoo as this long-standing evil that coursed through my blood like a curse. I can't say that this is a happy ending...but I do love my children and the years we had. Before everything fell apart Tony and Faithview was my loving home."

"I never had any idea." Michelle trailed off. "I just never thought of things that way."

"Of course not! My life choices are not anyone's burden to bear but my own." Tisha sighed. "I don't regret loving your father. We had three wonderful children and over thirty years together. I was a hardheaded eighteen-year-old when all of this started. I just don't want you to live with any regrets."

"So, are you saying to follow your heart? To use your head? That your choice of mate could determine your entire future?"

"The last one, mostly." Tisha clicked her tongue. "Tony was the riskier choice for me, but he was more acceptable than a multi-generational seeker of spirits. I wanted to travel outside my bubble and being a pastor's wife was an experience. Christians would not have accepted me as easily without my salvation story: the girl born in evil turning to God and cutting ties with all that she's known and loves to be a Christian. Powerful stuff for sure. I don't regret most of my choices, but I always wonder about what could have been."

"Even after all these years?"

"Yes." Tisha sighed. "Tyrone is your safe choice. The church loves him. Your father loves him. He's handsome, Christian, a bit dense but that will be remedied with time. He's not a bad choice besides the cheating and the other obvious flaw he seems to have. For the pastor's, and possibly future mayor's daughter, he's the safe one out of the two. He's also the one that doesn't resonate with your heart, but you can learn to love someone over time."

"So, like tolerating him until I do love him?" Michelle cringed. "That's kind of..."

"Off-putting?" Tisha laughed. "Your other option isn't a bad one. A handsome artist from another land that you've known for years. You two are so tight that being hit by a bullet couldn't break you two apart! That's one hell of a connection...plus you find him extremely attractive. Osirion is a good man that's been raised well. However, if you two do get together it will be hell before anyone accepts the two of you. Your father hates him and his family. His family dislikes you obviously. The church will hate him seeing that he's not Christian at all. Your relationship with each other will be easy because everything else around you is going to be a struggle."

"Those are two drastically different options."

"Very much." Tisha laughed. "Enjoy being a young woman but keep these things in mind. I'm not telling you what to do but think long and hard about it."

"Thanks, Mom." Michelle checked the time. "I have some things to do but I'll give you a call when I'm free."

"I'll be here." Tisha kissed over the line. "Take care, and I love you Zaria."

"Love you too, Mom."

S oft brown curls are the first thing everyone notices, then a dazzling smile and olive toned skin. Even as the sun sat on front campus Michelle saw the tallish figure in front of the small gaggle of instrument holders. "Gregory."

He showed her his pearly whites. "Zaria, since you want to use my government name and everything."

"Alright, Greg." Michelle fiddled with the pads of her flute. "What's good with you?"

"Just getting ready to graduate." He sat down alongside her. He opened a large case on the wooden stage and started to rearrange his saxophone. "The final project for our major is to be published or to give a public reading of a work, just so you know."

"Makes sense." Michelle sighed. "I just got here and you're on the way out. Do they have your replacement for drum major?"

"Tryouts will be held in the Fall." He shrugged. "If you're not too busy you should think about it. It's not too different from what you did at your Pop's church."

"Assistant music director and drum major are two different things." She looked out at the moving crowd. "What are we playing for Homecoming?"

"A few songs. Nothing too serious that you shouldn't be able to play, Preacher Girl." He grinned. "You'll be joining everyone else within ninety minutes."

"My Dad is the preacher, not me." The two stopped their chatter to warm up for their performance.

Michelle didn't expect to see Lisa as she walked between the various booths and different smells of grilled food and sweet drinks. The other woman had bags starting to form under her eyes and her once blonde hair was now a shade of bubblegum pink.

She's not looking too good.

"Go to hell Tyrone!" Michelle saw Lisa douse her boyfriend in a red punch before storming off into the crowd. All she could do was sigh at Tyrone's shocked expression as everyone jeered at his humiliation.

Am I even surprised at this point?

"Tyrone." Michelle called him over with a finger. "We need to talk."

"Babe." She stood aside as he tried to wring out his shirt before the drink dyed it too much. "I don't know why she went crazy on me."

"Did you have sex with Lisa?" She cut off whatever story he was about to spin. "I heard you apologizing when we went to visit. What are you sorry for?"

"How can you say that?" He sucked his teeth. "I don't know—

"Just stop." Michelle held up a hand. "You're not getting it from me for almost a year now. I know there's self-care, but you don't seem to have the patience needed to last for that long solo."

To his credit Tyrone stopped before letting out a deep sigh. "Yeah, I slept with her. For a minute but the last time was the worst one. I didn't mean to do all that but I kinda...lost control."

"The last time?" Michelle turned into the news. "How long has this been going on?"

"Like six months." He shrugged. "Before we transferred here but yeah."

"So, the second half of our relationship?" Michelle thought back with a frown.

That makes sense. Things were less annoying in the beginning...

"Right." She saw him bounce on his heels. "That makes sense when I look back at it. You are trash."

"Spare me you hypocrite." He turned on her. "You didn't think I noticed that piece you suddenly started to wear after November? I know he fucked you at least once!"

She laughed. Michelle let out a light laugh at his anger. "You really think I had sex with Osi with the way we act around each other?"

"Yeah!" He pointed to her jewelry. "That's a couple of stacks, at least. Looks like solid gold around your neck. That's like 12k? 14k?"

"It's 18k." Michelle corrected him. "And he wanted me to have it. I tried to give it back, but he refused."

That's a reasonable assumption.

"If we had sex, don't you think he would rub it in your face?" She asked him. "He hates you. If he bent me like a pretzel I know Osi would be petty enough to tell you, in detail at that."

"Well..." Tyrone stopped to think.

"Even better, he would draw it out and send it to you through the mail or something." She chuckled. "He's a very talented artist, after all."

"Shit." Tyrone nodded his head. "I hate to say it but you're right. I would never spend that kind of money on a woman I haven't bust wide open yet."

"I can see." Michelle sighed. "We're done Tyrone. Let's just break up now and go our separate ways."

"Michelle..."

"It's over." Michelle walked away before he could respond.

At least it's done.

I know I broke up with him, but he could have taken me back to my dorm. I caught the shuttle here and they stopped running due to mechanical issues...

Michelle kept to herself as she sat in the backseat. Osirion didn't mind giving her a ride to his place, since their buildings were close enough that they shared the same parking lot. Apparently, she was intruding on the couple's free time, but it wouldn't be that long of a ride...

"He just left her at the concert **this** late?" Beth shook her head. "I wonder what happened to make him leave her without a second thought?"

"He's just an asshole." Osirion's tone was tight, cutting with short answers. "Just wait until I see him."

"You're going to do what?" Beth cut him off. "Tell him how he should treat his own girlfriend?"

"Beat some sense into him." His voice was thick with anger.

I'm not trying to cause them trouble.

Michelle wore glasses but wasn't blind. Beth didn't hate her, but she had plenty of reason not to like her either.

I am definitely the other woman in this situation. Maybe if I close my eyes and zone out this ride will go faster?

Homecoming weekend was guaranteed fun. Her older brother Michah usually came over to link up with old friends and ogle the new batch of freshmen that came in. Disturbing, especially with his leadership position back at their home church, but their Dad was happy that his trouble-making son was doing something positive with his life.

It was all good until Tyrone and Michah got too much drink in their systems. Michah was a single man, and Tyrone was definitely enjoying his new single status under the influence. The concert was lots of fun until she realized that her brother was too drunk to drive, and Tyrone had left in his car without any indication.

I know I caught the bus over, but he did say he would give me a ride...before I dumped him.

Ty was too drunk to be on the road in any capacity, but Michelle was good to get behind the wheel. She prowled around the parking lot, assuming that he just went to sleep in his car waiting for her. She had to call him three times, just for him to tell her to walk to her room because he was almost asleep in his dorm.

Faking sleep in the back of the car third wheeling was better than walking the streets after two in the morning with campus being two miles away.

That small walk in the day is much different than in the middle of the night.

"Look at you!" Beth cackled in her seat. "I've never seen you so angry before! Your arm is shaking!"

"Shut up." His tone was low and steady.

Beth laughed some more. "You still owe me a night, remember? I'm cashing in."

"Tonight?" He sounded surprised.

"Of course." Michelle could hear the slyness in Beth's voice. "Michelle can sleep on the couch, and you can take her back in the morning if she doesn't want to walk. You're going to need some relief before you burst a blood vessel."

Osi made a dismissive noise but didn't reply. The rest of the ride was quiet and short as they came to a stop.

Let me just fake being asleep and sneak out while they're busy in the bedroom.

He propped the seat up and gently carried Michelle bridal style into the large dorm, only pausing to open the door. Her dorm was a short five-minute walk from his and the full moon would illuminate her path.

It's not even that cold outside right now. Just a quick hop and a skip.

"So much for getting over..." She heard him whisper as he laid her on the couch. He gently cradled her head and placed a pillow underneath. The heavy blanket he draped on top of Michelle was comforting, leaving her with a gentle kiss on the forehead before going into his personal room with Beth.

The silence hung in the air like static electricity before a storm. Michelle heard a long groan coming from the cracked door, followed by a slew of slaps against skin. Beth was moaning loud enough for Michelle to hear as she covered her eyes on the couch.

Petty, but I can't begrudge her.

In her shoes Michelle would have left it wide open so that the other woman could see the production.

It's not like we were waiting on each other. I have Tyrone constantly in his face day after day. I can only be mad at my own inability to take action, after all.

Their moans and grunts were getting louder with no regard to their guest in the shared living area. Michelle closed her eyes, hearing Osirion pant and curse in the next room. His voice was deep and strained, a cruel edge to his usual gentle cadence. She felt her face heat up, electricity traveling up and down her body under the blanket.

Oh God, am I getting turned on right now? Why...

Michelle groaned from mortification, careful not to catch the couple's attention. With the speed and sound of skin slapping against one another she could walk in and not get their attention. Her hands traced her body as the rhythmic thumping increased in tempo. Her mouth went dry as the couple was screaming through the wooden door.

If I walked in with them, could I join?

Michelle squashed the errant thought before her body could act upon it. Her fingers cupped her wet panties, her middle finger thumping against her heated lips in beat with the other two. Her imagination was running wild as she bit her lip to keep quiet.

Looks like another entry for my document of erotic writing. I should be thinking of a pen name to publish these under.

The clapping noises suddenly stopped; a pair of loud shouts filled the air. They had finished together, leaving Michelle frustrated and thirsty. She didn't dare finish herself and catch their attention in the now quiet dorm. The door swung open as Michelle snapped her eyes shut in the awkward position, hand still stuffed down her pants.

Don't look at me...don't look at me...

"That was fun." Beth laughed. "Do you feel better?"

"A little." Osi chuckled. "I appreciate it."

"Well, you know the saying: if you can't love the one you want, love the one you're with." The other woman sighed. Michelle didn't dare move.

"You should tell him before it's too late." His voice was quiet. "I know I'm not the one your heart sings for day after day."

"Follow your own advice." She laughed. "See you around or not. I might just go and confess later in the week. Who knows?"

The main door quietly shut. Michelle struggled to not open her eyes. She felt his stare on her burning through the blanket. His footsteps circled her until she could visualize him standing in front of her.

Should I let him know I'm awake or...

"Look at you." His voice was soft and closer than she realized. "Do you dream of me like I dream of you?" She felt his hands massage her scalp, fingers brushing through her loose coils. A moan slipped out of her making him freeze. She tried to even out her breathing once more to give the illusion of sleep.

Uh oh.

"Aishi teru." *(I love you.)* He whispered softly against her temple, breath caressing her skin. "If only I can tell you when you're awake..."

She felt his body heat move away from her, followed by the soft closing of his bedroom door. Michelle opened her eyes and stared at the plain ceiling in a state of shock. His voice played over and over in her head as the sound of rushing water cut through the silence.

Do I stay here? Do I get up?

Michelle suddenly had the urge to get some water. Her chest was tight like a snake was coiling around her body, slowly squeezing the air from her lungs.

How could he say that after having Beth like that? How could he touch another woman and then make such a sweet confession?

She grabbed a glass from the kitchen and filled it with cool water. A frown marred her features as she gulped down her drink.

Am I jealous? That's ridiculous! I don't get jealous, right?

Michelle could identify the anger and irritation that had filled her veins. It was a burning, sick feeling in her stomach akin to a tensing animal waiting to strike. She wanted to grab him by his long hair and...slap or kiss him.

Why not both?

"Oh, you're awake." Her eyes snapped to the deep voice. Osi was standing near the fridge wearing a pair of sweats and smelling of fragrant soap. "Did my shower wake you?"

Your shower?

"You did wake me up, but it wasn't your shower." Her voice was bitter even to her ears. "But I'm glad you cleaned off after your...activities."

"Ah." He crossed his arms over his chest. She saw his little smirk on his lips. "You were awake then."

"Yes, I was awake." She looked over at him. Long, wet hair over a satisfied face and a sturdy body. He wasn't too bulky or lean either way, but he was very attractive.

It's not realistic to think he wouldn't get with other women.

"Are you upset?"

"No." Her voice was sharp. "Why would I be?"

"I don't know." He slowly walked closer to her, leaning on a counter. "But you are."

Great. We know each other too well.

Michelle glared at him for a minute, but he didn't back down from her eyes. "Be quiet. I'm not upset."

"You're jealous." His voice held a bit of surprise. "I can't believe it, but you are."

"Happy about it?" She decided to give in. "You seem to be."

"A little." His smile irritated her even more. "Nice to see you're not immune to such feelings."

"I'm not made of stone, you know." She glared at him.

"I know you're too soft to be made of stone. I thought you were too *holy* for such thoughts to enter your mind." He rolled his eyes. "But are we not *just* friends? You have no reason to be jealous in that case."

"You're right." Michelle suddenly smiled. "I have no reason as your friend. Just as you have no reason to be jealous if I went over to Tyrone's place and got some tender care."

Now his own warm brown eyes darkened as he sneered at her. Osi leaned close to her ear. "Why would you need some 'tender care', Zaria? Get a little excited when you were eavesdropping?"

He put two and two together huh? Damn it.

"What business is it of yours?" She whispered into his ear. "It's not like you could do it instead."

They both knew she was bluffing but her comment had its intended effect. He pulled back from her ear and stepped forward to tower over her. "Try me."

She looked up at him and her throat went dry. Everything was a lot. Breaking up, third wheeling, jealousy issues, and now Osi was ready to rip her clothes off? Her eyes pricked at the corners as she squeezed them shut.

"Michelle?" She heard his question after the first tear traveled down her cheek. "I didn't mean to make you cry."

"It's just everything." Michelle sniffed as another tear traveled down her face. "I'm just...overwhelmed."

His arms wrapped around her shoulders and Michelle was pressed into his warm chest. She relaxed into his body as he spoke. "It's alright. I'm right here."

"Thank you." Her voice was muffled but it was worth taking in his scent of sandalwood and lavender. "Especially after all of this."

"You really were jealous, weren't you?"

She groaned. "I mean I broke up with my cheating ex and almost got off that couch and did some...unholy things with, or to, y'all so sure."

"Wait, cheating ex?" She felt him tense. "When did this happen?"

"I mean he cheated a while ago, but I broke up with him tonight." She nuzzled into his warmth. "If you have some ice cream I can tell you about it on the couch."

"I have ice cream." His lips touched her ear. "We can talk and—

"You're not getting lucky tonight." Michelle laughed. "You already dipped into the ocean once. Don't be greedy."

"Alright." He laughed. "Not tonight."

He annoyed her. He annoyed her more than poorly written soccer mom control porn being passed off as a romance story. She groaned in frustration while being splashed by the bouncing rain. The weather was just as bad as her mood, and she managed to get stuck outside the Le Marché Créole in a storm.

Tyrone doesn't take no for an answer, does he?

Streaks of lightning danced around in the night sky. She had made the reservation for their one-year anniversary over a month in advance, before Michelle found out about his infidelity. Le Marché Créole translated to 'The Creole Market' and it was the fanciest restaurant within walking distance from campus. The small eatery was in high demand for graduations, visiting parents, special events, and anniversaries of all kinds.

Dinner was going to be on my dime, and it would've been a shame to waste my reservation because of Tyrone.

For a while Michelle ate alone at her table for two. Some might see it as sad but with all of her romantic drama going on a little quiet was a nice change. A few minutes into her appetizer a gentle hand was placed on her shoulder.

"Hey chica." Angel gave her a gentle smile. "What are you doing here alone?"

"Just eating." Michelle greeted both her roommate and the pale Goth that Angel had brought with her. "You two can join if you want. I'm flying solo for the night."

"Sure, if you don't mind." Angel sat down as a waiter came with a third chair. "Michelle, this is my girl Raven I was telling you about. Baby, this is my roommate."

"Nice to meet you." Michelle took in the pale woman's dark makeup. Raven wore an almost overwhelming amount, but it was flawless on her.

"Nice to meet you too."

The three women had a good time talking and eating on a warm Spring night. The weather was perfect for walking and Michelle waved the couple off when they decided to leave for the evening with a smile.

I should have taken them up on that ride before they left.

Michelle sighed. Tyrone had texted her once afterwards about 'being more feminine and giving' or some shit like that. Nothing about an apology or any other explanation for his actions. He had plenty to say about her lack of interest in him and how they should 'fight for their love' and not give up so easily. . Was it childish that she didn't want to call Tyrone on their one year anniversary to get her out of a raging storm? Sure, but she didn't want to see his face. She didn't want to hear his reasoning. She didn't want to petition her point of view on every little thing like he was her long-lost son.

I need to either start walking or text a ride to get out of the rain. Let's see if he's free right now.

Hey Sweetie. Are you free?

I'm just relaxing in my room. What's wrong?

I'm just stuck outside Le marché créole in the rain.

Why? You didn't invite me!

I'll tell you about it. Please come and pick me up?

I'll be there soon. You better have a good reason.

Yeah, yeah. I'll see you soon, Sweetie.

See you soon, Love.

"There you are!" She jumped from the closeness of his voice. "What are you doing out in this weather in a dress?"

"It was my anniversary, and I didn't want to waste a reservation." She let out an awkward chuckle.

"Ah. Well, that's actually nice that he didn't cancel it." Osirion walked up to her holding a large umbrella.

"I'm the one that made it." She took his offered arm as they walked towards his car. "It would have been a shame not to go, and it did give me some needed 'me time.'"

It's been two weeks since her courses have taken their revenge, and her workload seemed to double. Between the two core classes she had left over from tech, the two courses in her Creative Writing major, tutoring in the Writing Lab, and using what little time she had for food, sleep, and martial arts practice Michelle hadn't seen Osirion in a minute after Homecoming. The plus side was that she also didn't see much of Tyrone as well. She figured that everyone was swamped with mid-terms as the late March transitioned into April.

"I'm glad you got the chance for a peaceful night." She quelled the flutter of her heart as he helped her in his car. He closed the door after her and circled around to get in the driver's side.

He's still the same sweet guy I've always known. I hope I'm as perfect for him as he is for me.

"Thanks for getting me." The ride back was short and pleasant. Traffic made it longer than it should have but neither seemed to mind.

"I wasn't going to leave you stranded." His fingers tapped against the wheel. "Next time I pick you up, grab me something to eat."

"I can do that." She looked at the water running down the window.

"Do you want to go to my room for the night or your own?"

"Angel already left with her date, so your place will be fine." Michelle laughed. "I would hate to interrupt their time together."

"You don't want to walk into something that would scar you for life." He let out a laugh.

"You are hilarious." She rolled her eyes. "I must preserve my innocence."

"Oh, really now?" His voice carried something that she couldn't figure out. "You can't run forever. Everyone loses that eventually."

You can't run forever.

"Perhaps." Michelle gave him a smile. "At least I know someone I trust enough to...help me lose it."

"Ah." She saw him clear his throat as his hand tightened on the wheel. "You should be more careful in what you say."

"Why is that?" She used as much charm she could to portray complete innocence. "I'm just a young, church going girl."

"Keep pushing me and you'll find out."

That made her ears heat up pleasantly as she smiled. "I can't wait and see."

They both walked into his dorm. He flipped the lights on in the kitchen and rummaged through the drawers. He walked over to start a pot of coffee. He poured them two cups, fitting her coffee the way she liked it before they walked into his room. "How have midterms been treating you?"

"I've been so busy lately. Adala is more challenging than Tech. I haven't had time to hang out with anyone to be honest." She took a seat on the corner of his bed. His room was simple and spacious but what caught her eye was a hanging curtain blocking her view in one of the corners. She was curious but knew not to be noisy.

"That's a shame that he can't give to you the way you give to him." Osi shook his head. "If I knew you were free, I would have taken you out myself."

"That's really sweet but I'm sure you're glad for the opportunity to rest." She gave him a smile. "I've missed you."

"I missed you too." He took her cup and set it on his desk. "You're still wearing the necklace I gave you."

Her hand touched the solid gold serpent wrapped around her neck. "Of course. It's a beautiful piece and it really goes with a lot of my wardrobe. Why would I take it off?"

Guilt suddenly crossed his face, and he looked down. "Maybe you should."

"Oh?" She didn't hide her surprise. "You did insist that I accepted it in the first place."

"I know." He stood up and gently took the necklace from her.

How is he going to take something back months after giving it to me? Oh nah!

She balled up her fists to keep herself from hitting him. "If you didn't want me to have it in the first place…"

"That's not it. I gave it to you because I was selfish." He turned it around in his hands with a sad smile. "I meant it for you but…"

She saw he was conflicted as a brief silence filled the room. Her anger tempered down just a little bit to mix with concern. "What's wrong with it?"

"Nothing!" His ears were turning red. "I should have given this gift in front of our families…and you would give me a gift as well."

She tilted her head, bells going off in her head already. "Why? What did I accept from you?"

"It's not anything bad." He went to defend himself. "Plus, I took it back so as far as you're concerned the engagement is null and void."

Her face went blank as it suddenly clicked in her head. This was something that happened in romance novels or fantasy stories that pitted star-crossed lovers against each other, not in real life.

The way our families hate each other I'm not surprised to be honest.

"Osirion." She got up and gave him a short slap across his head. "You gave me a betrothal gift before we even started dating?"

"Hey!" He rubbed the back of his head. "That's why I took it back! I just...forgot myself for a minute."

"For several months." She glared at him. "Halloween was over four months ago. A whole season has passed."

"I remember the entire night, thank you." He smirked at her. "Definitely my favorite birthday so far."

"You better try God before you step to me." She crossed her arms with a smirk. "I remember just how sweet and vulnerable you looked."

"I'm glad you have a good memory." He laughed right at her. "Do you remember begging me to take you on the floor? You were pleading so sweetly—-

She felt the smugness leave her body as she cut him off. "You don't have to remind me; I was there! It was just for one night."

"I know." He placed the necklace in the middle of his desk. "I did say one night only. It was a good night, but still just one."

It could be more than one, you know. We could have a part two...you know you want to...

"You're doing it again." He chuckled as he stood up. "Arguing in your head."

"I'm not arguing again." She let out a chuckle. "Just remembering, that's all."

He leaned down, taking a whiff of her perfume. She smelled like toasted caramel, and he tensed up. "You never did answer my question."

I guess it's about time we got this out of the way finally. I don't want to right now, but we can't keep running around each other.

"Go on." She placed a hand over his, giving him a gentle squeeze. "Say what's on your mind."

"Why did you start dating Tyrone?" It looked painful for him to push the question out his mouth.

She took note of his appearance. His eyes were searching for something in hers. His hand kept tapping on his knee almost like a nervous tick. His black tank top stood out against his skin; the color seemed to match his darker mood. Michelle had to put him out of his misery. "You really want to know why?"

"I asked, didn't I?" His patience was shot as he looked back at her. "Go on, tell me the truth."

"I wanted to forget you." She stepped back at his shocked expression. "It's true. He asked me out, but I accepted because I wanted you out of my head."

"You could have told me if you didn't want my friendship anymore." The pain in his eyes made her heart ache. "I can take rejection."

"That's not what I said or wanted." She took off her glasses, massaging her temples. "I always want you around silly. I just—

I'm going to have to spit it out, but why is it so hard?

"Just what?" He leaned in closer to her. She felt her face warming up as she observed the moonlight from the window falling on his face.

"I needed to forget you." Her heart sped up in her chest, but she continued. "No woman should be pining after a taken man. I saw that you were happy with Beth and...I knew my jealousy would eventually get the better of my emotions. So, I set out to move on."

Reasonable logic.

He listened to her reasoning, not showing any emotion on his face. "Did it work, at least for a short time?"

"For a little bit it did work." She locked eyes with him. "For a while I could be happy for you and be happy for myself. At least until I got to know Tyrone better and realized this wasn't going to be an easy way to distract myself..."

"You hide it well." He looked her up and down. "All this time you were just seething with jealousy then. Why not steal me away from Beth if you felt that way?"

She narrowed her eyes at him. "What goes around, comes around. Besides, I try to be a decent person."

He gave her a small smile. "You're better than me, I'll admit that. You should take your clothes off right about now."

Her eyes darted around the quiet room back to him. "E-excuse me?"

"You're wet." He motioned to her spot on his bed. "I don't mind changing the sheets, but I don't want to soak through the mattress with rainwater."

He did that on purpose.

"Oh right!" She jumped up. She obviously forgot about that, shuffling out of her blouse, pants, and shoes. "Do you have a washer and dryer?"

He stared as she stood in her purple sports bra and matching boxers, cut to show off her pear-shaped body. It wasn't until he licked his lips that she thought about how standing half naked was affecting him. "...yes. I'll go and start the washer."

I am really that comfortable around him to get half naked without a single thought about it.

"Your undergarments?" He motioned at her.

She patted herself down and groaned. They were damp as well, but they were all she had to cover herself. "What am I going to wear?"

"You can wear one of my shirts. It'll cover you." He shrugged. "My boxers probably wouldn't fit you though."

"I'll take a shirt and a shower." She went over to his dresser, bending over to go through for a shirt. "If you're going to stare at my butt you could try to hide it."

He snapped the band of her boxers with a laugh. "You're wet. I'm sure it's the rain, right?"

"No actually it's from that erection that wants to pierce me like a needle." She bumped him with her hip, making him back up. "I'll be in the shower. You can get my bra and panties at the door."

I know I shouldn't tease him, but I can't help it. I enjoy seeing him squirm.

His bathroom was a standard one. The shower had a frosted glass door so you couldn't see completely through it. Michelle stripped nude and cracked the door. "Here you go."

"Thank you." He took her clothes from her hand and walked away.

She turned the water on and adjusted the temperature until it was steamy in the small room. She got in and let the hot water ease her chilled body. "Oh, this feels so good. Now what soap to use..."

Right. This isn't my shower.

She groaned at her forgetfulness but paused as the door opened. She peeked out from her end to be greeted with a washcloth and an amused Osi.

"I put a towel on the toilet lid. You can use the blue body wash." He chuckled. "I'll be waiting so I can take my turn."

"Why wait when you can join me?" She moved over with a cackle. "It's your bathroom, after all."

Osi was about to reply but a loud noise made both of them jump. He went out of the bathroom as the pounding continued from the main door.

"Open the damn door!" The voice was male, loud enough for Michelle to groan from the bathroom.

Damn it, Tyrone! What do you want now?

Breaking Up

Two distinct voices were arguing back and forth, increasing in volume. She jumped out the water and dried herself furiously.

How did Tyrone even find out where I was?

Michelle looked herself over in the mirror one last time. Messy updo, wearing a large T shirt, no socks, and coming out of a steaming hot shower. The optics right now were horrible on her anniversary.

From the jump he's probably going to call me a cheater or some variety of whore. I can deal with this. Let's hope he's not drunk.

She walked out of the bathroom and stood in the living room. Tyrone and Osirion were having an epic stare down while Darius stood on the side, poised as if to stop any physical confrontation if needed.

"Tyrone!" She caught his attention. "What are you doing here?"

"It's our anniversary, you hoe!" His voice was strong and full of hurt. "I know you were mad at me but damn!"

Didn't even last five seconds!

"We broke up stupid." She rolled her eyes. "How did you find me in a raging storm?"

Lighting came crashing down from the skies, illuminating the room for a brief second. The pouring rain would be soothing if not for the drama inside.

"I called around obviously." Tyrone glared. "Angel picked up and told me to go to hell, but she slipped where you went earlier. I just asked how you left and traced you back here".

"Well, you know I'm safe now." She motioned to the door. "You can see your way out."

"Michelle...I'm sorry." Tyrone swallowed hard. "I messed up. I know that but we can talk this thing out. I shouldn't have done what I did."

His sincerity caught her attention. Michelle rubbed her temples. "Now you wanna say all of this?"

"Yes! I know that we don't always get along but who does?" Tyrone paced nervously. "I care for you, and I know that I test your patience but I'm still learning every day. I walk you to class, I eat lunch with you, and I even hangout with you during my free time. We could be a good couple, even a great one, but you have to meet me halfway."

Her curiosity was piqued just enough not to dismiss him. "Why do you even want to be with me?"

I guess this would be the great love confession you would read about in books. I wonder what he has to say.

Tyrone steeled himself with a shaky breath. Either he was about to say something profound or absolutely idiotic. "You're **my** woman."

The silence afterwards was filled with vast amounts of confusion on Michelle's end, while Tyrone sat there like he won the greatest prize of all.

"What?" Both Darius and Osirion questioned, confusion evident on their faces.

"You were made for me, to help me become the man of God that I am destined to grow into." Tyrone cleared his throat, eyes glazed over. "Every man has to be tested to grow and change into the leader he's meant to be. You, Michelle, are my test. The Tomboy Princess that needs a strong man to lead her to being the beautiful, **feminine** woman that's hidden inside all along. We will bring out the best out of each other..."

Tyrone was still talking but Michelle just zoned out, his voice became nothing more than a muffled noise instead of clear words. *He couldn't think of anything endearing to say at this time? I'm just a tool for transformation, a way for him to evolve by forcing me to change. This is below the bottom of the barrel.*

"...and the Bible says—

"Tyrone!" She cut off his rambling. "Leave."

"Huh?" He blinked. "What—"

"I've broken up with you!" She motioned towards the main exit. "We will never be a couple again. It's over. C'est la vie. Goodbye. Au revoir."

"You're not giving me another chance?" He looked in shock as he stood there. "Did none of that move your spirit?"

"Are you stupid?" The words came out before she could censor herself. "I'm sorry but you failed the test. Please leave."

It took a minute for realization to dawn on Tyrone. His face slowly changed as his eyes darkened, a frown set in his brow, and his posture straightened. He went from a bumbling boyfriend to an angry man.

"You're leaving me? No, you can't do that." His fists were shaking at his sides. "You're mine, and until I put you through the mattress like Lisa we **will** be together. You do—

One solid fist to the throat muted Tyrone's rantings as he held his neck on the ground. Osi opened the door and threw him out, all while wearing an unnaturally wide grin on his face. He probably enjoyed throwing Tyrone out like trash in the hallway. Michelle had goosebumps on her skin from the way her friend looked.

Ah, there's that temper he used to have when we were younger. He's gotten more patient as an adult...

"That's how you take out the trash." Darius shrugged before he retreated back to his personal room.

"Are you alright?" Osi gave her a warm smile.

"Yeah, I'm okay." Her mind was still reeling as she rubbed her temples. "I'll be okay."

"I'm going to take a shower." He gave her shoulder a gentle squeeze before he walked away.

I hope Tyrone gets the message now.

She walked back into Osi's room and took a seat in his chair. At his desk is the same golden serpent necklace laid out like its real-life counterpart. The golden necklace was absolutely beautiful as she admired the craftsmanship.

This was a lavish gift for a friend to give out. I didn't think it would be equal to asking for my hand but its telling that his mind went straight to marriage instead of hooking up.

Michelle turned it over in her hands. Her face flushed at the thought of putting it back on. A gift of courtship. A gift one would give their **fiancée**. A gift that translated the intent to marry.

The opening of the door made her smile. "You're clever Osi."

"What do you mean?" He softly closed the door and sat on his bed. His black hair was wet as he toweled it dry.

"You waited until we were in person to give this to me." Michelle holds up the necklace. "If you mailed it to me, I would have sent it right back."

"I wouldn't feel comfortable mailing something like that to you." He let out a nervous chuckle. "I didn't know I would be seeing you on my birthday either."

She gave him a sideways glance. "So, you had this made and just held on to it?"

"Yes." He grabbed a brush in one hand and ran the teeth through his locks. "I guess I was just hopeful that I would see you soon."

Michelle laughed at his response. It was earnest and sweet and so very much Osirion. She wrapped the necklace around her once again with a smile. "Where did you learn how to disarm someone like that? You were quick on your feet!"

"You put it back on." He stopped brushing his hair, eyebrows raised in shock. "You are aware of what that means, right?"

"This would be equal to a proposal?" She stared at him, fingers grazing the metal. "Like your fiancée?"

"Yes." He stared at her fully. "As in my future wife."

"I know the meaning of fiancée." She gave him a soft smile. "I decided to wear it voluntarily this time around."

A grin split on his face as he took her in. "So, you accept?"

"Yes." She smiled. "I wouldn't want to marry until after we graduate so we can use this engagement to see if we're a good fit?"

He gently took her face in his hands and gave her a warm kiss. His lips were soft from the lingering moisture on his skin. "You're mine at last."

She answered him with a kiss of her own, her voice light and musical like her beloved instrument. "At last."

Michelle was back in her dorm, freshly showered with her coffee and vanilla body wash and changed into some comfortable clothing when her break up with Tyrone had almost immediate consequences. Her phone was blowing up before noon the next day, different people leaving various voice messages.

"Hey there!" The door opened to see Angel strut into the dorm. The blue haired woman sat her bags on her side of the room and gave her a smile. "How was your night?"

"It was illuminating." Michelle greeted her roommate. "Made some choices that were a long time coming."

"Oh, I've heard some interesting rumors since class this morning." Angel smirked. "Is there any truth to them?"

"With all the calls I've been getting I can guess what Tyrone has been saying." Michelle glanced at her phone. 10 messages and five missed calls from him alone. Three from Mother Ruth, one from her Dad, and one from her older sister.

It looks like the whole church is going to call me today.

"Oh!" Angel smiles. "About time. What about your boy Osirion?"

"About time?" Michelle arches an eyebrow. "Well, we're together."

"Aww, are you two finally dating?" Angel cooed.

Michelle pointed to her necklace. "We're engaged."

"Que??!" Angel almost screamed at her. "Wait, your necklace was an engagement gift?"

"It was. He told me and took it back." She laughed. "I broke it off with Tyrone and accepted Osi's proposition. What kind of rumors have you heard?"

"Oh Sis." Angel cringed. "It's pretty bad. Everyone from you being a cheater to being a frigid monster to...well, some are better left unsaid."

"Damn it." Michelle groaned. "This is ridiculous."

Her phone lit up with another call. It was Tyrone yet again as she saw his picture on the screen. She hit the button and glared. "What do you want?"

Outside of the dorm's double locked doors Tyrone banged his fist against the metal. It was still early in the morning as she saw people give him odd looks over her screen. "Zaria Michelle Winderson!"

"What is wrong with you?" Michelle glared at him. "Go away before security gets you."

"Come out here right now!" His voice raised higher and higher. "We are not done yet."

"Are you crazy?" Michelle pinched the bridge of her nose and pressed the red button with her finger. The call ended and the two women walked to the front of the building.

"Me, crazy?" He paced back and forth, hands flailing. "You haven't seen crazy yet! Do you know who I am?"

"The idiot that put Lisa in the hospital!" She spat at him. "The moron that won't let go of a woman that doesn't want him!"

"Hoes like you can never be trusted." He paced once more. "Playing the good girl all this time. Girl, when I come in there..."

"Tyrone!" She cut him off. "Get over yourself! You weren't even a decent boyfriend in the time we were together! Where's security?"

"You still tripping over that?" He sucked his teeth. "Get over it! I don't give no bitch head. Especially one who won't fuck me to begin with!"

Michelle almost passed out from embarrassment. She heard everyone talking and laughing around her. "You airing out all my business!? Get the fuck away from here!"

Angel took her turn, cursing in Spanish as two security officers escorted Tyrone away from the area.

"Well, there goes my social life." Michelle groaned as she walked back to her room.

"I'll pray for you." Angel whispered as the two women retreated. "Cause that's only more fuel to the fire."

The video came through on her laptop as Michelle accepted the call. The sky was clear as a warm breeze caressed her face. All of that couldn't prepare her for this conversation that had to happen one way or another. "Good afternoon, Princess."

"Hi Dad." She tried to be chipper but failed miserably. "How can I help you now?"

"How's classes?" He was attempting small talk at least.

"They're keeping me busy." Michelle cracked a smile. "Midterms were rough but now I'm preparing for tests and finals week."

"I'm glad you're adjusting to university." Tony gave her an honest smile. "Always glad to talk to my daughter...but you know why I called specifically."

"I have a good idea." She frowned. "I didn't think my romantic life would be such a topic of discussion."

"I try to be a good father when it comes to my children dating." He looked pained just talking about the topic. "The congregation is not happy with your breakup with Tyrone. Honestly neither am I."

"Well, they will just have to get over it." She rolled her eyes. "People break up all the time."

Tony squinted in the camera before he gave her a deep frown. "Off topic, you never told me who gave that necklace to you."

"We went over this already." Michelle could see him figuring the math out. "It's a gift from a friend."

"A friend that I happen to despise." He was barely holding it together in his office. "You broke up with Tyrone to get with...that boy."

I guess I should rip the band-aid off now instead of later. This is not how I planned to tell him but oh well.

"Osirion." Just her saying his name made Tony recoil. "That's his name, Dad. And yes, I did all of that. He gave me this necklace."

Pastor Tony let out a deep, spiritual sigh at her words. The last time she saw him so uncomfortable was when he told the family about the divorce. "I figured that he was at the center of all this drama."

"Dad..." Michelle warned her father with her tone. "I can date who I want."

"Not really." His hands twitched with emotion. "You can but you *can't*. You're my daughter and that comes with certain responsibilities. Do you know how many people know of you through me? You can't have this family looking like anything out here, especially with my campaign run."

The church and politics...two realms that are big on image.

"He's my boyfriend, not yours." she replied. "It's not like Osirion is a bum! He's a hard-working college student from a close family. He treats me with respect. He doesn't make waves around here. What more do you want?"

"A fellow Christian would be the bare minimum." His voice was laced with anger. "Someone who has English as their first language would be expected. You know, someone with a good father figure is also part of that baseline."

"I can't help **you** were throwing hands with his daddy." She rolled her eyes. "Secondly xenophobia is not a good look on the possible future mayor of Atlanta."

"I don't give a damn about no xenophobia. The fact of the matter is you cannot date that boy."

"Dad, I'm not a pedophile like you. I'm dating a *grown man*." She coughed. "I'm sorry. Linda was nineteen, almost twenty, when you two started dating right? You're pedophile adjacent at over fifty years old."

"Zaria Michelle Winderson!" His harsh tone made her flinch. "Talk to me like you were raised with some respect. My love life isn't threatening to fracture my congregation into pieces."

It should have. Michelle kept the thought to herself.

"Break up with Osirion, today."

"I need to tell you something important." She cleared her throat. "We're not dating at all. We are betrothed."

Her father stared at her through the screen, eyes locked on the golden serpent around her neck. He stared so long it made Michelle uncomfortable. "Dad? You're not frozen, are you?"

Tony laughed in her face. "That was a betrothal gift then? No wonder you wouldn't tell me…"

"Aren't you going to get angry?" She looked at him. "Blow up? Hang up the call?"

"No." He smiled at his daughter. "I love you, Michelle. You are my youngest and my baby princess. No man would ever be good enough for you, but I thought Tyrone could come close. I'm actually happy for you."

"Why?"

"You got Osirion to propose without even trying. You weren't even dating him last semester. For a woman that is an impressive feat." Tony chuckled. "I'm also very sad for you."

"Why sad?" She frowned. "We have time before we plan on walking down the aisle. I get to date my best friend in the meantime."

"Because this love story is going to end so badly." His eyes were looking in her direction, but his gaze went straight through her. "It will be a tragedy instead of a love story. A broken heart is so hard to recover from, especially when it's your first one."

He has that distant look again, like he's talking to my soul instead of my physical body.

"Do you really believe that or are you just hoping?"

"I would never want you to have a broken heart." His face turned up. "Yet with you two it's inevitable. Difference is exciting but you two are just **too** different to work out."

"Thanks for the vote of confidence." Sarcasm laced her tone. "What else should I know about while you're chanting prophesy over there?"

He shrugged. "That I love you dearly, and when you two do fail I will be here to help you rebuild that wonderful heart of yours. Have fun now, and I'll talk to you later sweetie."

He ended the call, leaving her to stare at her blank screen. Michelle didn't know if she should have been angry or scared after this conversation.

The thing is, Dad is rarely wrong in these matters.

"Michelle, your work has really taken a turn." The older man handed Michelle a red journal. "Your use of speech and description really adds to the character's spiraling depression and struggles with mental health."

"Thank you, Professor Poe."

I wonder if there's any relation for him?

"Your poem *Morning Comes* is personal, isn't it?" He paused as she nodded. "It's a beautiful and tragic observation on married life. You didn't happen to get married, did you?"

"No, it's something inspired from my mother." She sighed. "Bits from my observations, her own admittances, and just a few other things."

"That's quality work. You don't shy away from the tragic, darker side of emotion. You should think about entering it in the writing contest coming up in the Fall." He handed her a flier. "There are a few prizes if you place first, second, or third plus a public reading at the Grind House."

"Really? You think it's that good?"

"I would consider it!" He smiled at her. "You'll have good competition, and the department is doing a blind judging. This seems to be a good creative direction for you. Loving it."

"I appreciate it, Dr. Poe." Michelle grabbed her bags. "Anything else before I go?"

"Yeah..." He coughed in his hand. "Sorry to hear about the whole campus thing...that's brutal."

Wow, even the professors know? Wait, this seems wildly inappropriate right now.

"...it is." She face-palmed. "It's been a month and people **still** talk about it. There are so many versions even I forget what really happened."

"They will stop soon, at least?" He shrugged. "It doesn't beat someone pooping themselves in class today."

This man can't hold water to save his life. Why did they hire him in the department?

"That's true." Michelle shuddered. "I'll take your advice on the poem though. Have a good one!"

If I can't get my personal life together then at least my academic one doesn't have to suffer.

The Cost of Love

Osirion opened his eyes, angry as he stared at the ceiling. He was in the living room, stretched out on the common area sofa. With a groan he rose and walked into his bedroom.

He loved Michelle with a burning passion. He had spent years dreaming about holding her, kissing her, giving her any and everything he could mentally, physically, and emotionally. He knew that being with her would have a price that he would willingly pay for her.

His bed was neatly made up with a fresh change of sheets. The tidbits of things were neatly arranged on his desk. The curtain covering his Kamidana was undisturbed. He gathered his clothing before heading into the bathroom. He turned the water on as hot as he could stand it before he went inside.

Kanojo wa boku no teian wa ukeire ta. (She accepted my proposal.)

He rinsed the lather away, turning off his shower and wrapping in a towel. Slowly the beginning of the night came back as she told him about the fight she had with Tyrone in the first place.

Osirion wiped down the fogged-up mirror with a glare. He went about lathering his face, going over the textured scar with care before rinsing off and applying moisturizer. Tension filled his body as he investigated his face.

Kore ijou yoku nara nai yoi. (It's not getting any better than this.)

He walked out the bathroom to put on a simple outfit for the day. Every step felt light as a tune started in his mind. It was a sweet and sensual song that Michelle accidentally showed him at one point.

Walking back into his room he slowly unveiled his Kami-dana. It was a simple shrine with his Ofuda displayed in the center, along with a few other items and a couple of white ceramic saucers. He kneeled on the floor, bringing the shrine level to his eyes. He bowed twice to the shrine, clapped twice, and bowed once more before praying to the Kami. There were times where he would go straight into prayer, but this was not one of them.

He prayed for Michelle. He prayed for her light and airy smile to never leave her face. For her to love him and never let him go. He prayed that her father wouldn't have a heart attack after finding out he was engaged to his daughter.

I don't want him to die but if Pastor Tony fainted, I wouldn't complain.

Raising his head, he opened the small shelf. There was a bottle of sake halfway drained. He steadily poured an offering in one of the ceramic saucers before capping the bottle and putting it away.

Rising from his position he pulled the curtain back in place, shielding the Kamidama from view. At times maintenance will come in the dorms for inspection and repair, and he didn't feel like explaining to the weary eyes what he was doing in his personal space.

Nanbu no shintou wa sonzai shi nai yoi. (Shinto here in the South is nonexistent.)

The thought gives him a pang of longing in his heart for home. Not where his family relocated here in Georgia but Nagoya all the way across the sea. His heart longed for home and its comforts, but he didn't want to leave Georgia either. The humidity was unbearable as it was heating up this time in the Spring but he liked the chirping of those odd insects that would keep everyone up at night. He liked peach cobbler and boiled peanuts. He liked a certain woman that he could never stop thinking about. There were good things here that he would miss as well.

Jugyou no jikan desu. (It's time for class.)

"Moshi moshi!" The older woman on the video call adjusted her phone, zooming out of her chin. She fiddled around until her face was fully visible. Osirion couldn't help but to laugh.

"Moshi moshi okaasan." The sound was a bit choppy but easily adjusted to suit his tastes.

"How is life treating you? Are you keeping up with your studies? What about your paintings? You know your Father wants you to go into the family business, it wouldn't hurt to minor in some management classes." Here came the slew of customary questions and statements in heavy Japanese. He waited until she ran out of steam with a smile.

"I'm doing well. Yes, I just got done with midterms a while ago. I've sold a couple of paintings since last time. I was thinking about getting a minor, maybe business would be good. I'm not taking over the family business from him." He rattled off updates as she smiled. Her black hair was pinned up on her head and he could see small streaks of silver at her temples and forehead.

"What's the matter?" She cut him off. "You look sad."

"I'm not sad...just conflicted." He coughed into his hand. "Personal things, not anything related to my studies."

"Girl trouble?" She saw right through him. "Is this the one you love or your replacement girl?"

"Excuse me, Mother?" He told her about Beth in a roundabout way that she was his 'special friend' but he wasn't ready for this type of conversation. "What do you mean?"

"Oh, this is going to be fun." She gave her son a knowing smile. "Have you sorted out those long-term feelings for that man's daughter or are you still using pointless sex to cope with potential heartbreak?"

He was quiet, staring at the screen. His mother was patient in the video call, an eyebrow raised as she waited for answers. "I think I made her life a bit harder."

"How did you do that musuko?"

"She accepted my gift." He sighed before starting the story from where he last left off. He did tell his mother that Michelle transferred over but left out a few important details. Like him taking her to his place and 'working out' those frustrations on Beth. Like what he wanted to do before Tyrone interrupted their night.

"Musuko..." She gave him a sad smile. "Much has happened in a short amount of time."

"I didn't realize how intertwined her father's church population would be in her love life." He tapped his fingers on his desk. "Even with the little she tells me I know their constant questions weigh on her."

"Nobody can escape the legacy of their family." She placed a hand over her heart. "You can accept or reject it but you can't hide from it. I'm sure she is aware of that fact. Do you want to break it off with her?"

"No!" He looked away, aware of his outburst.

"Do you want my advice?" She gave him a small smile.

"Mochiron, okaasan." *(Of course, Mother.)*

He could always count on his mother to be by his side with solid wisdom from years of learned experience.

"Tell her how you feel about it. She's been by your side for almost seven years now." She let out a tired sigh. "I knew you two would eventually find each other. The church is a large part of her life and if you're going to be with her, be sure you're ready for any ire directed your way."

"That's true." Eventually he would have to go with her as well. He wouldn't convert to her religion, but he couldn't let them think they can push the two of them around like pawns.

"Absolutely." She smirked. "So, when are we going to have dinner with Michelle? I need to know all of her intentions for my eldest son."

"Okaasan." He rolled his eyes.

"You're my chounan, I know you." She stared him down. "She has my respect for breaking up with her boyfriend before being your fiancée, but I remember her high school 'confession.'"

"You remember that?"

"I'm the one that caught you two red handed! You were laid out in a hormonal puddle unable to move. She was going to take advantage of you!" She huffed. "You two were such children. I'm glad to see she's grown a bit since adulthood."

"I'll make sure to ask her about that dinner."

She smiled. "That's what I like to hear. Please, tell Michelle to invite her mother along instead of her father. I don't need to remind you about the last time those two were face-to-face."

"I remember." He smiled. "I thought no woman would be good enough for me?"

"No woman is good enough for you." She cooed. "...but I might be able to accept her. Of course I would love to talk to her alone first, but after things settle. Just do me a personal favor?"

"Nani ka." *(Anything.)*

"Use protection. I want grandchildren but not this soon." She laughed. "Although when it comes to relationships, you're like your Father. Sweet and charming until you start losing the clothes and then..."

"Haha!" He blurted out with a red face.

"I know you two are going to have sex." His mother rolled her eyes. "You probably already have! Don't be so coy over this line."

"We haven't!" He protested. "Not yet anyway."

"You've tried it." She smiled.

"I have not." He coughed. He didn't tell her what happened on his last birthday or the phone call in the middle of the night.

"Are you sure she likes men? You're handsome, kind, artistic...and she hasn't tried to make you lose your mind?" His mother clicked her tongue. "Isn't sex a sensitive subject for Christians? Maybe she doesn't like the act?"

"I don't think that's it." He tried to hide his face. He saw her on top, slowly grinding all over his throbbing erection with **that** look on her face.

"Son." She cleared her throat. "You're...."

"Mou shitsu teru yoi." *(I already know.)* He placed a pillow over the tight area in his pants. He didn't need to see her face to feel the smug expression.

"Don't forget your brother will be coming to spend a year with you soon. It'll be good for you two to be in the same place once again."

"Right!" He smiled. "I'll make sure he keeps his head on straight."

"Please do." She laughed.

"Of course." He sighed, placing a hand on his head. "I have dinner to start on. Dewa nochihodo." *(Talk to you later.)*

"I have the rice cooling down for the onigiri." Osirion pointed to a cooling pot on the stove. Michelle peeked over his shoulder. "And this is the breadcrumbs for the tonkatsu."

"Rice balls and fried pork?" Michelle washed her hands before she gave him a smile. "That doesn't seem too hard."

"I wanted to start off slow for your first time with me." The statement hung in the air for a moment making both of them giggle.

"Any veggies or appetizers I can help with?" She shrugged. "I might need some directions though."

"You can help with the main dish." He pointed to the pounded-out cutlets and egg wash. "I'll make the miso soup since I know your aversion for tofu."

"I tried it once!" She huffed. "You want me to fry this like chicken fried steak?"

"Yes, and the horrible restaurant Downtown doesn't count!" He went into the refrigerator to get the miso paste, tofu, and green onion.

"What can I say, I'm an American." She dredged the meat and placed it in the hot pan. "I'll try it this time since you're cooking it from scratch though."

"Thank you." A smile crossed his face. "My version is much better."

"I'm sure it is." She grinned at him. "Did you season your breadcrumbs at least?"

"Of course I did." He looked offended. "I don't have a weakness of seasoning."

"I just had to ask!" She flipped over the cutlet. "I never cooked with you before! At least I know when I want to make you some soul food that I can use my family measurements."

"Family measurements?" He placed a pot on the other side of the stove.

"Yeah. I just shake until I hear the ancestors tell me to stop." She giggled. "I've had to modify the amounts for different palates."

Osirion laughed as he turned to his side of the stove. His eyes wandered over to where she was standing. Michelle wasn't wearing anything unusual today with her jeans and oversized shirt. She had tied her twisted hair back to avoid the heat and oil of the stove. She had pulled back her shirt and tied it off behind her so the extra length wouldn't catch anywhere as a safety hazard. It unintentionally exposed a patch of her lower back and the white band of her underwear.

He cut his eyes back to his dish, licking his lips. Now he was hungry in two different ways, but he really didn't want to mess up the soup. Miso soup deserved respect and adoration, much like the woman he loved.

"I'm done with the main course." She plated the juicy pork off to the side. "Do you have the fillings for the rice?"

"In the fridge. Feel free to make a few the way you would like them." She pattered over and bent down to get the various containers of fillings.

He stared her down as she rose up with the bowls, and she let out a small squeak. "Are you okay?"

"I'm hungry." He was blunt to a fault as he put the lid on the soup.

"Aww you poor thing!" She cooed. "Dinner will be ready soon."

"Dinner?" His stare intensified.

"Oh." She started on a rice ball before her face flushed. "**Oh**. You're going to make me blush!"

"Good." He undressed her with his eyes, watching her squirm. It felt good to make her so nervous. "I'm glad I have an effect on you after all."

"You always do." She whispered as he joined her to finish up.

"Oh?" He arched an eyebrow. "Must be a Southern thing to not show it then."

She sputtered, becoming even more flustered. "You have no idea."

Osi laughed. "Dinner is ready. We should eat while the food is still hot."

Osirion knew he could be patient. He had experience in waiting until the right moment to strike. He has to wait for his paints to dry before layering oils on top of another. Walking on front campus near the end of the day was a testament to his patient nature.

Two weeks is long enough for what I need to do.

He wanted to be patient before making his move. His heart drummed in his chest every time he thought of hunting her down and pinning her to the ground.

Is it normal to want someone this much? To caress her skin? To pull her hair? To make her stutter and stammer all over her words?

Osi tied back his long hair into a lazy bun on the top of his head as a few loose strands ticked his face and neck.

The sun was setting as he strode on main campus, walking past the manicured grass and heading into Downtown. The weekday meant that campus security was rather lax as they saved all their manpower for the rowdy weekends. He turned the corner and went inside the bar as it was just setting up for happy hour.

In the corner, leering over some poor woman, Tyrone lounged like a lazy leopard. He was motioning at his lap with the woman looking uncomfortable. Osirion took the seat in the booth across from him.

"Hello."

"What the fuck are you doing here?" Tyrone leveled him with a heated glare.

"Do you not remember what I told you?" He slowly smiled at the taller man. "About if you hurt her, you'll get a visit from me?"

"So?" Tyrone glared as the woman walked away from the duo. "Look at you fucking up my game!"

"So?" Osi arched a brow at him. "You do realize what I'm going to do now, right?"

"Who do you—"

His fist slammed into Tyrone's nose, breaking the cartilage with a clean strike. A fight broke out immediately, which was expected. Tyrone had longer reach with his arms but a swift punch to the throat stopped him from trying to bash Osi's head against the table. Osi dragged Tyrone out the booth and onto the floor, getting popped in the eye for his efforts. Even through the pain Osi felt himself laughing, kicking him in the ribs for good measure.

With a steady laughter Osi ran out of the business before the actual police could come. He only gave Tyrone a broken nose. Everything else was either bruises or scrapes. His tongue ran over his lip, tasting blood from the cut.

A black eye and a busted lip. Thank Kami I didn't lose any teeth.

If anything, he was a man of his word.

Thirteen

Coffee and Kicking Back

"Angel..." Michelle rubbed her temples. "How have you been? I haven't seen Raven recently." She sucked her teeth. "We're on a break."

"Why?"

"It's complicated." Angel turned to Michelle.

"You wanna talk about it?" Michelle offered. "I can just listen or whatever. No pressure."

"Girl..." Angel paused. "It started at the PRIDE alliance meeting the other week. Someone was talking about what we should do for Pride month and bisexuals got brought up. Everyone is dissing, having a good time but I wanted to include something for bisexuals. I would run that part since I'm bisexual—-

"Wait." Michelle interrupted. "You are?"

"Yes." Angel deadpanned. "99% of dudes irritate the hell out of me but...some of them are fine, not going to lie. I just don't like talking to most men...ugh."

"This is new info." Michelle clicked her tongue. "What does Raven have to do with this?"

"Shh. I'm getting there." Angel chastised her. "Raven thought I was just a lesbian so she kinda...lost it when I said that. She started yelling, I started yelling...the whole thing blew up. It's a mess."

"Oh. Damn, I'm sorry."

"Yeah. I know she's waiting on me to apologize but for what?" She grumbled. "Being bi is not a crime. How is she going to feel lied to when I never said I was a lesbian, I like women! I also think a few guys are attractive too but big deal!

"I can't advise you on this one." Michelle fiddled with her hands. "Is she afraid you'll leave her for a man?"

"That..." Angel started but stopped. "I don't know! She isn't answering my texts. I stopped trying on the second day since she wants to ignore me. We don't have any classes together and I haven't seen her in the cafe at her usual times."

"Sounds like you need a distraction." Michelle patted her on the back.

"Yeah. You want to hit up the club tomorrow night? Drinks are on me!" Angel smirked. "We can have a girl's night out."

"I have work in the Learning Center all this week." She declined. "5-9, and you know I have my last core class early morning Monday, Wednesday, and Friday."

"Right, right." She groaned. "What about Friday night? I know your weekends are free."

"I'll be doing a reading at the Grind House but after that we can turn up. You should come along and vibe."

"You artsy types." Angel chuckled. "Alright, I'll vibe with some coffee. See what y'all be talking about over there."

"Oh, this is nice." Angel looked around, assaulted by the smell of roasting beans. "The coffee smells expensive."

"It's less than a five-minute walk from campus but yeah." Michelle nodded. "They do have a rewards program though. Every fifth cup is free."

"That's pretty cool." The blue haired woman swayed as she walked, drawing a few eyes. "Why are they staring?"

"They just haven't seen you before." Michelle waved to a few. "Mostly the English department hangs out here long term. They'll warm up in a minute."

The two women walked towards the back, going downstairs. The lighting was dim but warm, giving off a pleasant mood. The stage was well illuminated with a microphone and seat in the center.

"Smells like cheap incense." Angel held her nose. "Why is it so strong down here?"

"I don't know." Michelle laughed. "You'll get used to it quickly but it's very strong."

"Oh Michelle, you're here!" Someone flagged her down with a wave, pointing to an open journal. "You should sign up for a slot! We got room tonight!"

"That's what I planned to do!" Michelle clicked the pen, writing her name. "Oh, Lena is going on stage too?"

"Yep!" The signer smiled. "It's going to be off the chain tonight! We got two out of the Big Three on set!"

"Big Three?" Angel quirked an eyebrow.

"It's a nickname." Michelle shrugged. "A silly thing really. We're just competitive in the writing department."

"She's modest!" The signer waved at her. "It's Lena, Michelle, and Greg if you go to the Creative Writing department. Those three always have something different in their heads. I'm curious about your 'new direction' I've heard whispers about."

"Ah." Michelle scratched the back of her head. "You'll have to wait and see then."

"This is going to be fun." Angel snickered. "You've got some friendly rivalries you didn't tell me about."

"I'm cool with both of them." Michelle covered a cough. "Most of the time."

"Unless we get a few drinks in our systems." A deep voice cut in the conversation. Soft brown curls were the first thing everyone noticed, then a dazzling smile and olive toned skin.

"We were just talking about you Greg." Michelle gave him a friendly hug. "Are you joining me and Lena tonight?"

"Nah." He shook his head. "I'm still working on too many things. I'm just here to enjoy myself."

"Oh really? You two are here as well?" A wavy brunette walked through the gathering crowd downstairs. "Michelle and Greg, my inspiration for staying on top! How nice of you to come by and hear me tonight."

"Is she serious?" Angel blinked in confusion. "Are you a celebrity or something?"

"You haven't seen my IG?" Lena pushed her phone in everyone's face. "Lena Swartz. 150 thousand followers. Goes LIVE constantly. Get with the program."

"Lena is good at marketing; I'll give her that." Michelle grumbled. "I need to do better with that."

"Yeah." Greg agreed. "Unfortunately, me too."

"Maybe I'll put you two on one day." She laughed. "But it won't be today. I'll be reading some new material, never heard before!"

"Well we're about to start." Michelle motioned to the stage. "Let's get it."

"Good evening." Michelle sat down on the stage, holding a small leather-bound journal. "How's everyone? Tonight, I'll be reading a newish piece of mine. It's called *Puppeteer* and hope y'all enjoy it."

Remembrance can be a strong psychosis

fluttering as a wing's beat in humid air.

His fingers dance across moist lips

creating haunting melodies for a private show.

Twisting a tongue rocks my exposed core

leaving me vulnerable to his minstrel song.

Snagged by loyalty and split open by lust

my heart lays exposed to the maelstrom

called love.

His lucky soul entangled with mine as we

clash in the bedroom performing skillful pup-
petry

padding our strings.

A beautiful story is made against the

breathing backdrop as the audience cheers

and boos.

As panting performers we celebrate this art

gifted by God called life.

"Tragic love here." The audience let out a chorus of claps and snaps. The speaker nodded with a smile. "Always a great subject in poetry. Thank you, Michelle, for that piece. Last but not least, we will have Lena taking the stage."

"Hello everyone!" Lena takes the stage. It's been around thirty minutes of performances, and the night is drawing to a close. The curly brunette walked on stage, flipping a very expensive moleskin journal in her hands. "I'll be reading my brand new piece called *Garden* from my personal collection. You can find me on IG @lenaswartzpoetry to look at some of my older work. Now I'll read."

What use are of men?

Some you just like and pick them like a flower
then they die.

Some you adore so you plant them outside.

They grow, multiply, until they are choked by
the weeds.

Then there is one you love so you caress his
petals but leave him be,

so he can grow unbridled.

So how useful are men?

Should a gardener have just one or many?

Each gardener is different with her garden;
there is no room for shame.

And like gardens each flower's purpose is never the same.

"That was good." Michelle let out a few well-timed
snaps.

"She's not all talk." Angel let out a small clap as the
brunette took a bow on stage.

"Lena can run her mouth, but she has the skills to back
it up." Greg snapped. "She makes our writing department
look good, and they use her videos to attract potential
students. A win-win for the school."

"Thank you everyone." Lena sat down, turning to
Michelle. "Yours was good as well, just kinda obvious
based on your life. Too much of a self-insert for my
tastes..."

"Self-insert?"

"Loyalty and lust? Dancing together like a performance.
The loss of free will as you both complete your assigned

roles." Lena smirked. "A woman torn between two suitors, forcing herself to behave in a respectable way instead of becoming lost to your desires. Self-insert."

"I can't dispute you there, although that wasn't my initial intention." Michelle laughed. "Yours can be the same as well with your recent break up."

"Mine is about exploration, thank you." Lena balked. "College is the time to see what you like and dislike. What will you put up with and what will make you walk away. My matter is deeper than having a love triangle."

"You wrote about collecting men like pretty flowers." Angel interjected. "Sounds like a...lover's garden. Real deep there."

"You're just not cultured enough to understand it." Lena rolled her eyes. "Most people that grew up under a certain...tax bracket has a hard time relating to art."

"Oh, Angel understands it, and her parents make more than yours." Michelle interjected. "Does your garden also include your seventeen-year-old ex?"

"Seventeen?" Greg interjected, almost spitting out his coffee. "Like one of the college prep high schoolers?"

"Excuse me?" Angel blinked. "You can't be serious."

"Men are lived experiences for women." Lena rolled her eyes. "Plus, the legal age in Georgia is sixteen so I don't see an issue."

"You don't?" Michelle gaped. "Why do you know that off the dome?"

"Oh Lena..." Greg turned his head.

"She's just an admitted pedophile?" Angel stared in confusion. "This tea is hot!"

"Wasn't the *whole* campus talking about your unsatisfying ex relationship?" Lena glared at Michelle. "You coming for me cause your former man can't get you off!"

"Keyword is *man!*" Michelle shook her head. "Being a certified pedophile is much worse than my lack of sexual fulfillment. We are not glossing over that!"

"Seventeen is legal in this state!" Lena huffed. "He was not a child when we were together!"

"She just doubled down?" Angel cringed. "This is just sick!"

"What do you mean sick?" Lena glared at her. "Me loving a young Black man is not *sick*! Racist much?"

"Soy negra, idiota!" Angel shot back. "How are you not in jail?"

"Money," both Greg and Michelle stated.

"It was just once." Lena turned away from the group. "Making mistakes is a part of life and everyone has some. I will not be shamed for being attracted to the opposite sex."

"Even if he's still a minor."

"He was six foot one! Strong enough to tackle a grown man on the football field. That is not a child anymore, alright?"

"That is some of the most pedophile logic I've ever heard." Michelle frowned. "Developing early makes your behavior acceptable?"

"It just one mistake." Lena rose from her seat to leave. "Don't judge me!"

They all looked at each other as the night came to a close, partially disturbed and partially entertained by the turn of events.

"Boys, how are y'all doing?" Michelle and Angel both walked into the dorm. Darius was in the kitchen spooning something into a mug. Osirion was fingering through the movie selection on the sofa.

"Good evening, ladies." Darius pointed to a slow cooker. "I have some spiked punch if you want some."

"What happened to your face?" Michelle gave Osi a kiss on his lips, noticing his bruised face.

"Just a small accident." Osi smiled at her. "Nothing to be worried about."

"Small accident, my ass." Darius laughed and Osi turned his head to stare at his roommate. "Your man should be fine in a few days. Anyway, the punch is rather weak. Your fiancée told me about your low alcohol tolerance and your daddy is not going to beat me up because you got drunk."

"Everybody has jokes." Michelle grabbed a cup before joining everyone on the sofa.

"It's okay chica." Angel pulled out a flask from her purse. "We'll make sure you don't do anything you will regret...probably."

"Angel, we just came from the Grind House." Michelle laughed. "You just had something to drink."

"After hearing about that pedophile, I need another." Angel shuddered. "There are some creepy folks out here."

"What?" Both Darius and Osi gave blank stares. "A what?"

"It's a long story." Michelle shook her head. "Let's just say one of the writing majors likes to date high school boys."

"Oh, I didn't need to know that." Darius took a long swig of his drink. "Like at all. Is that tequila in your flask?"

"Yeah." Angel smiled. "You want some?"

"Hit me cause this is weak." Darius held out his cup.

"Why are you getting drunk anyway Darius?" Michelle rolled her eyes. "Having a hard time with coursework?"

"His girlfriend dumped him." Osi popped a movie in the game station. "Not exactly but close enough."

"She left me because she didn't want to call me Daddy in the bedroom." Darius huffed. "Crystal said it was too creepy and broke it off with me."

Oh my. Michelle giggled while Angel gagged on her drink.

"What?" Darius stared at the women. "Is that too much to ask? Is it really weird?"

"I wouldn't say weird." Angel shrugged. "It's a bit odd but it can be sexy. You're a giant of a man with those arms and barrel chest...you're a 'Daddy' to someone."

Michelle managed a smile. "Everyone isn't as adventurous as you. I'm sure you'll find the right playmate soon."

"Like you have with Osirion?" Darius gave her a tell-tell smirk.

"What do you mean?" Michelle tilted her head.

"Shut up, Darius." Osi snapped at the other man. "He's just talking, that's all."

"Oh, you sweet summer child." Darius grinned like a wolf showing off its fangs. "I can't wait for you to find out."

You and me both cause Osi is a freaky one. Saying his fantasies in Japanese trying to be slick. Those four semesters of Japanese are definitely paying off right now.

"So, we have *Dracula Dead and Loving It*, *Candyman*, and *Black Adam* to choose from." Osirion cleared his throat. "What is everyone in the mood for?"

"Candyman!" Michelle was the first to pick. "Is it the original or the remake?"

"Original." Darius spoke up. "Give me Dracula. I love a good comedy."

"Hmm...I vote for Black Adam." Angel took a swig of her flask. "I haven't seen it yet."

"A three-way split." Osi tapped his fingers as he paused. "I'm going with Dracula."

"Wow!" Angel groaned. "Sticking by your boy? Classic man behavior."

"Ugh." Michelle rolled her eyes. "I'll give it a shot. I haven't seen it."

"It's really good." Darius took a large swig of his drink. "Be prepared to laugh."

The four students got comfortable as Osi flipped the lights off and brought out a large bowl of popcorn to share. To the men's credit, Michelle found herself laughing early in the film. Angel stared at the glowing screen wide eyed, fully caught in the story.

Michelle cuddled up to Osi as the movie went on and on. After an hour everyone was tired and a bit loose if the empty punch bowl was anything to go by but the movie still had almost an hour of playtime left. She cut away from the screen to stare at the man she was cuddled up against.

His eyes were a beautiful shade of brown and were the second feature that always caught her attention. Even if his face was wiped of emotion his eyes always gave him away. She nuzzled against his jaw, cheek brushing against the small hairs that were trying to grow through his skin. Her action made him laugh, exposing her to a lovely smile as his hands tightened over her waist. Osirion was a charming man she had to admit.

I have to look at my favorite part of him.

Her eyes cut down from his face, tracing over his neck and chest. As handsome as she found him, it was his hands that set her face aflame. They were simple hands with short cut nails. Sometimes he painted them different colors, other times they were bare. At times they were coated in paint while he held a brush. Other times they would be holding planks as he worked in the crafting station on campus in his woodworking class. No matter what they were doing, his hands were just plain sexy.

Those strong hands can hold me down and—

Michelle cut off her thoughts with a quickness. She knew her face was warming up rapidly as she closed her eyes. For the most part their relationship really didn't change once she accepted his gift. They still walked together in the mornings. She still rubbed out the knots in his back because he refused to sit properly over an easel. He still made her coffee the way she loved it. To anyone watching they were still easy-going best friends.

That wasn't a problem. The thing is now when she teased him, he teased her back. Relentlessly. He made her blush and stammer over her words like she didn't grow up giving Easter speeches every year. When he touched her back, she arched into him without thinking. An innocent mistake, sometimes. He would retaliate by leaning into her ear and letting out a low growl just to see her melt into a puddle in public. He was enough of a gentleman to help her if she stumbled, at least, but enough of a man to keep doing it after seeing her reaction.

I guess I can't be the only one teasing him all the time.

"Chuuibukai." *(Careful.)* His voice rose over the movie. His fingers thumped against her waist as he smiled. "Kiniitsu ta mono wa ari masu ka?" *(Do you see something you like?)*

Yes, and his habit of slipping into Japanese when he wanted to say something she shouldn't understand. His voice was deeper than when he spoke English, and the syllables twisted around with more fluidity in his mother tongue. It would mess with her more if she couldn't translate his phrases, but his audacity made her laugh.

She appreciated the cultural differences they had...and he couldn't say anything if she teased him just the same, right?

He really thinks he's slick with it. Oh man I can't wait to burst his bubble.

"What was that sweetie?" For now, Michelle played the role of the obvious lover.

"Oh, nothing important." He kissed her on her forehead. "Just saying how cute I find you."

"That's so nice sweetie." She traced his hand with her fingertips. "You're cute too."

"Thanks." His smile was sweet and genuine. The sight made her heart melt.

Despite his cheekiness he really was a sweet guy.

"Sweetie." She looked over to see Darius asleep on the other side of the couch. Angel was texting on her phone, not paying them any attention. "I have to tell you something."

"What is it ai?" *(Love.)* He turned to face her.

He's getting cocky nowadays being such a tease. I got something for him.

Her hand crawled up his back before grabbing the top of his tied hair. "I love my serpent necklace but if you ever trick me into something serious like that again...I will peg your cute little ass with no remorse."

She saw his mouth open in surprise, but no words came out. His face flushed a pleasant pink as her words registered in his mind. The distant look in his eyes told her he was envisioning what that would look like, and he didn't seem to object from his facial features.

"Oooh someone's in trouble." Angel cackled. "Do you need the monster strap cause I can show you where I bought mine."

"Maybe." She smiled as he gave her an impression of a gaping fish. "I'm glad you can help me, Angel. Are you more of a width or a length type of guy, sweetie?"

He made a flustered noise as she flushed as well. The idea made her sweat underneath her clothes, and she licked her lips before releasing his hair. Desire ran through her body like a lightning bolt as she worked to calm herself down. She got her point across from the way he reacted.

Serves him right. Might be a bit much but I can't resist seeing him so flustered.

Angel got up, waving at the two. "I'm going to turn in for the night. Please don't break that poor man."

"I'm not!" Michelle got up and hugged her. "He learned his lesson. I'm not cruel."

"Sure, you're not." Angel waved at Osi who nodded at her.

"Good night, Angel." Michelle walked her to the door before closing it behind her roommate. Her back was turned to the sofa as she walked into the kitchen. "Do you want some water, sweetie?"

He didn't answer. She looked over at the couch to see that he was gone.

She poured some water in a glass, then took a good long sip. She could feel his presence behind her as she stood in front of the sink. It was almost overwhelming as she felt his body heat on her back.

She turned around to look at him. He stood in front of her, but she saw it all over his body. Darkness. Not an evil look as he stood there but it was like seeing someone's aura or maybe spirit or inner intentions. He looked *dark*.

Dad was always going on about seeing spirits within people, almost like a sort of possession. I guess I caught the same ability too.

"Hey sweetie." She smiled at him all chipper. "Water?"

The smile he gave her was sweet and wicked as it warmed her insides. He pressed against her and kissed her on the lips. It wasn't a sweet kiss as he moved against her mouth, opening her up and thrusting his tongue into her mouth. She moaned against his mouth as he held her in place, eyes fluttering in response. He explored her to the point where she needed to breathe, but he pulled away before she did.

"For a woman that talks about sex so much, you have such an aversion to the actual act." He whispered close to her face. "Are you a virgin, love?"

Her eyes fluttered at the tone of his voice. "No, I'm not."

"Ah." He smirked at her. "You tease me all the time, yet we haven't had sex yet. Are you nervous to be with me?"

"Uh..." She looked away from his dark eyes. She fought the tremble in her body as he pinned her to the sink with his lower body, pressing his hard erection right against her. "Not nervous per say."

"Are you repressed?" He licked from her collarbone up towards her ear, leaving a wet trail on her skin. "Or do you enjoy giving men blue balls without doing anything to help like a sadist?"

Her mind was scattered to the winds as not one word left her lips. Being struck mute was a new experience as she let out a shaky breath. "I..."

"You're a good girl but you have a whore's mouth." He smiled at her flabbergasted expression. His hand came up and pulled her hair until her neck was exposed to his greedy lips. "When you tease me, I want to do horrible things to you. Things I shouldn't do to you, but I will."

Ah. This is getting interesting.

"Blah blah blah." She mocked his voice as she stared at the ceiling. "You're all talk yourself."

"Am I now?" His voice was dangerously calm as he released her hair. She caught his gaze and almost fainted. He looked evil with a twitch near his eye.

"Isn't Darius still on the couch?" Michelle peeked over into the living room. She couldn't see his large frame on the sofa.

"He woke up and retired for the night while you were drinking water." Osi chuckled in her ear. "It's just you and me, Love."

Maybe I pushed him a little too far?

Those strong hands she was just admiring moments ago pulled off her shirt with ease, followed up with her pants in a quick and efficient manner. There went her socks, her sports bra, her boxers...he stripped her naked within a few blinks of her wide eyes.

"Do you not realize what I can do to you?" He whispered right in her ear. The air was so thick she felt she would choke on the tension in her wound-up body. He stripped off his clothes easily, before staring her down as naked as he was born. "Little church girl, I can **ruin** you."

He's serious...and sexy...and...where is my self-preservation?

Her gaze caught his eye before traveling down. She touched his bare chest, and a moan escaped his lips. Her hand ghosted over his stomach and the muscles twitched under her touch. Her nails tickled the short hairs below his navel, and he chuckled.

"Look at what we have here." She grinned like a cat that finally caught her prey. Her hand brushed against his erect penis, starting at the base and tracing the vein underneath. She grasped his shaft and pulled down, exposing a bright swollen head pouring clear liquid from the very tip. "You're uncircumcised, aren't you?"

She grasped him and pumped up and down and he almost crumbled at her touch. "Yes."

"I've never seen an uncut man before." She rolled her thumb on the top, watching him writhe in her hand. She watched him shake as he used his hands to steady himself on the sink behind her. She watched his eyes close as her hand glided along his shaft as he dripped on her hand and down his foreskin. She watched his teeth dig into lip, almost drawing blood as a strangled grasp tore from his mouth. She watched him unravel under her touch. "You're so close...I can feel you throbbing in my hand."

Having such control over him feels good. I can't explain why but it just does.

Then she stopped. Pulled her hand away completely. She saw him jump in the air from the lack of contact.

"Zaria?" His face was full of concern as he opened his eyes.

"You must have been on that thin edge." She kissed his cheek gently, scooting outside of his reach. "But what do I know? I'm just a little church girl."

Her sarcasm cut him deep as his face changed almost immediately. He was a half-step away from losing it and it was all on his face. "You little..."

"What?" Michelle felt that goading him would be a bad idea but did it anyway. "Go on, say it."

I wonder if he's at the edge of losing his self-control yet? Why do I want him to go off the edge so badly? Am I the drama?

"You little brat." He smiled too hard. He lifted her off the floor with ease and marched into his room, slamming the door shut. He tossed her on the bed and caged her in with his long arms. "You want a villain, don't you?"

Her face burned as she took him in on top of her. "A villain?"

"Yes." He grasped his shaft in one hand and rubbed his head up and down her swollen lips. She jumped at the contact, but he held her down with his free hand. "You're such a **good** girl. A church girl. A chaste girl. You wouldn't tell me to fuck you senseless...well, not for our first time."

"Ah..." She tried to string a sentence together but the electric shocks from her pussy stopped any and all thought.

"Admit it, that's why you taunt me all the time." He poked and prodded against her wet folds enough to keep her on edge. "You're just taking advantage of my kind heart.

Trying to stay a good girl but you're really my bratty little slut underneath it all."

Oh, I mean he's not wrong, is he? I want him so bad right now.

His filthy words just burned through any sort of rebuttal she was trying to let out. It was a miracle she remembered her own name at this point. "...yes."

"I can't hear you." He opened her legs further before slapping his hand against her clit.

"Fuck yes!" She screamed it at him, body twitching against his hand. "Please fuck me."

"Now you want it?" He sneered at her from above. "Are you really sure? Do you want to think about it? Maybe tomorrow or the next week or the next year..."

She would have kicked him in the shoulder if his hands didn't catch her leg. "You're so petty!"

He lined up perfectly and pushed his head inside of her with a smirk. "But I can also be nice."

Her eyes went wide as she stretched around him. Inch by inch by inch she gaped at being filled from the inside. Her legs wrapped around his waist and pushed the last few inches deep inside. "So good."

His hands rubbed her legs, feeling the muscles underneath flutter and strain. His hands traveled up her hips and waist to settle on her breasts as he leaned forward. "*So good.*"

Osirion slowly pulled out to see her open her eyes and thrust back in just as slow to see her grasp at the sheets underneath. His hands kneaded the small mounds on her chest, fingertips dragging over her pebbled nipples. Each thrust was as slow as he could stand it as she mewed under his touch.

"C-could you pinch them?" She held his hands on her chest. "That feels nice."

"Of course, Love." He rewarded her request and her back bowed. "Like that?"

"Yes." He traced them gently before pinching her again. She clenched around him with a strangled gasp. His hips snapped into hers as that tense coil pooled deep down in her groin. He leaned down and lapped at her left, taking special care to pull at her nipple with his teeth.

"Where do you want me?" He choked out as she fluttered around him. She wasn't going to last any longer and he was close to follow. "You better tell me…"

"Inside." She choked out before she arched off the bed, hands running through his hair. Her walls clenched and pulsed as she came with a rush of warmth splashing on his thighs. That was all he needed to lock his hips with hers, painting her white with each throb and swell as he came with a groan.

She tapped his nose, eyes glazed over as she laid out on the bed. He slowly pulled out of her and settled down next to her with a smile. His hand lazily traced across her breasts as she twitched. "That's sensitive."

"Your breasts are that sensitive?" He palmed a mound, and she moaned. He traced along her collarbone, and she grinned. "That's good for me to know."

"Keep it to yourself since you're the first to know." She closed her eyes. "I'm sorry for teasing you all the time."

"Thank you." He traced over her right breast watching her squirm. "I'll admit I do like it though so don't stop."

"Oh, okay." Her breath caught as his hand trailed underneath her gentle swells. "I'll try to be nicer about it though. You were about to lose your mind."

"True." He agreed, giving her a sharp pinch. "Am I really the first to touch these? You have two perfect handfuls."

She licked her lips, trying to talk. He was using both hands to squeeze with an observant look. "Don't look so surprised...you've seen my ex."

"He was selfish." He added pressure to his hands as her back gently bowed underneath. "You've been so deprived all this time."

She nodded as one hand trailed down her stomach to circle around her bundle of sensitive nerves. Her legs opened to let his fingers push inside.

"You're so close." He grinned as she fluttered around him again, body tense before going limp. "You're full of surprises."

"I keep making a mess because of you!" She shooed his hands away from her body. "Why is your bed so wet?"

He gaped at her. "Because of you. Don't tell me you never had an orgasm before!"

"Of course I have!" She flushed in embarrassment. Her arms flapped around as he waited. "I just...not with someone else with me!"

"Wow." He was stunned as he realized she was telling him the truth. "Let's clean up first but that's interesting! We need to have a conversation."

"Really?" She groaned but nodded.

Michelle heard him in the bathroom turning on the shower. He gently picked her up and carried her like a princess. He let her lean in the shower, taking his time cleaning every inch of her before she returned the favor. He dried her off and wrapped her in a pink robe that he apparently bought just for her. She stood in the doorway while he changed his sheets and wiped down his waterproof mattress.

"What's that?" She pointed to the gray blanket he placed on top of the fresh sheets.

"A waterproof blanket." He smirked. "Keeps me from changing the sheets again."

"I don't squirt that much!" She crossed her arms with a smile. "You're so dramatic."

"You can touch the sheets and find out."

She peeked into his hamper but declined the offer. "I'll just trust you on that."

He picked her up and placed her on the bed much like a fairytale princess. He walked out only to return with two bottles of water and a few small snacks. "Here you go, your majesty! You need to keep your strength up."

"Don't you have to pick up Toshi from the airport in the morning?"

"I do, after we go to the pharmacy first." He blushed with a smile.

"Oh right." She laughed out loud. "That was...a lapse in judgment."

"It's not going to be the only one we'll make tonight." He smirked at her. "Do you know about safe words?"

"I do." She nodded.

"That's great. How do you feel about blindfolds?"

"It's going to be a long night, isn't it?" She moaned as he leaned in and kissed her.

"A very long night."

"Ani-ki!"*(Older brother!)* Toshrio walked into the dorm, dragging some rolling bags behind him. His black hair was tousled and spiked and he sported a neat beard along his jaw. "Did you miss me?"

"Oniisama." *(Little brother.)* Osirion grumbled, rolling his eyes lightheartedly. "Welcome back to the States."

"You could have helped with my luggage!" The two men embraced. "I'm going to have to loosen you up over the year."

"You have arms, Toshiro." Osi led the younger man down the hall. "Let me walk you to your room."

"That's nice since you were **forty minutes** late picking me up." Toshiro ruffled his hair. "Were you busy brushing the tangles out of your ponytail?"

"You know how important brushing is for my hair." His face flushed a bit. "I'm shaving as soon as we get back to my room."

"You didn't say anything about Big Sis, I see." He smirked before sliding his key card at the door at the end of the hall. The door opened with a click and they started to put bags inside the empty room. "I heard that you two are together finally!"

"Yes we are." Osi rolled his eyes with a smile. "She accepted my gift I had made for her."

"Your expensive golden serpent necklace?" Toshiro chucked a bag onto his new mattress. "Alright! I bet you two had a fun night afterwards."

"You're a pervert." The older brother shook his head. "We're taking things slowly, at a leisurely pace."

"Leisurely pace? How long have you two known each other?" Toshiro laughed and wiggled his eyebrows. "Going from best friends to engaged is not taking it slow."

"You're hilarious." Osi motioned for his little brother to follow down the hall. "We can go whatever speed we want."

"You're sweating and it's not that hot in here." Toshiro pointed to his hands as Osi opened his dorm door. "Why were you so late this morning anyway?"

"What is this, one of your soap operas?" Osi laughed at his brother. "A slow burn romance drama?"

"I don't like slow burn 'ramas." Toshiro flopped on his brother's bed. "I like my stories fast, hot, and heavy."

"Ah, so like elite porn?" Osi walked into the bathroom, taking out his razor and shaving cream. "That sounds like you so I'm not surprised."

"Better that than a burn that's so slow the fire goes out." Toshiro heard his brother rumble in the other room. "You didn't answer my question!"

"I rather not fuck a woman the same day I get serious with her." He eyed Toshiro, sticking his half shaved face out the bathroom. "I was in traffic. It happens to everyone."

"It's fine with me, ani-ki!" He snickered. "I just hope for Big Sis's sake you're not out of practice on satisfying a woman, that's all!"

"Toshiro." Osi gave his brother a heavy glare before returning to shave. "You never called Beth 'Big Sis'."

"I didn't like Beth." Toshiro countered. "Pretty face, nice body, but vapid. You wanna guarantee that your kids are going to be a dull bore, she's the one."

"So critical."Osirion rinsed off his blade before going back to shave.. "You didn't like Michelle when you first met her either."

Toshiro sucked his teeth. "Her brother tried to beat me up but she was cool once she got me that ice cream...plus she ragged on you so our friendship was a done deal after that."

"I'm glad I could bring you two together." Osi walked out the bathroom, facial hair removed. "Come on, let's get something to eat. I know your flight was long."

"Hope the food here is good." Toshiro smiled. "You still didn't answer my question."

"Is traffic not a good enough answer for you?" Osi arched an eyebrow.

"You're never late to **anything**." Toshiro laughed. "Except for today."

"Traffic was bad." Osi shrugged.

"Oh and the fact that your bed was unmade **must** be a coincidence." Toshiro pointed out the wrinkled sheets. "Especially for someone that always made his bed before leaving the house."

"Ah. College got me to relax a bit?" Osi gave him a lopsided smile. "Isn't that a good thing?"

"Of course, of course." Toshiro shook his head with a smile. "It's not like someone was here when you left your room to pick me up and they left before we came back. Never that."

"Shut up, baka." Osi laughed. "Now let's go and get something to eat."

"This food is trash." Toshiro prodded a pile of greasy fried rice around. "The drinks are amazing though. I'm glad they import the good stuff."

"I told you." Osirion gulped down a bit of beer. "Alcohol is where the money is at anyways. Almost anything tastes good if you're drunk enough."

"I'm glad you two are finally dating." He poked his older brother. "Better late than never!"

"At least we finally took that plunge." A small smile graced his lips. "It's cute seeing her get flustered *because* of me."

"Usually it's the other way around." Toshiro snickered. "She has you blushing at least three times a day."

Does she? I do blush a bit when I'm around her...

"Real funny."

The restaurant door opened and two familiar women walked inside. A smile graced Osirion's lips as his newest love walked over to their table, with Angel escorting as well.

"Hey guys!" Michelle gave him a kiss on the cheek before grabbing Toshiro in a hug. "Hey Toshi! You made it here at last."

"Hey Big Sis! We were just talking about you!" He patted her on the head before extending a hand to the other woman. "We haven't met. I'm Toshiro, the better looking younger brother."

"Roasted by your little brother." Angel chuckled at the older brother's eye roll. "I'm Angel."

He raised her hand to his lips, giving her a small kiss. "Pleasure to meet you."

"Someone's smooth." Angel laughed as she took a seat. "Charming, but I'm not interested playboy."

"Shot down the same day you met her." Osi shook his head. "At least Angel is nice about it."

"It happens." Toshiro shrugged his shoulders. "What can an international student do for fun around here? I saw a coffee shop, a dance club or bar, and the college book-store downtown."

"It's a small town Toshi." Michelle skimmed through the menu. "Um...the club is always packed because it's walking distance from the dorms. The Mediterranean spot has the best food, but this place has the best drinks. The mall is a five-minute drive away if you want to shop. There's some random stuff further in Downtown as well."

"The random stuff might be the most interesting." He grumbled. "I'll be so bored that I won't have a choice but to study."

"That's a good thing." Osi gave him a glare. "I won't have to hear about you from Mother and Father this year at least."

"You're my older brother. You're supposed to look after me, ani-ki."

Osi shook his head. "At least I'll have someone worth sparring with finally."

"Hey, I'm right here!" Michelle cleared her throat. "I'm in the MMA club and you never come and spar with us!"

"The club is mostly women." He rubbed the back of his head. "I would be uncomfortable sparring with them."

"You can spar with me." She cocked an eyebrow. "I've taken you down before! I would give you a decent time, at least..."

"She's taken you down before, eh?" Toshiro interrupted. "The thing is that would be the problem. It wouldn't be a sparring match for long..."

Angel grabbed a napkin, almost spitting out her drink. Michelle chuckled, face turning red as her mind wandered. Osirion glared, face burning bright red.

"Oh I'm going to get you for that."

"My guy, are we seriously looking at a political debate on a Wednesday night?" On the large couch Darius scratched his head in confusion. "You sure you don't want to play a few rounds of Xtreme Beach Volleyball?"

"I'm sure." Osirion replied with a pained look on his face. "Michelle's father is supposed to be debating tonight."

"That guy?" Toshiro frowned. "Why are you interested?"

"He's a pain in our lives." Osi clicked his tongue. "She also loves him, and I can't avoid him for the rest of my life if we're going to be together."

"Do you not get along with her father?" Darius shoved a handful of popcorn in his mouth.

"He shot me in the face as a child." Osi deadpanned, pointing to his face. Darius squinted until Osirion moved his head and the light revealed the white textured scar spanning from his cheek to his ear. "The bullet grazed my face and that's how I got this scar."

"Shit." Darius blinked. "I'd plow his daughter too if that's the treatment I got."

Toshiro shook his head. "It's not like that, right ani-ki?"

"It's not like that." Osirion sighed. "If I was still an idiotic teenager sure but I love Michelle for Michelle. Her father hating me is just a bonus."

"That's the guy?" Darius pointed at the screen. Pastor Tony was walking on stage in a fitted suit showing off his average build and large arms. The camera panned to the audience where Yvette, Michah, and Michelle were seated.

"That's him." Osirion answered as he looked at his lover. Michelle was dressed in a modest black sleeveless dress wearing a rose gold jewelry set with sea blue aquamarines, from earrings to a tennis bracelet.

"He looks like a jerk." Darius commented. "Is there some weird meaning with their jewelry?"

Osi squinted as he took in Yvette and Michah. Michelle's older sister was wearing either silver or white gold adornments with square emeralds while Michah sported yellow gold with square topazes. Michah had the most detailed jewelry of the three but still fit on his masculine frame.

Reminds me of metals. Gold, silver, and bronze. That's ridiculous. No father would rank their children like athletes.

"Not sure." Osi frowned as the camera panned back to the two mayoral candidates on stage. The two men had their cameras adjusted on their clothes before the event began.

"Can you give a summary of your platform before we get into specifics?" The host turned to Tony. "You first, Revend Winderson."

"Thank you." Tony cleared his throat. "My platform is one based on common sense. One that puts marriage in the forefront of our culture once again. Commitment to one another instead of lifeless one-night stands and broken homes. I am looking to work with the people to give incentives to married couples and promote marriage among single minded people...

"He sounds conservative and old-fashioned." Darius sighed. "Like we need more of those."

Osi rolled his eyes as he listened to Michelle's father go on and on for five minutes about his religious based platform. He didn't have a problem with Tony's system, but the man wielded it like a sword, ready to slay a dragon at all times. Osi listened to half of the debate before the moderator asked a question that made him pause.

"Pastor, what is your position on immigration?" The question made both Osirion and Toshiro perk up from their phones.

"Citizens should be in our great country." He stated without blinking. "Those with a visa should stay for their allotted time then leave. If you want to stay longer, get another visa or become a citizen."

"What about those that gain citizenship through marriage visas?"

"I have no problem with people that marry for American citizenship, as long as they are family oriented." Tony smirked as he looked directly into the camera. "Of course, the prospective couple should be interviewed to make sure they are not taking advantage of any loopholes in the law but after the ink dries on their wedding license I don't see a problem with it."

"So, the rumors are true about your youngest daughter's fiancée then?" The moderator went in for the throat.

"Her boyfriend." He cleared his throat with a frown. "Her left hand is bare, but I digress. I am welcoming of all people, as long as they have good character."

The television zoomed in on Michelle's bare left hand. Her face was full of embarrassment as she hid her hand after a beat.

"Too bad she wasn't wearing that necklace you got her tonight." Darius frowned. "Although he does have a point about the ring thing."

"That necklace is a more thoughtful gift." Osi sighed. "Still..."

Ringu wa kanojo no ji no ookina present ni naru yotei da. Ima sugu ni demo. (Rings were going to be her next big present. Sooner now than later.)

"We have good character!" Toshiro frowned, motioning towards the screen. "Our family has great character, liar!"

"What can you expect? He's a religious leader of a large following that hangs on to his every word as if it was blessed before passing his lips." Osi snorted. "We can watch something else now."

"About time." Darius turned on the gaming console. "He didn't surprise me with his answers growing up here. He's just like a lot of other people here. Maybe with time he'll warm up to you?"

"I doubt it, but you never know." Osi grabbed a controller with a frown. "You never know."

*P**ress right here into the center. Get some more oil. Rub it in and press right here...*

"Oh!" Michelle was on his back, massaging his flesh here and there. A gasp escaped his lips as he relaxed back on the bed with a deep sigh. "That felt nice."

"I've told you about your posture, Osi." She hummed as she found another spot to press and prod. "You need to take more stretching breaks. Put the palette down for a minute."

"Like I tell you all the time hunched over the desk." He groaned.

"Your shoulders are so tight." She countered. "I take breaks, sweetheart. You're the one getting rubbed down."

"Ah..." He let out a long moan. "That hurts a little..."

"It'll feel better in a minute." She kneaded; face scrunched in concentration. "Give me time to work."

A few curses filled the air as she rolled and kneaded. More sandalwood oil and a few more rubs before he was purring in her hands, suddenly relaxed. "Oh yes.... that's nice. It feels good again..."

"I told you." She moved down his back. "You should take better care of your posture."

"I know." He grumbled. "Oh, I love you so much."

"I love you too sweetie." She chuckled. Her hands mapped out his back as she worked. His breathing deepened as she adjusted the pillow underneath his hips. "Pants a little tight?"

"I can't help it." His moans were of pure pleasure. "I love being touched."

"I didn't say it was bad." She pressed harder into a knot. He quivered under her with a whine. "The band isn't the only thing I can make stand at attention."

"You already knew that." He purred in her hands. She pressed a kiss to the nape of his neck, feeling him gasp in surprise. "Don't stop, Love."

I can do this for a long time. I know his back aches from all the knots and stress...

"Osi..." She whispered after a time of working in comfortable silence. His back rose and fell but otherwise no response. She dried off her hands and gently got off his back. "Oh...rest up dear."

Michelle gently closed his bedroom door and went into the kitchen. She put the water in the kettle and grabbed a cup for tea. The large dorm was quiet and peaceful as she smiled.

I'll chill for a little bit before leaving him to rest. I know his projects take up so much time, and he needs sleep.

She placed the loose tea in a small strainer, letting it sit at the bottom of the cup. She poured hot water over the tea before her phone started to ring.

"Hello?" She kept her voice low, reaching for the sugar.

"Princess!" A gruff, older male laughed over the speaker. "It's been a minute!"

"Hi Dad." Michelle chuckled. "How are you?"

"I'm doing good, praise the Lord." He paused. "Brother Davis pulled me to the side the other day after the sermon."

Oh, this is going to be fun...let's get it over with.

Michelle held back a groan. "Oh, what did he want?"

"Just talking about his son and stuff at the university." Her father waited. "He gave me a *very* interesting update about you as well."

"Besides what you already know?" Michelle sighed. "I think I told you everything."

"Did Tyrone cheat on you?" He started the questions. "Abuse you? Was he a disgusting creature, cause men can be that way until they get used to a woman's presence. Just because he sleeps with Lisa doesn't mean he hates you."

"Dad..." Michelle stopped him. "How do you know about Lisa?"

"Word travels, especially when Tyrone keeps talking about you." He sounded bored. "Love ebbs and flows sweetie. He misses you."

"That's too bad." She cut him off. "Did you forget that I'm engaged?"

"I was hoping you forgot or changed your mind." She knew he was upset. "The unbeliever. We had dinner with his family before, so I remember him well. His father was about to get the beating of his life, if I remember correctly."

"Dad, don't be this way."

"What way? I'm just stating an observation." He sneered. "I mean he's not Christian, right?"

"You already know the answer to that." She deadpanned. "You already asked Mr. Makoto about his family and their Shintoistic beliefs."

"I know, but I was wondering if you forgot," he asked. "Since I think you still are one, so I'm just confused on how you two got together in the first place."

"After seven years you really don't see it?" She tried not to be short with him, but her patience was waning. "Do you want the cliff notes version again?"

"I'll admit he's a good friend." He cleared his throat. "For a romantic relationship you need different compatibility."

"Tyrone and I weren't compatible on that level." She fought the urge to blush. "I'm not going into detail, but *you know* what I mean."

"Young people and your obsession with sex." He sighed. "You can teach the important things...after marriage. If that's the only thing wrong with the boy, then that's nothing."

"He can't stay faithful, we don't get along, and we have no intimate relationship." She stirred her tea before taking a sip. "Why would I force him to love me? Isn't that sad to you?"

"My suggestion is to pray on it. Remember, you're single until you're married." He flipped a few pages over the phone. "I was calling you to remind you about the Gala coming up this Thursday evening. I'll send Deacon to pick you up outside your dorm at 4pm. All you have to do is grab a nice, evening dress and have a date to escort you."

"That doesn't sound too bad…"

"Please ask Tyrone if he can still come and be your escort. I like the young man and you two were such a cute couple."

"Or I can invite my current fiancé and have a great time," she countered. "Maybe you can be open and have a grown conversation with him too?"

"Or I'll give him a call and extend the invitation. That way you'll have a guaranteed other half and the press won't hound you as usual." He chuckled, a dark and foreboding one. "Can't forget you're in the public light as a Winderson."

"Like I can ever forget." She grimaced. "I'll have a nice dress ready when I get picked up but I'm not riding along with my ex-boyfriend. You're weird for even inviting him."

"No, you're weird for giving up on love so casually." He countered. "You can't be afraid of a little hard work."

"It's not a crime to break up with someone, Dad." She tried to keep her rising voice low.

"It's not," he agreed. "I'm getting fitted at the tailor's…we'll talk later sweetheart. See you soon."

"Yeah…" She hung up the phone, letting out a long sigh. Even the warm tea couldn't comfort her aggravated nerves. "Is he fucking serious…"

"That went well." She jumped at the sound of Osi's sarcastic voice. "I already know who you were talking to."

"Did I wake you?" She finished off her drink. "I tried to talk softly."

"I was getting up when I heard your phone call." He gently rubbed her shoulders. "Is everything alright?"

"Yeah…no." She groaned. "My Dad has this fundraiser coming up Thursday. Wants me there."

"That doesn't sound too bad…"

"He's also inviting Tyrone to be my plus one." She felt his hands stop. "I told him I could invite you and see if you could come but he's being a pain about it."

"…you told him we were engaged?"

"Of course!" She laughed. "I gave him the update and everything. He's actually inviting Tyrone himself…that's so creepy."

"That's very troubling." Osi sighed. "It's good to know that he still doesn't like me."

"I'm sorry." She winced. "You would think he would get over it by now."

"It's not your fault, love." He kissed her cheek. "So, what time do I need to be ready?"

Toes painted, nails done, hair is pressed and wrapped. I have the dress, heels, and purse. I got some new makeup for my skin. I think I have everything. She unwrapped the towel from her body and started her regimen.

A few pumps of cocoa butter lotion to the hand before rubbing it across her arms. More lotion as her hands moved to her shoulders. Palms rubbed her chest, moisturizing hardened nipples and soft mounds of flesh. Massaged the lotion in before trailing down her stomach and waist. She smoothed the creamy white lotion into her skin, getting some more for her thighs and neatly trimmed triangle below.

"Angel, are you staring at me?" She turned her head to stare at her roommate.

"What?" The other woman looked away from her screen. "I wanna see your dress! It's so pretty!"

Michelle laughed, rubbing down her legs and supple rear. Next were her legs and feet to complete her moisture ritual.

I can't be out here ashy.

She grabbed her matching bra and panty set with a smile. Nude colored, actual nude for her tone, and lacy bra and matching bottoms. She slipped the garments on with a smile.

"Wow, you're wearing a thong?" Angel commented. "You have to be all femme tonight huh?"

"Yeah." She motioned to her painted nails. "**Very** feminine so I don't stand out."

"You'll stand out but in a beautiful woman way." Angel smiled. "Your Pops might regret asking you to get all glammed up."

She smiled, sitting down to roll on the sheer stockings on her legs. They went on like a second skin, blending in perfectly. "That's the plan for tonight."

"Too bad your dad got Tyrone to be your escort." Angel grimaced.

"I took care of that." Michelle gathered the dress in her hands before stepping in. Gorgeous shades of green and silver are weaved together in a flattering mermaid style. "At least I hope he went for it."

"This is so nice!" Angel walked behind to help zip it up. "You can do your own makeup?"

"Yes, I can." Michelle readied her primer. "Just because I don't wear it often doesn't mean I can't do it."

"I just asked!" Angel laughed. "I don't see you going complete glam, so I was curious."

Swipe. Swipe. First sunscreen, primer, then foundation. Now some soft glam for the eyes and something bold for my lips. She paid extra attention to the area where her glasses rested on her nose and underneath her eyes.

"Oh, you're gorgeous." Angel helped to spray the setting spray. "Everyone is going to flip when they see you! Is Osi coming with you?"

"He's the one I invited." Michelle chuckled. She fanned her face until it was dry, then unraveled her silk wrap. A quick shake and a few brush strokes unleashed her hair, pressed as straight as a bone. Black tresses fell down her shoulders and collarbone as she swept it into style with her comb.

"Pretty silk press." Angel adjusted a hand mirror, so she had a better angle. "I won't be in when you get back."

"Thanks." She pinned the longer side out of her eyes to make space for her silver frames. "Spending some time with Raven?"

"Nah." Angel frowned. "Not with Raven. I can't with her right now, even after we talked. I'm just hanging out with some people."

"Okay." Michelle pulled on her silver gloves to complete her outfit. "Is it something you need to talk about later?"

"...I don't know, girl." Angel shrugged her shoulders. "I'll tell you over the weekend. Now you go and 'be good' for the cameras."

"Yeah, yeah." She grabbed her purse and gave Angel a hug. "Stupid fundraiser. I'll catch up with you."

Michelle walked out the door and headed upstairs towards the main exit. Her eyes lit up catching her fiancé pace outside.

He looks amazing. She slowed down to take in his black suit, white button down, and red tie. The fit was simple, but it wrapped around him like a glove, highlighting his shoulders and long legs. His long hair was free and framed his face before spilling over his shoulders.

You know he's clean shaved and smells good. Oh I gotta keep my hands to myself...

"Oh wow..." He opened the door for her, smiling in amazement. "You look..."

"...amazing." She finished his sentence. "Turning heads, Osirion."

"Not like you." He kissed the top of her hand. "You are beautiful. You look like a goddess of the forest, of nature itself."

She smiled, face heating up in a blush. "I know you are going to steal the cameras tonight, especially with the older ladies."

"Won't they be married?"

"Probably, but would that stop anyone?" She chuckled. "Women love eye candy. I'll have to hang around you for sure."

"You'll have all my attention, love."

A black limo pulled up to the two and the window rolled down. "Sister Zaria?"

"Hey Deacon." Michelle waved at the man through the open window.

Osirion opened the passenger door, allowing her to get inside. Michelle spoke up to inform the driver. "Osirion is my plus one for the event."

"Ah..." The older man frowned but said nothing as the two closed the door. "Pastor is not going to like this, young lady. He likes that Tyrone boy."

"Well Tyrone and I are no longer together so he will have to adjust." The limo pulled away from the dorm. "How long is the ride, Deacon?"

"An hour away." He put on some soft music. "Relax, Sister. It's going to be a good night."

"Are you ready?" Michelle leaned in to whisper in his ear. The limo was retreating to the lot, leaving the couple to walk to the open doors. She wore a perfect, imperfect smile, showing a bit more teeth than necessary.

"As ready as I'll ever be." His smile was more subtle but just as tense. Camera flashes were going off, almost blinding the two.

"Zaria!" Her father caught her in the doorway, his genuine smile shifted into a frown before he trained his face to appear happy. "You brought a different date for tonight?"

"Hi Dad!" The two embraced. "I'm sure Tyrone just got the times mixed up. You know how busy college students are in a week."

"A mix up." The older man turned to Osirion. "Osirion, how have you been?"

"I've been doing well, Mr. Winderson." The two shook hands, the elder squeezed far harder than necessary before letting go. "You seem to be doing well. You're running a strong campaign."

"Ah, thank you. The battle isn't over yet, but things are looking up." Tony turned to his daughter, whispering. "Tyrone will be here within the hour. I can't believe you would do something like this..."

"You know me so well," she whispered, not letting her disappointment show. "That's why you're my Dad!"

"That's right. Your siblings are already seated at the table." He pointed in the direction. "Linda is also there so behave."

"Of course, *Linda* is here." She couldn't keep the spite out of her voice. "We're going to take our seat at the table."

"My Lady." Osi held out his arm for her. "Let us go and join your family, shall we?"

She hooked an arm with his, walking toward the dining area. The place was beautifully decorated in golds and silvers, from hanging matte balloons and steamers to the warm light refracting off the chandelier.

Michelle waved over to brother and sister at the table. Yvette was wearing a long silver dress clashing against the warm tones in her darker skin. Her hair was straightened and pinned in an elegant updo littered with silver and pearl adornments. Michah has his hair short, lined up to perfection complementing his dark, neat facial hair. Gold rings adorned his right hand, and a glimpse of a gold chain could be seen in the gaps between his shirt and skin.

"Hey Little Sis, Osirion." The elegant woman rose to embrace them both. "It's a pleasant surprise to see you here with my Michelle."

"Hey Sis." Michelle returned her sister's embrace.

"Nice to see you again, Yvette." Ever the gentleman Osi kissed the top of Yvette's hand. "You're even more beautiful with age."

"Oh, you have a charmer with you this evening." Yvette laughed. "I'll give you credit for being on your best behavior. I know Dad was not happy."

"He's still mad." Michelle sighed. "Hey Michah."

"Hey *Zaria*. Nice to see you here." He empathized her first name. "You've grown, Osi. Almost as tall as me...but still under six feet I see."

"I might be five-nine, but I'm tall where it counts." Osi smiled with a straight face. The women both laughed as they took their seats.

A harsh tap caught Michelle's attention, making her jump. The light skinned woman behind Michelle cleared her throat. "Good evening, Zaria. It's been a while."

"Hello Linda." Michelle turned to address the young woman. "It's only been two years since I last saw you."

"Two years too long." She huffed, pulling down her very short black dress. "Who is this handsome young man?"

"Hello ma'am. I'm Osirion Najimi." He held out his hand for her to shake "I'm Michelle's fiancée."

"Like engaged? How much did I miss?" She looked him up and down before crushing him in a hug. "We're *family*...or will be shortly.

"Ah, of course..." He gently peeled her off. "It's nice to meet you Ms. Linda."

"You can call me Mrs. Winderson. It will only be a matter of time." Linda flashed a large cluster diamond ring before taking her seat next to her father. "Tony told me to go sit down while he finishes with the press."

"That's nice." Michelle stated. "You two are settling down finally?"

"We will be." Linda twisted the band around her finger. "Your father gave me this promise ring just this week."

"That's nice." Michelle smiled. "Honestly, it's a nice ring. Diamonds, white gold, round stone setting."

"Oh, you know something about jewelry?"

"A little something, something." Michelle shrugged. "Summer job. Taught me some useful things."

"Our Little Sis is like a walking Libra scale." Yvette smiled. "A steady balance of both the masculine and feminine. The Tomboy Princess."

"Yvette, not the nickname!" The two women laughed. "I'm not a kid anymore!"

"Finally, and you're dressed like an adult." Michah laughed. "A very beautiful adult **woman**."

"I swear, you and Dad are the same." She stuck a tongue out at her brother, which he brushed off.

"I'm just saying." Michah held up his hands. "I'm sure your fiancé would agree with me that you look better in feminine clothes."

"Actually, I don't have a preference between masculine or feminine." Osi shrugged. "I love both looks on her."

"Liar." Michah narrowed his eyes.

"Why would I?" Osi shook his head. "Masculine clothing takes nothing away from her. If she's comfortable with her self-expression then so am I."

Oh, that is so touching! I just want to give him all the massages but that would be inappropriate right now.

A waiter stopped by with a menu, pointing out the substitutions for the evening. A good main entree selection of chicken, beef, or fish with two sides and two different soup selections. Michelle observed her other half carrying conversation with Yvette or clapping back at Michah at passive-aggressive comments.

He seems so relaxed, fitting right in place. I'm glad I brought him along.

A loud throat clearing broke the friendly lull over the table. True to her father's word there stood Tyrone, dressed in his own black suit and green and silver tie. There was a moment of awkwardness, as the only empty seat was already reserved for the patriarch of the family.

"Ah, Tyrone." Yvette broke the air. "Didn't think you were coming tonight. We just started putting in our orders for the courses."

"He was just running late." Pastor Winderson walked up to the table, carrying an extra chair. "Linda, can you scoot over a bit? I want to put this chair to Zaria's right."

"Oh, alright sweetie." Linda moved her chair over with no fuss, feeling the tension in the air. "Is Tyrone another family member?"

"He's my ex-boyfriend." Michelle dropped the tea on the table, to the annoyance of her Dad. "Dad invited him."

"...oh." Linda stood up. "I'm going to the Ladies' Room. Can someone put down my order for the fish and the lobster bisque?"

"Sure lovely." Pastor Winderson placed Tyrone in his seat personally, giving his youngest a glare before taking his own seat. "Yvette, you didn't bring a plus one?"

"He's not feeling well so no." She gave a tight smile. "**Both** of them are better off home this evening."

"It's a shame really." He tutted. "I guess Osirion could fill that gap for the night…"

"Dad!" Michelle admonished him. "You're being so rude!"

"Oh, I'll take Tyrone instead." Yvette cut in the conversation. "He's closer in looks to Brandon anyway. I insist, as the big sister."

He opened his mouth for a rebuttal, but the waiter came back to take orders for food and drink. The waiter wrote down the orders before popping the bottle, serving champagne and wine to each one's preference.

"Thank you." Michelle mouthed to her elder sister as Yvette grabbed Tyrone's hand. She smiled back in response before Michelle turned to Tony. "Dad, stop being so inconsiderate."

Her father sighed, looking from his youngest daughter to the man she'd chosen. "…you're right Zaria. I do have a few questions for your guest."

"You've met my mother, father, and brother, Mr. Winderson." Osi looked at her father. "You know what they do for a living and how long they've been in the States."

"I remember that." Tony chuckled. "I have questions for *you*, however. After all, you are now a grown man, and we can talk about certain things that were once off limits when you were in high school."

"You want to do that here, Pops?" Yvette cringed. "In public? At a highly **photographed** event?"

"Oh, I'm sure these questions won't be any trouble for two college aged adults." He brushed his eldest off. "As a father I just have a few concerns for my youngest child, you understand?"

It's never good when he agrees so easily. Michelle looked at her father, trying to see his true motives through his eyes.

"That's fine, Mr. Winderson." Osi shrugged. "I don't mind being questioned if it eases your mind a bit."

"That's great." The older man chuckled. "How long have you two been engaged?"

"A few months so far." Osi cleared his throat. "Since we made it official."

"Wow, a brand new relationship." He smiled. "You've been friends for years, but this is all new territory. I'm guessing you're having a good time?"

"Yes." Even Osirion gave him a suspicious look. "I love your daughter very much."

"That's good to know." He was still smiling. "If you two did make it to the altar, what would the ceremony look like?"

"Excuse me?"

"Surely you two have discussed it at least once?" He leaned in, going for the kill. "You're not a Christian, as I know. I was just curious about if it would be in a church like my own or somewhere else...where does your religion gather for these types of things?"

Oh, I see the plan now. Michelle narrowed her eyes at her father. *I can't tell if he's genuinely curious or using our differences as a division tactic.*

Osirion stared at him for a moment, eyes narrowing. "Well in Shintoism we have shrines. Since it's only been a few months, we haven't talked about the specifics of a future wedding, but I don't object to a church wedding either if that is what Michelle wants."

"Deferring to the woman, interesting." Her father rubbed his chin.

"Simp alert!" Michah stated, taking a drink. "My radar is going off."

"Shut up, Michah." Michelle rolled her eyes. "Dad, we haven't got to those conversations yet. We're only *a few months* into our romance."

"Hmm...what better time to learn than early on?" He countered. "With Tyrone I already knew what to expect. Male Christian plus female Christian equals little Christians. The math is simple, but with Osirion here it's more complicated."

"Pops, they just started seeing each other. This is a peaceful dinner, not a shotgun wedding," Yvette butted in. "You can ask your questions another time; this is highly inappropriate."

"Am I not the father here?" he questioned. "I am entitled to ask these questions of *any man* that wants to be involved with my daughters, no matter how long you've known each other. Being friends is nothing like becoming a couple...especially in the spiritual realm."

"Dad." Michelle spoke up. "I've already told you these answers to some of your questions. Take it at that and leave it."

"You've told me years ago, sweetheart!" He chuckled. "Young people may not like traditional roles nowadays but they have purpose. As a man to another man, I want to know what direction my daughters and future grandchildren could possibly move in. What about children, by the way?"

"What about them?"

"Will your family allow for them to be saved, or will they have to grow up as atheists...or Shintoists first?" Tony paused to shake someone's hand, getting a quick picture in before the food was served on the table. To his credit Osirion closed his eyes, breath coming out of his nose in a heavy rush. He inhaled several times through the mouth, holding the air for a second before exhaling through his nose. She could see his knuckles turn white under the table, but on the outside he passed as collected.

He's barely holding it together. This has to stop.

"Dad. Stop it." Michelle waited until the waiter was done refilling the drinks before she spoke.

"Should have seen this coming..." Tyrone whistled, cutting his steak. She resisted the urge to snap at him, instead opting for her fish.

"Mr. Winderson." Osirion opened his eyes, giving the older man a cold look. His voice had dropped an octave, but the volume remained the same. "Kami, you are a special type of hater."

Did he just steal one of my expressions?

"Did you just cuss at me? Don't make me—

Osi snorted. A full, undignified snort erupted from his mouth, turning into covered laughter from deep within. "No, I didn't. Again, *we haven't discussed this* but since you want my opinion so badly, I can indulge you this one time. Our future children **will** have the freedom of choice. As citizens of two distinct cultures, faiths, languages, worlds...they are entitled to learn about both and choose their birthright. Black and Japanese. Augusta and Nagoya. Christian and Shintoist. What I won't have you, or anyone, do is force them to draw battle lines in an attempt for your simple minds to understand how the hell we organize our home in the first place or which spouse is *more dominant*. Respectfully, do you understand...my position on the matter?"

Well, damn.

Everyone was silent, all looking towards the Winderson patriarch. Her father was angry, eyes narrowed, and a deep frown marred his face. The older man closed his eyes, sucked his teeth, and gave the younger a sardonic smile. "Seems like you and my daughter share a love of words. Don't worry, I got the message loud and clear, Osirion."

"You know..." Linda was the one to break the silence. "This food is really good."

"Despite everything, I have to thank you for inviting me." Like a gentleman, Osi held the door as Michelle stepped out of the limo. The dinner was a bit awkward after everything, and the ride home was muted but pleasant.

"The night isn't over." Michelle kept a straight face, not giving away any emotion. "Come with me."

"Oh..." She could see his worried expression as she carded the two back into her dorm building. The event stretched longer than expected with a variety of speeches and her father's generous contributions to the cause.

"Come on." She fished out her room key from her purse. True to Angel's word, the room was unoccupied as she flipped on her small desk lamp. She held up her hair and looked back. "I need help with my zipper."

"Ah." He grasped the metal zipper and slowly pulled down. "You're not upset?"

"You...you stood up for yourself." His fingertips trailed along the length of her spine, making her shiver. "I wasn't surprised that you got angry but the way you did it was very eloquent to be put on the spot."

"You get those questions being different..." He placed a kiss to the middle of her back. "I'll be heading to my room if you don't need me."

"It's almost 3am." She showed him the time. "You can nap here for a couple of hours. Angel told me she'll be out for the night."

"Her and Raven made up finally?"

"Nah. It's deeper than that." Michelle shook her head. "I'll go to the bathroom and change into a night shirt."

"What am I going to sleep in?" He motioned to his suit.

"Place it on my wooden hangers." She smirked. "You have something underneath, don't you? It doesn't matter to me if you don't..."

She left him to sputter and turn red, carrying a mid-thigh shirt with her. She took her time taking off her makeup, wrapping her pressed hair and tying it with a silk wrap before shimming out of her form fitting dress and *finally* getting out of those high heels.

Relief! I'm proud that I was able to hang on for those hours.

She exited the bathroom and hung up her dress in the closet.

"The next question is where will I be napping?"

"Oh, please yo...."

Michelle locked eyes with Osi standing in her bedroom and trailed off. The moonlight accentuated every muscle in his arms, chest, and stomach as she felt her mouth go dry. He looked firm but not hard, smooth skin stretched over impressive arms, a broad chest, and semi defined abdomen. He looked like he would have a small squish of give before taut muscles could pick her up and twirl her like a baton. Long black hair, dusky brown nipples, and the cockiest expression she's ever seen on his face completed her fantasy come true.

*A fine man that **knows** he's fine is a dangerous creature. Again, I set myself up for this.*

"Michelle?" He chuckled, breaking her intense staring. "Where should I sleep?"

"J-just you k-know." She stuttered. "On top of my bed. I'll be under the covers."

"Oh, the stuttering and the outfit." He whistled at her. "You are too adorable...and with the smooth legs...*adorable.*"

She rolled her eyes. "You look like you want to eat me."

His face started his signature blush, but he didn't look away. "I can make that happen if you want..."

"Oh, someone is smelling himself." She chuckled at his confused glance. "If you're going to do that, at least take me out to dinner first."

"We just came from a very expensive dinner." He stepped towards her, their shoulders touching. "Technically you took *me* out so this should be the reverse."

"In that case." She smirked. "You should be getting on your knees for me then. A good rush of endorphins would definitely relax me enough to sleep."

He stared at her, mouth slightly ajar and eyebrows raised. A red blush stained his cheeks such a pretty color. She let out a low chuckle as she sat down on the bed.

Now this is more like it. Tomato Osi is a classic best of feature...wait, what is he doing?

He suddenly shrugged, a teasing smile on his lips. He raked a hand through his hair before he kneeled down at her feet, fingers running along her stocking wrapped calves. "You talked yourself into some trouble, love."

"M-me?" She choked out as he ran his hand along her arch.

"Yes, you." He painted her with an obvious look. "I'll give you a rush, dear."

His hand traveled up her leg, pausing to tickle behind her knee to draw a laugh. His hands were hot as he started along her inner thigh, a wicked smile drawn on his face.

He is not...oh.

A tremble went through her leg, making her right involuntarily twitch. His finger stopped mid way on her left, right at the band of her sheer stocking. He gently held her thigh in his hand, leaning forward until his breath caressed her skin. His hair shielded his face, ticking her thigh as she felt his teeth catch the band.

His tongue touched the inside of her thigh, almost making her lose her composure. She was deadly still as he dragged the band down to her shin with his mouth, then removed the garment with his hand.

"Shall I remove the second one, Zaria?" He looked up at her expression. A pool of heat was settled low in her belly, threatening to spill over. She didn't dare speak, too stunned to mentally formulate words. "Can't talk now?"

His right hand repeated the ritual, trailing up slow and steady towards her band. She let out a gasp, almost deafening in the quiet room. His head tilted slightly at the noise, eyes concentrating on her lidded expression.

He rubbed her thigh, warmth spreading through his hand before inching further upwards. A heady gasp tore out of her mouth as he touched her bare skin. Her hands clenched the sheets tighter as she bit her bottom lip.

Oh, please don't stop now...

His hand inched further and further up, leaving a heated trail in his wake. Less than an inch away from her heated core, his hand stopped. A dark chuckle filled the room as he leaned his head up to stare right in her eyes. "Now you know how it feels...the things you slip out of your mouth, the looks you give when you think I don't notice. The things I want to do...every single...time. Now, sit here and be a good girl for Daddy."

He curled his fingers inward, dragging his blunt nails down her thigh until he reached the stocking she was still wearing. His eyes were wide and black, a look as dark as the unfathomable sea reflecting directly at her. The sting of his nails caused a loud groan to leave her lips, eyes filled with disbelief.

An intense longing filled her as she stared down at his expression. Before he could catch her stocking again, she rushed forward, a hand twisting in his hair forcing him to look up. "You're a good tease as well but you are meant to serve me."

She saw him part his lips to speak but nothing came out. She twisted her hand again, catching his long ponytail. "Make yourself useful and eat this pussy."

The room was silent, save for their labored breaths. He felt that part of himself, always sealed away from the light, clawing to come out under her intense gaze. The part he indulged in his darkest paintings, the part that does not turn from pain or pleasure or pressure but instead reveled in the intense fantasies of his mind all with her as a glowing co-star.

What if my good intentions are depriving her of something essential? He saw the darkness in her eyes and instead of worrying him, sparks of excitement surged all over his body.

"What was I thinking? Of course, I'll serve you." With beautiful clarity he realized he could be free around her with no judgment.

His hand shot up, cupping her warm, lacy covered mound. She released his hair from shock, and he worked his thumb on her clit, middle finger stroking the puddling moisture at her entrance. She threw her head back as his thumb nudged her hardened bundle of nerves.

"Look at you, so wet and needy." He rose up and kissed the column of her neck. He let his pointer and ring fingers thump her swollen outer lips.

She groaned out something not of words but of a baser need. He fondled her wet underwear until he slipped his middle finger inside. He took turns kissing the left and right sides of her neck, nipping here and there to go along with his thrusting hand. Her hands gripped his forearms, panting with the mounting pleasure.

"Do you want more?" His voice was ragged against her ear.

"Y-yes." She closed her eyes, trying to form words. "I want more."

"So, demanding." He eased her glasses off onto the bed, bringing her face to look him in the eyes. Her mouth was open, small pants coming out with a flushed face and dazed expression. This was the most unraveled he's ever seen her, and she was absolutely beautiful. "Beg me."

She bit her lip, eyes shifting away for a moment before coming back to him. "Osirion, please don't leave me like this. Don't be so cruel..."

"That was good." He rubbed her face. His thumb swirled small circles across her clit, and she jumped. "I like the way you say my name."

"You're enjoying this, aren't you?" She laughed, body twitching in pleasure. "Bending me with just a single hand."

"Of course I am." He smiled. "I've dreamed about you for years, eyes closed as I fucked myself to insanity and shame. I will be enjoying all of this."

"Ah..." She cried out as he curled his finger deeper. "Well, now you have my full attention, future husband."

He withdrew his hand, glancing at the wet digits. A whimper filled the air, making him smile. With a gentle kiss, he picked her up and placed her body across her bed. "At last."

She leaned up on her elbows, breath catching in her throat. He was standing between parted legs, gently peeling away her underwear while placing her leg on one of his shoulders. Her eyes traveled down to his red boxer briefs, the large wet spot making her blush. "Someone's excited."

He kissed her thigh, his face bending down. "I'm not the only one either."

He held her legs open, tongue lapping from her parted opening up to her swollen, engorged nerves. His lips kissed and wrapped around her clit as his tongue swirled and traveled around. She threw her head back as her thighs clamped around his head. His hands massaged her legs, getting her to loosen enough to breathe again.

She's finally unraveling after all this time.

He kissed her outer lips before using his fingers to expose her inner parts. He tasted and explored to his heart's desire, finding out what made her legs twitch and eyes roll with an uncanny patience. "You're so beautiful, you know that?"

"T-thank you." He alternated his hand, curling two of his fingers against a squishy bump inside of her walls.

"No really." His thumb circled her clit at just the right speed and pressure. "You're so flustered and shaking..."

"Ugh." Her right leg started to tense, thigh muscle flexing with a tightness.

"...teetering so close, I feel you clenching around me..." He increased the speed of his curling fingers. "...so far away..."

Her eyes fluttered as the tension wound tighter and tighter. "I-I—

"I know, love." He felt her shake as he applied steady, constant pressure. "You're going to come for me, my good girl. Just let go..."

A new wave of heat rolled down her stomach. "A good girl?"

"Yes." He spoke with reverence. She cried out, grabbing hold of his arms. "My bossy, teasing, good girl. Now, come for me you little brat."

That tension building up in her leg finally snapped, a flood of warmth gushing from between her legs. She cried out, eyes shut as her back arched with her release.

He should be demanding more often because I can get used to this.

"Oh yes." She heard him groan above her. "You taste delicious."

"Wha?" She turned her head to look at him, watching his tongue trailing his arm to collect her lingering juices.

His other hand was palming a rather impressive erection through his wet underwear. He was as erotic as he was wicked, staring her down with a smile. "...don't do *that*."

"Do what?" He chuckled, scooting closer to tap himself against her unsteady legs. "Giving you fuel for your dirty little fantasies later?"

"You ass..." She laughed, thoroughly wet and embarrassed. She heard him rummage through her table. "I don't have any rubbers dear. Threw them out with the breakup."

I didn't think about refreshing my stash for a while now. Gotta use this brain for more than writing storage.

"We didn't have them the first time you were under me." He walked back over to her, kissing her stomach.

"Plan B is for emergencies, not frequent happenings." She cursed her luck, feeling coming back in her toes. "You're not a submissive, are you?"

"I can be." He smiled. "But not usually. I'll make you a deal though."

"What kind of deal?"

He gently pulled her up to a sitting position, still in between her legs. She was eye level to his stomach, and just a little lower than his crotch. He kissed over her face, moving down her neck with gentleness. "I'll gladly be your submissive..."

"But?" she whispered as he leaned in for a kiss.

"Just know that any moment, I can toss you in my lap and show you how dominant I can be." He smiled. "I remember you calling me, what was it...tic-tac sized?"

Of course, he would remember that...

She let out a nervous chuckle. "You didn't forget that."

"Of course not." His grin grew. "Many times, you have alluded to me being small so it was easy to remember."

She laughed, throwing her head back. "Have you forgotten you've been inside of me a few times now?"

"Not in that pretty little mouth of yours." He smirked at her. "I know you don't like the act itself, so I'll leave the choice to you."

Michelle cringed as her memory reminded her why she hated it so much. *Especially the soreness afterwards.*

"Are you alright?" He kissed her cheek, concerned. "You can turn me down if you want."

"I'm curious to try but..." She pointed to her throat which was actually bare for the night. "...without the pain of an aching throat."

His eyes flickered as he realized what she was saying. "I should go and punch him in the throat again."

"You should, but not right now." She ran her fingers down his stomach, making him laugh. She hooked her thumbs under the band of his clothes and pulled down. "Show me how it's supposed to feel."

She wrapped a hand around his shaft, giving it a squeeze. It twitched in her palm, hardening under her touch. She pushed back the foreskin, exposing his bright rose-colored head. She stuck out her tongue, giving him a swipe. His hips bucked forward but her hand caught his hip just in time.

"You know it doesn't bite..." His face was flushed but he was smiling. "You're doing good so far."

"Be careful or I might give you a nibble." She gave him a slow hand pump, running her thumb underneath his shaft.

"You're the one who put his dick in my face to begin with, so now I get to run a few experiments."

He was about to reply but she hushed him with another long lick, hand pumping at a leisurely pace. He tasted salty but also smelled faintly of soap. She smiled before taking him a few inches into her mouth. He grabbed her shoulders and forced his hands to stay still.

How considerate to not shove it down all the way.

Michelle nudged him over to the bed, waiting as he stretched out on the covers. She wrapped her hand around him again before opening wide, taking him all the way to the base. She relaxed her throat as he stretched her a bit, tongue flat against his underside as she hummed.

"...say something." She looked at his gleeful expression.

"Mm." She rolled her eyes at his chuckle, realizing what he was referencing.

He's big enough after all. Congratulations.

She cut off his mental glee by bobbing her head up and down, getting into a steady rhythm. One hand rubbed and rotated his foreskin, while another came to palm the two heavy balls tapping against her chin with every down stroke.

He groaned, hand rubbing her shoulder as salty fluid leaked into her mouth. She removed his swollen head with a 'pop', a strand of saliva breaking. He protested with a low moan, more clear fluid running down her fingers and puddling to the sheets.

"You are making a mess." She chuckled, swirling her thumb over his head. "You'll be cleaning up after, understand?"

"Ah..." He sputtered, opening his eyes.

"You understand?" She gave him a hard squeeze, pumping him faster.

His face was turning as red as the head she was rolling around with her hand. "Y-yes, just don't stop..."

"Yes what?" His hips were bucking, meeting her thrust for thrust. Just from his expression he had to be close to going over that edge...

"Michelle..." He was gasping, hips rolling with her movements.

He's going to lose his patience, but he has to learn.

She let out a dark chuckle. Shoving down his hips, she took him all the way down her throat in one move. She felt him swell in her mouth, squeezing his base tightly just before he could orgasm.

"Zaria!" He glared daggers as she took him out her mouth, hand still pumping in her grip.

"Say **'Yes, Mistress'** and I'll let go." Her hand glided up and down the shaft and skin, feeling him pulse and drip in desperation.

He was floored, hips trying to buck off her grip. "You—you..."

"You must not want to come, Osi." She grinned at his expression. Was it mean? Yes. Was she also having fun at his expense? Definitely. Would he get her later for denying his orgasm? She had no doubt, but for now she had the upper hand.

"...Yes, Mistress." He managed to ground out clenched teeth, sweat running down his face.

"That wasn't hard, sweetheart." She stopped pumping to observe his now purple head and bulging veins. She leaned forward a little too far, mouth open to slowly tease him.

"No, but I still am." He grasped the back of her head, tangling his fingers into her hair. "Open your mouth nice and wide."

She followed his directions and closed her eyes. He led her down slowly, filling her throat until her lips bottomed out at his base. He massaged the nape of her neck, slowly thrusting with a deep groan.

"Did that hurt?" He pulled her off to stare at her face.

"No." She was a bit dazed but unharmed.

"Now back down." He eased his shaft back into her mouth with a tight hold on her hair. He rolled his hips slowly as he thrust inside her mouth. Her hands rubbed along his hips and she dragged her nails against his skin.

"Oh...fuck yes." His voice was lovely in her ears. She felt him quiver under her touch. His grip on her hair was secure but she saw he was about to lose it. "Keep doing that."

He's starting to unravel. Is this how it's supposed to go?

His strokes became shorter and faster but he didn't go overboard with force. Her face flushed at the mews and whines filling the room. A fine sheen of sweat made her hands slippery against his skin and caused her to dig her nails harder near his thighs.

"I'm gonna come down your throat." He growled into the room as he came, thick and salty semen forcing her to swallow. His yell filled the air as he poured into her throat, riding out his orgasm until its end.

Oh that was a lot.

He released her after a long moment, letting her come up for air. "Are you alright?"

A small trail of white leaked out the corner of her mouth and down her chin. "That was...something. I love the sound of your voice."

"Oh yeah?" His voice was rough and pleased. "How was it?"

"I want to do it again." She savored the aftertaste lingering in her mouth. "I want to see you shake and shiver under my touch."

His teeth caught his bottom lip as he flushed. "If I wasn't so worn out, I would punish your little ass."

She blushed, not expecting his choice of words. "I touched a nerve, huh?"

He pushed his sweaty hair back. "I touched a bundle of them and you came apart."

"That's a good one." She collapsed next to him. "Don't forget to dry off my mattress and change my sheets when you get up, okay."

"I won't." He kissed her forehead. "I know those rumors are false from personal experience now..."

"Oh God." She groaned. "Never trust the words of a broken hearted boy. Let's just say he doesn't know me as well as he thinks he does..."

I almost forgot about that.

He nuzzled against her, spent for the evening. He let out a yawn as he willed himself off the bed. "Oh, and my parents finally decided on a date to interrogate you."

"Oh really?" Michelle felt a wave of nervousness set in. "Tell me when and where."

Eighteen

Dinner with the Parents

Michelle walked through the large glass doors with her Mom right at her side. The small black box was steady in her hands but she was sweating bullets on the inside of her pants suit. She wore a colorful floral pattern with a flattering cut for a modern and unisex look for the evening.

Intimacy will always win out over sex. Over time, a close bond will win out over a relationship held together by late night encounters.

Her now silver haired Mom always drilled the simple rule into Michelle ever since the young girl started to get crushes on boys. If Michelle had to bring anyone with her to this warmly lit restaurant it would be her Mom.

Seated in the very back of the calm establishment was her beloved and both of his parents.

I usually don't have to do things like this.

Being a Winderson came with a few good perks in the area. Everyone that wished to date Pastor Tony's children had to go through the patriarch first, with Osirion being the exception to the rule. Suitors tripped over themselves for Pastor to even like them enough to allow a relationship, and being the youngest, Michelle was always the prized one as she grew into womanhood. Her father's reputation would actually be a negative tonight instead of an overwhelming boon.

"It's lovely to see you both again." In the middle was his father Makoto, who stood up as the two women approached. The graying man had the stature of Osirion but reminded her of a mid-50s Toshiro. "Michelle. Tisha. It's been a while since we've seen each other."

Michelle gave his offered hand a firm shake. Tisha smiled and gave him a small hug which he readily accepted.

"Michelle." The even tone of his mother caught her attention. His wife Akiko was a few shades darker than husband with her olive brown tone and just as gorgeous as the former First Lady of Faithview Baptist.

I wonder how often she tans for that beautiful color, if at all.

"Hello Ma'am." Michelle gave her a polite bow to which the older woman returned. She didn't smile at Michelle but that was to be expected. Tisha walked over and gave a quick kiss to her cheek.

How did they get so friendly and I get the cold shoulder?

"Good evening, love." Osi bent down and kissed her on the lips. It was a polite kiss they could do in front of parents without getting into trouble.

"Hey sweetie." She kissed him in return before everyone took their seats.

Suddenly the busy room was too quiet as Michelle tried to quiet her beating heart. The lights were hot and a sense of unease came over her. Michelle politely looked over the menu as she cleared her throat. "How have you two been over the past few years?"

The older couple looked back and forth, speaking in quick Japanese before Akiko answered. "We've been doing well. Since our children are in college we've been traveling across the States."

"Kanojo wa musuko no neckless wa kubi ni mai te i masu." His mother leaned over to her graying husband.

(She's wearing our son's necklace around her neck.)

Michelle tried not to look obvious as she translated their conversation.

"Naruhodo. Kanojo wa kare no okurimono wa ukeire ta,oboe te i masu ka?" Makoto replied.

(I see that dear. She accepted his gift, remember?)

"Karera wa konyaku shi te i masu! Naze kanojo wa chounan ni fusawashii to omotsu te iru no desho u ka?" Akiko almost barked at her proper husband.

(They're engaged! Why does she think she's good enough for our eldest son?)

Michelle let out a deep sigh. *Oh, this is going to be an uphill fight.*

"Ah, well!" Tisha smiled before looking at her daughter. "Michelle here just transferred for her creative writing program this semester. It set her back a semester or so but she'll be able to get her bachelors here."

"Creative writing?" Makoto stared at her. Sarcasm flowed from his lips like water in a stream. "That's one of those majors that you should be really good at or you're just wasting your time."

"Considering I'm the top transferring student of this semester I would say I'm good at what I do." Michelle gave him a smile. "There is always room for improvement. That's how you remain the best, right?"

"Aa, kanojo wa taido ga ari masu." His mother's tone was clipped in low tones.

(Oh, she has an attitude.)

"Kanojo ni ijiwaru wa shi nai de kudasai." Osirion broke up his parents respectfully.

(Don't be mean to her.)

"Ima no tokoro kanojo ga suki desu. Kanojo wa gaiken yori mo backborne wa motsu te i masu." Makoto nodded his head slightly.

(I like her so far. She has more of a backbone than what appears on the outside.)

Tisha leaned into her daughter's ear with a whisper. "Do you have any idea what they are saying?"

"Give me some time. It's going to be hilarious." Michelle whispered back with a smile.

"This is one of my favorite style of restaurants." Tisha broke up the murmurs with a smile. "Korean BBQ is one of my guilty pleasures I must admit."

"I'm glad that hasn't changed over the years." Makoto was warm with Tisha as he gave her a smile.

Conversation stopped for everyone to order at the table. The waiter turned on the grill plate in the center of the table before he served drinks around the table. Michelle cleared her throat with a smile.

"I have a gift for you sweetie." She passed the black box to Osi. She placed her clammy hands in her lap as he gave her a bright smile. She heard her mother coo from her side of the table.

"Thank you." He unwrapped the silk bow around the box. Inside was a ring. Gold and white gold was twisted together in an artistic expression highlighting a wolf's head on the top with two dazzling gems shifting in shades of red, white and greens. "It's amazing."

She motioned to her middle finger, and he slipped it on his right hand. The style was different from what he usually wore but the craftsman managed to make it fit onto his hand. He tilted his head at her. "Why a wolf?"

"It's my favorite animal. Wolves also remind me of my huskies back home that I grew up with all the time." Michelle gave him a soft smile. "Also the wolf does represent my family. You remember I am a military brat right? I would be a cute wolf cub since my father was called the Midnight Wolf during his service."

"Something that is both personal to you and also represents your family." Osi nodded approvingly. "Also, it's something I can wear just like your necklace. What kind of stones are set for the eyes?"

"One of your birthstones." Michelle smiles. "Tourmalines. The different hues are called watermelon tourmalines specifically."

Beautiful stones. Hard as hell to find. Perfect hard stone for an artist.

Akiko grabbed her son's hand to investigate Michelle's offering. "This...is nice actually." The woman's English was thickly accented with her light, heavenly voice.

"Thank you so much." Michelle took the compliment with a gracious smile.

"Kanojo ga warui okurimono wa shi te kure tara ii noni. Kanojo wa oikaesu no wa kantan daro u." Makoto talked in the direction of his wife.

(I wish she gave a bad gift. It would be easier to turn her away.)

"Kanojo wa oikaeshi tai desu ka?" Osi frowned at his father.

(You want to turn her away?)

"Watashi wa sou shi taku nai no desu ga, sore wa ronri teki desu." The older man hushed his son.

(I don't want to but it's logical.)

His mother stared Michelle down, her eyes going through a plethora of emotions. She was quiet but her voice broke through the two men that were talking in clipped tones. "Why do you love my son? Surely there are other choices out there for you."

The question took Michelle off guard. Everyone quieted down to hear her answer. She was quiet for a few moments, eyes closed in concentration. She took so long one would think Michelle didn't have an answer to such a logical inquiry but then she spoke.

"Naze watashi wa kare wa aisa nai no daro u?" Her Southern accent was thick, as expected, but she pronounced the words a bit slower than one would for clarity.

(Why wouldn't I love him?)

This isn't my first language but it's worth it. I hope I can get my point across.

Michelle cleared her throat before proceeding. "Saisho wa kare ga uttoushiku te totemo hen da to omoi mashi ta. Sonogo, kare wa watashi no shinyuu to nari, cut sa re ta diamond no you ni, kono you na subarashii dansei wa tsukuriage ta fukusuu no fa set wa miru koto ga deki mashi ta. Nengetsu ga tatsu nitsure, watashi wa kare wa kai tai to omotsu ta .shoyuu mono no you ni de wa naku, partner toshite. Watashi to ni arui te subarashii monogatari wa tomoni tsukureru hito. Yousuruni, kare wa anata no musuko da kara, watashi wa kare wa aishi te i masu. Kare koso watashi ga aishi te iru hito desu."

(I first thought Osirion was annoying, and very strange. Then he became my closest friend and like a cut diamond I could see the multiple facets that combined to make such a wonderful man. As the years went by I desired to have him. Not like a possession but as a partner. Someone that I could walk alongside and...create a wonderful story together. In short, because he is your son I love him. He's the one I love.)

Tisha squealed, hugging Michelle in a tight hug. "Vous avez si bien fait!

(You did so well!)

Michelle laughed at her mother's joy. "Tu parles encore français."

(You're speaking French again.)

"Baby girl, look at their faces!" Tisha pointed out to her youngest.

Each member of the Najimi family had different reactions splayed across their faces. Osirion was gaping at her with wide eyes. The tips of his ears turned red as his mind whirled like dial-up Internet over the phone lines. Makoto started laughing at the table. The older man was turning red in the face from humor as he tried to hold himself together. His mother nodded in appreciation, her previously straight face breaking into some positive emotion.

"You understood us all this time, didn't you?" Osi turned to her.

"Yes." Michelle nodded excitingly.

"How long?"

"Oh I started four semesters ago." She waved at him. "I took all the 100 and 200 level courses and now I brush up to keep it fresh."

"So when I called on the phone and everything..." Osi waved his hands about. "You knew what I was saying?"

"I did."

The poor man was blushing so hard Michelle was concerned that he was going to pass out. "Oh..um..."

"Yes son." Makoto finally regained his senses. "She knew every dirty thing you said in Japanese. Thought you got away with it, but you did not."

"What kind of things were you saying to this young woman?" Akiko asked him with a stern look.

"Excuse me." Osi rose from his seat and walked in the direction of the restrooms.

"He'll be alright." Makoto waved off his son before turning to her. "You are full of surprises!"

"Very much." His mother smirked. "You're grown from that girl that was rubbing against my son like you were in heat."

Wow, why she gotta bring up old stuff!

"Well you know how teenagers get with their hormones." Tisha was cooking her selection of meat and vegetables on the grill. "Your son lived long enough to grow into a nice young man."

"Ah yes." Both of his parents cringed but Makoto spoke up. "I had to save him from your ex-husband Tisha."

"Tony can be quite intense." She plated her hot food. "He's a great father but he goes overboard at times."

"You are a good choice for my son." Makoto looked at the golden serpent around Michelle's neck. "We've been prepared for this for a long time. I have no objections to you alone Michelle."

"But?" She heard his hesitation. Everyone knew the elephant in the room.

"When you marry, you marry someone's entire family." He stared her down. "That includes your father. I cannot imagine myself related to that man that you have the unfortunate circumstance of being a part of."

"Hold up on the insults." She frowned. "I know you two have beef and all, but he's still my Dad."

"You're right." The older man sighed. "So how did he take your engagement? Or did he not figure that part out yet?"

"Oh he knows." She looked away. "He's waiting for the other shoe to drop. Not happy about it but besides being petty he's just waiting."

"Always good to know that your father wishes all the ill on your happiness right?" Makoto narrowed his eyes. "I bet you two have a wonderful relationship."

"Ha ha. We do but we don't agree on many things." Michelle deadpanned. "At the heart of it all we're just a normal family, bickering and all. You and my Dad already got the fighting part down so you just have to work on getting along."

I definitely sold that because not agreeing is an understatement. Let's say it's a work in progress.

"You talk like I've already given you my blessing." He smiled at her.

"You have." She smirked at the older man. "You have no personal objections to me. That means I'm solid as far as you are concerned. The question is are you going to hold me accountable for the sins of my father?"

"That's the big question isn't it?" Makoto chewed his food for a moment. Everyone sat in relative silence before he broke the vibe. "I'm not but I will beat that man within an inch of his life if needed."

"You really think you can take on an US war veteran in a fair match?" Michelle didn't mean to sound rude but she could tell he took it hard. Although in shape and put together for his age, Makoto was shorter than his sons by two or so inches. She couldn't see the details on his frame from his blazer and coat but she assumed he muscle definition was about average or below. "No offense Najimi-sama."

"You know about honorifics?" Osi had snuck his way back to the table looking better than before.

"Oh yes." Michelle smiled. "I used the right one. How can I not respect a man that faced off against an angry father with a gun to save his child? Plus you did move **thousands** of miles to come to Georgia with your family not knowing what you were going to get. I respect your father greatly so that's the reason."

"That's very kind." His mother smiled at Michelle softly. "So babies..."

Michelle felt her face heat up. "I want them but not anytime soon. What about them?"

Why does everyone want grandchildren nowadays? Do they know how expensive childcare is in this country?

She scooted closer with a large smile on her face. "Osirion is our eldest son. You know that means he has a responsibility..."

"Mother." Osi groaned. "We haven't been together that long to talk about children."

"You two are engaged." She deadpanned. "You have so much culture to absorb before that happens though."

Tisha chuckled. "Oh yes. I'll have to take you back home too so my grandchildren will have some NOLA soul in them."

Most people get their cultural practices from their mother and her relatives. It would make sense for her and my Mom to basically tag team me about any future grandchildren.

"I'm a new age Southerner at heart." Michelle gave both of the older women a smile. "But I'm willing to learn some things if either of you want to share them..."

"Oh, that is wonderful!" Akiko squealed at the table like a girl. "Tisha, we both have to help these young ones for our future bloodline!"

"Couldn't have said better myself, Akiko." Tisha scooted closer and they immediately went into planning mode.

This is going to be their long term project.

"My love." Osi's sing-song voice caught her attention. "Thank you for the gift. I love it."

"Really?" She blushed just a little, thankful for her dark skin. "I'm so glad you like it! I kinda matched the design from my charm bracelet."

She pulled up her sleeve to show off a thick rose gold bracelet. There were a few charms attached: a flute, a small doghouse, a typewriter, fists, and a wolf's head in white gold. They were small and dainty as they caught the restaurant lights.

This is going better than I imagined. Especially with the gun incident. Then a fight at a restaurant and the church parking lot. There's probably even more reasons than the ones I know.

She squinted her eyes. For a second she saw the same dark energy around the older man as he reminisced that reminded her of her lover. She took off her glasses and it was gone.

What was that about?

"So go ahead and be together. When I do come around I will try to be as civil as possible; I just ask for the same treatment in return." Makoto smiled as he caught her attention.

"Thank you." Michelle worked on her own food before her stomach could growl.

She felt his eyes on her as she chewed. Makoto was smiling but he was looking through her instead of just looking in her direction. He finished off his food and turned to his companions. "Should we go and give these two some privacy?"

"Oh?" Osi stared at his father with surprise. "You're leaving us alone?"

"Why not?" He clapped Osi on the shoulder. "Just don't forget to...let her know about that. I don't want you to scare her off."

"Let me know about what?" Michelle questioned with friendly eyes.

Osi swallowed hard before he addressed his father. "I will. Good night."

Makoto laughed. "You have a long conversation ahead of you. Good evening son, Michelle."

The three said their goodbyes as they went out on the town for the rest of the night, leaving Michelle and Osirion alone. She arched an eyebrow at him. "A long conversation indeed. Should we start on that right now?"

"Let us wait until we get more comfortable." Osi chuckled as he started to eat.

"Alright." Michelle smiled. "We can wait if you want."

At least they paid before dipping out on us.

Detangling Issues

Sex can feel wonderful if done right, but it doesn't compare to having someone's hands help you take loose the ropes of twists and freeing your hair from their stylish abodes. Michelle had grabbed a night bag and a bunch of supplies before crashing with her beloved for the evening. She was seated on the floor in between his legs as her hands deftly unraveled another twist. She didn't have any added hair to complicate things, and she smiled at his confused expressions.

"So, first the water." He misted the top of her head with the bottle. Osirion was a bit heavy with it but he had the spirit. "Then the conditioner, right?"

"Yep." She squirted a bit in her hand before handing him the bottle. "Work the conditioner in one twist. Then start from the bottom and unwind them."

"This smells like coconuts." Osi followed her instructions with a nervous energy in his hands. He struggled to unwind the two strands and she handed him a rat tailed comb after a moment.

"Take the point end and find where the twists can be parted." Michelle had detangled her freed section and already started on another.

"Alright." He has an easier time and is working his fingers in her hair. "Your hair is soft."

"Yes it is." She used a pad with lots of tiny bristles to work out the strands of shed hairs. "You know what I'm going to ask."

"I do." He groaned but continued to work. "Go ahead."

"What do you have to tell me that can scare me off?" Michelle started on another section.

"Ahem." He coughed to the side. "It's nothing unusual."

"Right..." She rolled her eyes. "Are you an international criminal running from the law?"

"No!" He blurted out. "Why is that the first thing you thought about?"

"I read it in a romance novel." She shrugged. "It sounds sexy on paper but it would be a logistical nightmare. I can't go on vacation because you might go to prison. Ugh..."

Osi laughed at her, leaning on her smaller frame. His laughter was light against her ear. "It's nothing like that. I just like different things, darker things than some."

"That's not a big deal." She sighed. "I thought you were a secret killer or a former incel. Now that would have been terrifying."

"That doesn't bother you?" He tried to detangle a patch of hair near her crown but she took it from his inexperienced hands.

"No!" She laughed at his shocked face. "I mean...you'll think I'm crazy but I see it around you. Like a shadow."

"A dark shadow?" He pondered for a moment. "Shinto also believes in spirits. Maybe I should go and get purified during the summer if it's visible to you."

"Purified? Is that like being baptized?" She elaborated when he gave her a confused look. "Dunked in a body of water after confessing your life and starting anew. Letting the blood wash away your sin?"

"In a roundabout way. I do purify my negative energy with water." He smiled. "There are no official shrines in Georgia so I have to do it myself."

"Don't you have a shrine in your room?" Michelle pointed at his door. "Or is that for a different purpose?"

"It's my personal shrine." He detangled a twist completely on his own. "I pray and leave offerings but other shrines are dedicated to different Kami and are more communal."

"Does it compare to worship online and worshiping in a church?" She asked. "In the sense of being alone versus being with others that share your beliefs."

"In a sense, yes."

"Ah, I think I understand." A wave of sadness came over her. "What do you want to do when you want to worship?"

"I pray at my shrine in my room and make offerings." He raked his fingers across her scalp. "The closest shrine in this country would be in Honolulu but there are so many tourists during that time of the year."

"Hawaii?" She gasped as he continued his ministrations. "There's no online option for you huh?"

"Sadly no." He sighed. "It's hard to explain Shinto without being back home. It's cultural. It's religious. It's—"

"You're homesick." She moved her head to kiss at his exposed thighs. Her heart ached for him as she peppered him with kisses.

"I am." His voice was light, tinged with sadness. "I want to go back after graduation...with you."

"I would love to see where you came from." A moan slipped from her mouth as he scratched her scalp. "But you'll have to lead me around like I'm a kid playing with a new toy."

"I would love to." His voice was barely above a whisper as she finished the last of her twists, freeing her confined hair.

She leaned her head back with closed eyes, savoring her freedom. Her face was at peace then she felt a strong prod at the back of her head. "You can't help yourself, can't you?"

"It's a compliment." He continued with her massage. "I love being around you, close to you, touching you. What do you expect to happen?"

She leaned even more into him with a smile. Stripped down to the least amount of clothing they both were relaxed against one another. She let out a low chuckle. "...for you to punish me I guess."

His fingers stopped moving along her scalp. She opened her eyes at the lack of stimulation to meet his black eyes and shallow breath. Osi leaned in close and ghosted a kiss upside down on her lips. It was nothing more than a brush against her own but sparks shot down her body at the simple contact.

"Should I put you across my lap then?" He whispered against the shell of her ear. "Bind you to my bed and have my way with you? Pin you against the wall and see if I can make you cry? I've been thinking about it for a long time."

This man has no shame whatsoever...

"Would it hurt?" Her eyes were half closed as she looked up at him.

"It could." He licked his lips slowly for her to see. "Pain and pleasure are better together. It wouldn't be unbearable."

Why am I even considering this?

Her tongue darted out to wet her own lips. The room was warming up the longer she held his gaze but she couldn't let it go. "What would you get out of it?"

"Everything." His hands continued their gentle ministrations. "Laying my hands on you. Watching you twist and turn. Seeing the expressions on your face. Making your skin turn a bright red under my touch."

Because it's interesting and it's something we wanted for a long time...

She saw him swallow as he described everything to her. She felt his hand trace her necklace, her gift on his hand touching her sensitive skin. Her heart drummed against her chest in a worrying way combined with the familiar prickles of apprehension.

...before Purity Camp...

"Was that too much?" His concern washed over her as he placed a hand over her heart.

"I want to but I shouldn't." Her tongue feels too big for her mouth but she gets it out.

"Why not?" His brow knitted together. "Am I scaring you?"

"I'm scaring myself." She gently broke eye contact by rising from his lap. Even after all this time Michelle still felt the tethers of her past cutting off the full depths of her desire. She pressed a hand to her eyes, parting her legs enough for the cooler air to temper the wet heat staining her underwear.

"It's alright." He touched her back. "I can see it's hard for you to fully let go."

"I'm so tired." She pulled her knees to her chest in a self-soothing attempt. "The constant strain makes me so tired. I just want to jump off the cliff of desire and fall..."

Thanks a lot Purity Camp for the extra trauma.

She felt him rise from the couch and she closed her eyes. She didn't want to see if he decided this was too much and had to go away. It wasn't logical to think he would leave her in the living room for the night but that voice in the back of her head wasn't based on logic.

"Hey you." His fingers cradled the sides of her head as he pulled her face out of her knees. He was kneeling in front of her, straddling one of her legs with a smile. His face was soft despite his erection resting on her thigh. "Look at me love."

"Yes?" She was already embarrassed and still had to wash and plait her hair for the night.

"You don't have to be ashamed." He kissed the top of her head. "You don't have to worry about me walking out the door either."

He kissed her near the corners of her eyes. "You chose to love me, so let me choose to love you." He planted a loving kiss on her lips before pulling away. "You're scared of intimacy, not sex. So, let me help you please."

"How can you help me?" Her heart was beating fast enough to come out her chest. "You're going to let me tease you all night?"

He snorted. "How would **that** help?"

"I mean...it does!" She shrugged. "I feel a bit bad afterwards but it's like training myself to have and accept these feelings."

He sighed. "What happened for you to feel this way?"

Michelle looked at his worried expression and confessed. She told him the horrible experience known as Purity Camp. The sexual shaming. The constant pitting of girls against each other to be the purest of them all. The sweet and unsettling Father-Daughter Balls. The mistrust and aversion of young men. The more she told him about it, the more her mouth flowed with story after story. It was something she had buried so deep in her tortured mind, she couldn't get it out, but she trusted Osi in many ways.

I mean we exchanged gifts and did the parental meet up. We're engaged, of all things! He has a right to know what he's walking into.

To his credit Osirion listened intently to her story. He forced his face to remain as neutral as possible. Of all people he couldn't judge her upbringing, but it lit a fire inside.

"That's inhumane." He waited until she was finished and silence descended on them before speaking. "To punish your daughter for having human urges."

Michelle opened her mouth to defend her family but nothing came out. Honestly a part of her was broken, or at least fractured severely.

"That's why you tease me so much." Understanding was on his face. "It's a way to claim a bit of what you lost."

"Yes." She closed her eyes with a heavy sigh. "I'm a lover but it's hard for me to give love."

"Yet you love me." He leaned in to nuzzle her cheek. "How do you feel when you're with me?"

She gave him a loving look. They'd known each other long enough to see the good and the bad in each other. "I feel safe and content."

Michelle gently held his face and kissed him. He let out a little hum of pleasure in response. First she gave him a peck, then another, then she gently pried his mouth open with her lips. He groaned when she entered his mouth and held the back of her head with tentative hands.

Is he nervous or just being gentle?

She trailed her lips away from his to his neck, pecking and nipping as she traveled downward. He held her with his hands but she was the more assertive of the two this time around.

"You can kiss me back." She whispered in the crook of his shoulder.

"I know." He kissed her shoulder once. "This isn't about me though. I want **you** to kiss me."

Her hands traced along his neck and chest, giving his stomach a small tickle. "You want me to kiss you?"

"I want you to be **comfortable** kissing me." He explained. "I want you but I can control myself for the time."

Her fingers traced over his nipples and he shivered. She went back to his face and gave him a full kiss on his lips. She held nothing back as she kissed him like her life depended on it. Her tongue explored every crevice she could touch as he responded in kind. It was sloppy, embarrassing, and highly erotic the way their mouths moved against one another.

Now she was even wetter and her panties were uncomfortable against her skin. Her fingers trailed down to separate the fabric from her swollen lips but he popped her hand before she could get there. Then her hand wandered down his chest to mess with his erection but he popped her again.

"Not tonight." He nipped her ear.

"It's uncomfortable." She lifted her hips to show him her issue. His hands twitched at her waist but he reigned himself in. "You can touch me at least, or pull my panties away from me."

"No." He spoke through his teeth. "I'm controlling myself."

"I am amazed at your control." She admitted, motioning down to his own soaked through garments. "But the air is making me cold and kissing you is making me hot."

"It evens out." He nipped her other ear. "Keep them on until you go and take a shower."

"I'm taking them off." She rose on her knees to shimmy them down.

"No." He narrowed his eyes before giving her one slap against her rear end. She moaned before she could stop herself as her face flushed.

"...did you just spank me?" She gaped at him.

He blushed and hid his hands behind his back. "Gomen-nassai!"

Michelle stared in shock before standing up and taking them off.

"You—"

"Nope." She balled up her soaked underwear and stuffed it in his mouth. "You can put me over your knee later but I'm going to shower and wash. You stay here until I get out of the bathroom."

"Hmhm." He made a few noises but didn't move.

"Aht aht!" She waved a finger at him. "Stay down and wait until I return."

Michelle grabbed her bag and walked out the living room. She took her time lining up her shampoo, conditioner, body wash, and other necessities before taking her soothing hot shower. She toweled off her hair, worked through her conditioner, and braided her hair into two boxer braids before walking back into the living room.

He actually stayed?

Osirion was exactly where she left him, fingers tapping away on his phone while a bit of her underwear peeked from his mouth. She grabbed a water bottle and a sweet snack from the kitchen before clearing her throat. "You stayed."

He gave her a 'duh' look, rolling his eyes.

She walked in front of him and gently pulled him to his feet. Her hands took out the wet cloth and gave him the water. "Your mouth is dry."

He gulped down a good bit before crossing his arms. "Really? I didn't know."

She chose to ignore his sarcasm. "Do your knees hurt?"

"A little."

"Come here and let me rub them." She sat down on the sofa. "Just put your legs across my lap and relax."

He relaxed across the sofa and she rubbed his legs a little bit at a time. She leaned over and kissed him here and there, lingering on the feel of his lips and the sounds of his moans.

"I think I like kissing." She felt her face heat up, which made no sense to her but she didn't question it.

"Do you?" He groaned as she raked a hand through his hair.

"I think so." She felt a surge of shyness as their tongues touched. Her heart was racing again in her chest.

Why am I so shy about a kiss? We've done much more than this together!

"Are you okay?" His hand rubbed up and down her arm. "You're tense."

"I feel...shy." She looked away with a small huff. "This is so silly."

"It's not silly." He gently traced the sides of her face. "It's nice seeing you like this. Soft. Sweet. Gentle."

She just blushed even more listening to his kind words. "I'm going to melt into the sofa if you keep up with the sweet talk."

"Would that be so bad?" He rubbed his thumbs across her cheeks and kissed her thoroughly. "Thank you for your gift, and you did great with my parents. Good job."

"I'm glad the restaurant was left in one piece." She blessed him with another kiss all on her own. She tried to push out that nagging voice in the back of her head as it got louder and louder with each touch of their lips.

Filthy. Dirty. Whore. Look at you all over him. Good girls don't do this.

Despite the pleasure warming her body, the persistent nagging over and over forced her to draw back with a grimace. "I wish I could stop thinking for once."

"It's alright." He held her in his arms as they leaned back in comfort. "We'll take it slow and steady. I can be very patient."

Michelle relaxed into his embrace as they made small talk. His hand traced circles on her back to try to calm her down. She closed her eyes with a sad look on her face as she started to doze off.

God, what is wrong with me?

"What is your finals week looking like?" Michelle was sitting in the waiting room, flipping through a worn magazine. Osirion was watching the television, a large band aid covering his arm.

"I'll be busy until Tuesday." He sighed. "Finishing projects, handing them in. All my professors will be gone by Wednesday morning."

"Lucky." Michelle sighed. "I have until Wednesday to finish revising my short story, finish an essay, and go take an actual exam Wednesday morning."

"Stressful." He gave her a sympathetic smile. "At least Wednesday night the band has that performance, then the summer semester starts for you."

"Are you still coming to see it?"

"Of course." He smiled. "Is it choreography with music?"

"A choreopoem with music." Michelle sighed. "We're helping with the music and the end performance."

A door opened in the office as a nurse stepped out, papers in hand. "Z-Zeria Winderson?"

"*Zaria*." Michelle sighed, getting out the chair. "Zar-ia is how you pronounce it."

"Sorry about that." The older woman led her to the back. "Is that your boyfriend? Such responsible young adults, getting your blood work together."

"Better safe than sorry." She chuckled. "Especially with the summer coming up."

"Right." The nurse laughed. "He's handsome too. I can understand those urges."

Finals week was always known as Hell Week, and for good reason. The whole campus was in chaos Monday morning. The petting puppies were on the front lawn with a line of nervous students pausing to play with soft, furry bundles like their lives depended on it. Free coffee flowed from the cafe to the student center. The smell of roasted, or burned, beans were everywhere. Michelle took off her glasses, giving her eyes a break from all the red ink of corrections in her papers. Angel was bustling in the corner, finishing up a presentation and emailing her group mates back and forth.

"This is horrible." Michelle opened the window to their dorm, letting in the fresh air. It was humid and hot, but still fresh.

"We can do it." Angel groaned. "Just think about our bigger apartment we'll be in this summer. Our own bedrooms. A large living room. An actual kitchen!"

"Living the dream." Michelle smiled. "Just so close. Gotta get through these corrections. I think we ran out of coffee."

"They got some outside the dorm, near the front door," Angel murmured. "Why does this man question how I computed the percentages correctly? Is he calling me an idiot?"

"You want some more?" Michelle grabbed her keys. "Coffee? Pastry? Water?"

"Water and a chocolate chip muffin." Angel frowned. "People are stupid."

Michelle laughed, shutting the door behind her. It was a short walk upstairs to the entrance and she groaned as the humid Southern air smacked her in the face upon opening the door.

Just a couple of more days before a full summer of leisure, paid for by my Dad. I'm surprised he offered so I didn't have to work this time.

She grabbed a few creamers and sugar packets, dumping them into the coffee cup. She was just minding her business when a voice caught her attention.

"Hey, Michelle."

"...Tyrone?" She looked at him surprised. "I guess your building ran out of coffee?"

"Yeah…" He waited until she moved near the coffee containers. "Someone saw you at the clinic this weekend."

"Okay?" She grabbed a bottle of water and a muffin for her roommate. "Why are you telling me?"

"Did you get tested?"

"It's none of your business." She stirred the hot liquid, dissolving her condiments.

"I just…" He filled his cup with a sigh. "I meant to stop by after the gala, but it was real late. Just wanted to talk about stuff."

"Stuff?" She stared. "What do **we** have to talk about?"

"Getting back together." He shrugged. "We just tossed away our relationship without really fighting for it."

"Tyrone." Michelle sighed. "We are not getting back together."

"Why not?"

"People are just getting over the whole 'she's bad at sex' fiasco you started." She glared. "It was a month of rumors!"

"Oh." He looked away in shame. "It wasn't supposed to be that serious. Just a little joke…"

"Your 'joke' evolved into me being labeled the Frigid Fish Bitch." She stared him down. "Who does that to someone?"

"Michelle." He walked after her. "I'm sorry for that. Really. We never had sex so I wouldn't know if you're good at it or not."

"Get out of my face, Tyrone." She glared. "Else I'll let it slip about **your** big little secret."

She swung the door open, walking through before he had a chance to respond. With a steady hand Michelle went downstairs and walked back into her room.

"What took so long?" Angel questioned.

"Ran into Tyrone outside." Michelle groaned. "He's still trippin..."

"Another rumor?" Angel exasperated. "You have to ruin his life at this point."

"Nah, not this again." She shook her head. "He was trying to get back with me."

"Weird." Angel cringed. "Maybe going to that event made him think about things...unfortunate."

"He needs to get over it." She sat down at her desk, sipping the elixir. "Still can't believe Dad actually did that..."

"That's wild." Angel agreed before wiggling her eyebrows. "How was that anyway? Did you have a good time?"

"Oh, it was interesting." Michelle sighed. "It was nice seeing my siblings again. It was awkward between my Dad and Osi though. Could have ended badly..."

"Your dad got into it with Osirion?" Angel gaped. "That's unexpected."

"I didn't think my Dad would be so rude, since the whole high school disaster dinner. The two didn't come to blows but it was just as bad."

"That's rough." Angel gave her a sympathetic look. "I'm sure the night got better when you guys returned to your room."

"He helped me out of my dress." Michelle chuckled. "I would have never reached that zipper on my own."

"I'm sure he was **very** helpful." Angel grinned. "Helpful hands, helpful mouth, helpful tongue..."

"You have a dirty mind." Michelle giggled. "We just got tested this week! Safety first."

Well not exactly safe but we're both tested and clean...now. I'll just keep that to myself.

"That's just wonderful." Angel snored. "You two had the whole room for a night and nothing happened? I don't believe that."

Michelle scratched the back of her head, heat coming to her face. "We found ways to entertain ourselves."

"In other words, we got naked and fooled around." Angel laughed. "At least you two got some of the tension out."

"So, what did you do while we were occupied?" Michelle changed the subject.

"I just hung out. Went to the student center. Played some games. Kept Toshiro company for a few hours." Angel shrugged. "It was surprisingly nice to get to know him."

"That sounds very relaxing." Michelle smiled. "That's all?"

"Of course!" Angel laughed. "That's basically all."

"Ani-ki..." Toshiro knocked on his brother's door. "I know you're in there!"

"Yes, I am here." Osirion opened the door, wearing a shirt covered in paint. "Don't you have a class to prepare for this summer?"

"I bought the book, flipped through it, checked out the syllabus." Toshiro made his way into the dorm. Darius was seated on the sofa, bent over typing away.

"Hey Toshiro." Darius spared the younger a glance before going back to his computer. "Here to be nosy about your brother's date or to tell him about your own?"

"Thanks Darius." Toshiro followed his older brother into his bedroom. On an easel there was a canvas, the smell of oil paints filling the room before traveling outside via the window. It was strong but not overpowering.

"What is it?" Osirion started to stretch. "I needed to get up anyway."

"I messed up." The statement caused the older sibling to freeze, looking at his brother with concern. "I did but I don't regret it."

"What happened?"

"You remember that night you left for the gala?" Toshiro paused. "Eventually I spent the night with her roommate, Angel."

"Alright..." Osirion nodded. "Did you two..."

"We fucked." Toshiro stated as bluntly as a dull knife.

"...wait." Osi paused. "Isn't she a lesbian?"

"She's bisexual actually." Toshiro laughed. "But that's where I messed up. I like her personality. Her sense of humor. The way we can go on about you two being clueless in a relationship and laugh about it..."

"Really?" Osi's lips quirked into a smile. "Everybody knew but us apparently."

"Yes, everybody literally did. We all just waited for the inevitable to happen." Toshiro laughed. "Anyway, I had a great time the other night. I just have one problem."

"Really?" Osirion inquired. "What's that?"

"The thing is she just wants to keep things casual." He pulled out his phone and showed his older brother.

> That night was an experiment. A pleasant one, but nothing good can come from this. I keep thinking about my ex, and that's not fair to you. Sorry.

"I thought Angel was dating someone but perhaps not." Osirion shrugged. "What's the problem?"

"Why don't you think she doesn't want more?" Toshiro sat down on the bed. "I don't want to brag but she's not crawling back for another round."

"Is that a problem?" Osirion stared at his younger brother. "She wants to keep it casual to get back with her lover."

"But why?" Toshiro groaned. "Don't you think that's odd? This is me you're talking about."

"Toshiro." Osirion paused in his sketch. "Just keep things casual. You're only here for a year then you go back home."

"I know." Toshiro whined. "I just want to have some fun in the meantime. She doesn't want that, apparently."

"Then find somebody else." Osirion frowned. "Why does this bother you so much? This is the perfect situation."

Darius stood in the doorway with crossed arms. "He likes her more than he wants to admit."

"No. I just want a repeat of the other night." Toshiro glared. "I wasn't talking to you."

"You might as well have been with how loud you were." Darius laughed. "Angel's a baddie. Be careful with that one."

"How would you know?" Both brothers stared at Darius.

"Look how Raven is still around her when we hang out again." Darius chuckled. "I know Raven from some of my classes. She's not happy with Angel's naughty behavior but doesn't know the man she laid down with. For now, you're a mystery."

"I'm not scared of someone's jealous girlfriend." Toshiro brushed him off. "I don't owe Raven any loyalty."

"True, but she might decide to take out some of her anger on you if she puts the pieces together." Darius shrugged. "You'll learn like everyone else."

Twenty-One

Square Up

I feel like I'm all over the place. I should get a planner to help with my time management skills.

"So, for the Fall we're going to split the club into two?" Michelle was walking inside the sparring area of the gym with the sun setting within an hour. It was the MMA club meeting night, which meant Monday was gone and now it was Tuesday. She had spent the entire night drinking coffee, revising her paper, and turning it in alongside her short story before crashing for most of the day.

"Yeah." Dante was walking along the ring shirtless. "It's going to be an even split between the men and the women."

"I think two women were interested in joining the sparring section of the club." Michelle fingered her taped hands, eyes slighting squinted. It was annoying to go without her glasses but a necessity.

"I can't technically ban them." He groaned. "But they will be fighting with a bunch of men. Stronger, bigger, and just as skilled as them, if not more."

"I mean we do sign waivers for this club." Michelle sighed. "In addition, the goal shouldn't be to send someone to the hospital. This is a sparring student pastime, not Fight Club."

"Yeah." He agreed. "But bad things happen. Even worse things can happen when you fight outside of your weight class."

"You can't intentionally target them because they're women."

"I wouldn't." He defended himself. "Other guys in the club might not share those feelings though. Please tell them it would be dangerous to join the sparring club."

Michelle sighed. "...I will. It's not right, but I will stress your point to them."

"Many things are not fair. Women are just at a disadvantage when it comes to physical combat though."

"I can beat you, and you're seven inches taller." She retorted.

"You can, but barely." He countered. "We are tied in a few spars, thank you very much. Those two are not as skilled as you are, and they *will* get hurt."

"What about new students?" She started to stretch. "What if a woman even better than me wants to join?"

"I will try to turn them down." He admitted. "But if I can assess their skill and it's acceptable, I would have to accept them. We are a public university, and I can't turn them away based on their sex."

"There you go."

"I will be calling you in for backup though." He added. "Lay it on thick. Get them to see a really brutal spar between some of the guys. It should help the point sink in."

"I guess." She shrugged. "I'll have to see about the Fall semester. I think I've gotten a bit over my head."

"So many clubs to join, and so little time." Dante nodded. "You're from Tech so I bet it's overwhelming. Definitely get a planner."

"I'll do that over the summer." Michelle agreed. "I have lots of interests but not enough time for all the meetings, along with courses and work."

"I would start with the orgs that go along with your major the best." Dante stretched his arms. "Like FBA for the business majors or journalism for the writing ones. Adala is huge so there's something for every major. Then maybe one for fun or your interests if you have the spare time...or not and just rest. Can't forget to sleep."

"You're right about the sleeping part." Michelle got into a ready stance. "Until then you have to worry about me. Ready to start?"

"Yeah." He laughed. "Let's break our tie real quick before this semester ends."

The two took opposing positions before she rushed at him. Being smaller she would close the space as quickly as possible. Most of the time he put up a defense before she could throw a kick but at times her quickness surprised him.

This was not one of those times.

She sidestepped a kick of his own before throwing an elbow. She caught his arm in a block, knowing that even using most of her force wasn't comparable to his strength. He threw a series of punches, forcing her to back away.

"Stay light on your feet, don't lose your balance. Let them do the work and observe. Catch them by surprise and end it quickly." Michelle focused as her Dad's voice whispered in her mind. *"Float like a butterfly, sting like a bee."*

She weaved away from his reach, trying to look for an opportunity. He would eventually get off a hit or two if she continued like this, and the match would be over as quickly as it started. With nothing else to lose she rushed him once again. He threw a swinging kick when she was in range, forcing her to duck underneath to avoid the hit.

Taking the chance, she came to meet his twisting chin with an uppercut. It was shoddy but she made contact, stunning him for a moment. She easily kicked his feet underneath his body, forcing him to the ground. She mounted his hips to go on the offensive, but Dante was aware enough to flip her over and ruin her sudden advantage.

Michelle managed to get her hands up in just the right moment as he rained blows to her left and right. It was only desperation that caused her to let down her guard as he was pulling back for another swing. She shifted her body just a tad, arms going out alongside his own. His fist smacked her shoulder hard, but he provided her with an opening.

She grabbed his arm with both hands, wrapping her legs around his neck and pulling his body down towards the mat. She unmounted the man, twisting their bodies until she had him locked in a submission hold.

"Oh, hell no!" Dante started to thrash, causing her to use her heels to dig into his body. A good kick or two to the side before she stretched out his arm, holding him hostage.

"Tap out." She pulled against his body, threatening to dislocate his shoulder. "Just tap out."

She saw panic in his eyes as he realized that she wasn't bluffing. A light realization made her smile as she kept the hold nice and tight.

He doesn't realize he could just break out of it with strength. You can't blame him, since I never use submissions at all.

The quick tapping came soon before she could add more pressure. A quick end to a quick match. "You did good!"

"Let me guess: your Dad?" He shook the limb out.

"Yeah." She chuckled. "It's not something I would do but you know."

"Next time you won't have the element of surprise." Dante helped her get to her feet. "I'm going to head out."

"I'll wipe it down and close up." She smiled. "Yeah, next time is going to suck though."

"Oh it is." Dante groaned. "We had an audience."

Michelle turned around to see Osirion gazing at her, eyes wide in fascination. She let out a laugh, turning towards him. "Were you entertained?"

"That was impressive." She couldn't read the full range of emotions in his eyes but his happiness did make her smile. "I was worried for a moment, but you pulled it off."

"Quick thinking pays off." She smiled. "I'll be done in ten or fifteen minutes."

"Even sooner since I'll help." The two grabbed some towels and disinfectant spray before working on the mat. Not the fun part of the club, but you can't leave your sweat to dry. She couldn't imagine how disgusting it would be if that were to happen.

"Thanks." Michelle jumped from the mat onto the gym floor. "What were you doing here anyway?"

"I came to give you something." He took the used towels and placed them into a bin. He went into his bag to pull out a box. A warm, steamy box at that.

"Aww." She smiled. "I was wondering what I was going to do about dinner after I left here. Thank you."

"I had a feeling you would be hungry." He motioned outside where a large fountain was running. The court-yard was filled with benches and places to sit on the soft grass, vacant due to overstressed students. "You want to eat outside?"

This man is such a sweetie. She smiled, opening her box. Chicken, rice, sautéed vegetables, and a brownie awaited her empty stomach. *A sweet, homemade bento box.*

"Well?" He was taking peeks at her while eating his own food. "I didn't think you had any food allergies, but I did use soy sauce and fish sauce cooking your food."

"Oh, I don't have any food allergies." She took a bite of chicken. "This is good. What's the brand of the sauce?"

"Oyster sauce, brown sugar, and a bit of soy." He chuckled. "I don't like the pre-made sauces. Most are too sweet for my tastes."

"This is really good." She moaned in appreciation, eyes closed. "Thank you."

The two ate in a comfortable silence as the wind blew across their damp skin. Even as the sun was setting it was uncomfortably hot, surely a sign of weather to come. He stared ahead for a moment, hands stilled. "You shouldn't have won that match."

"Hmm?" She blinked. "What was that?"

"You should have lost." Osirion turned to look at her. "Dante should have gotten out of that submission move."

"...yeah." She shrugged. "What he didn't know ended up costing him a win. Sorrow sorrow."

He gave her a confused look. "Sorrow?"

"It's a saying." She chuckled. "Think of me saying 'meh' at the end of a sentence."

"Oh."

"You say I should have lost." She sipped from her water bottle. "How do you know that? I never saw you spar in a ring."

His eyes widened for a moment, taken off guard. "...it's an observation. Being a man, he could have lifted you off the ground."

She stared him down through her glasses with a glare. "Really? An observation?"

A bead of sweat from his forehead traveled down his face. "Hai."

"Sure it was." She smirked at him. "And beating up Tyrone was just beginner's luck right?"

"You heard about that?" He sounded surprised.

"Oh yeah. People love to gossip around here." She looked him up and down. "People say you were...enjoying beating him in a restaurant."

He sighed. "I had to show him that I am a man of my word."

"By trying to beat him senseless?" She stared. "I'm glad I didn't have to bail you out of jail. I would have if you called but I would be upset."

"He had it coming." Osi frowned.

Her eyes softened as she laughed. "Thank you for defending my honor."

She leaned forward and gave him a peck on the cheek. Even such an innocent gesture made her body warm up but it was a pleasant sensation.

"Of course." He leaned in and placed a kiss on her cheek in return. "I couldn't let him get away with something like that."

Chivalry isn't dead after all.

"You're rather affectionate." Her breath hitched as he kissed her other cheek tenderly.

"And you're rather not." He didn't hide the yearning in his voice as his lips lingered on her skin.

"You know why." She closed her eyes as a bit of sadness overtook her. "This does feel nice though."

"That's good." He whispered in her ear before leaning away to eat his food again.

He's worked up again. I can see it in his eyes. Need a distraction.

"That's why Dante wanted to recruit you to the club." She snapped her fingers. "It didn't make sense in the beginning but he must have saw something in you."

"To my annoyance, yes." He sighed. "It's something I rather not continue in undergrad."

"You don't miss it?"

"I mean...it was enjoyable." He rubbed the back of his head. "I practice my katas alone to help stay in shape, but I've left sparring behind."

She sighed, finishing off her box. "If I had known this, I would have challenged you ages ago!"

She felt him stiffen like a cat on the edge. "You wanted to spar with **me**?"

Damn, I should be offended.

"Why do you say it like that?" She frowned, hands near her hips. "You just saw me take on someone taller than you."

"Yes, you did." He cleared his throat. "Bigger doesn't mean better. You just wouldn't win in a spar against me."

Her glare deepened. "Someone's full of himself."

"I didn't mean it like that." He held his hands up. "You're skilled. The odds are not stacked in your favor, however."

"If you're so sure then I'm challenging you." She smiled. "Shouldn't be a problem for you, right?"

He swallowed, letting her look at his bobbing Adam's apple. "I don't spar anymore..."

"So sad that you're so scared." She tsked, shaking her head. "Most men are all bark and no bite..."

"I know what you're trying to do and it won't work." He rolled his eyes at her.

She mimicked a chicken, flapping her arms around. "Someone was running their mouth and now wants to back out!"

"You're hilarious." His tone was dry.

"I know." She smirked. "It's fine, sweetheart. I wouldn't want to embarrass you, after all."

He arched an eyebrow in questioning.

"I still remember how flustered you got underneath me." She chuckled at his sudden surprise. "How breathy you were and so red in the face. A win over you would be too easy..." She rose from her seat in a long stretch. "All I have to do is straddle you in my short shorts and you'll melt into the floor."

When in doubt, tease him out loud.

She felt his eyes burning into her back as a groan escaped his mouth. His neck was already turning the slightest shade of red, surely to travel up his face if she continued. Shameful tactics but very effective.

He's just too easy.

Michelle felt an arm slide around her waist, pulling her down on his lap. A firm bulge pressed into her bottom as she wiggled to get comfortable. "On second thought, I'll indulge you."

"What?" She sat still as he kissed the back of her neck. He left tingles all over her skin.

"I accept your challenge." He laughed. "During the summer, I'll spar with you."

"That was easy." She gave him a suspicious look. "Too easy. What are you up to?"

"Up to what?" He feigned innocence, licking a path along her shoulders. "You challenged me, I accepted. I'll just put you in the ground once and for all."

"Excuse me?" She swallowed. "Put me in the ground? Like six feet under?"

"Not that deep, no!" He laughed. His grip on her waist was locked in. "I won't even bury you a foot...more like eight inches. That's not bad, is it?"

A heady throb made her mind go blank for a second, his ever pressing bulge pushing further into her thin workout shorts, pushing further into her center with a throb.

"This was not the time to go commando..."

"Oh?" She looked into his devious grin. "No underwear at all?"

I said that out loud, didn't I?

"I-I-I have an exam in the morning." She let out a flustered laugh. "I need a shower, I'm all sweaty."

"Then by all means, let me walk you to your building." He motioned to the brick building across the courtyard. "After all, that's what a gentleman does."

Twenty-Two

Semester's End

Michelle laughed, flexing her fingers. She finished her final exam of the semester. It was done. The move from cramped shared dorm to a more spacious, apartment style quarters was done. She finally had her own room! Angel was still her roommate, along with two other women that haven't arrived yet.

Having privacy in college was a beautiful luxury now that she was done with the last of her annoying core classes. A few didn't transfer over, causing her to take their 'equivalent' or something to have the credit on her transcript. Privacy meant time to lay out and enjoy her soft sheets...her peace and quiet...and her wandering mind.

This semester is in the bag. Finally.

Despite her raging hormones and active imagination, Michelle kept thinking about one particular look her love would give her. His eyes were kind as they went along their respective days but every so often, she would see a hunger flash across his face so strong he looked to be starving at his very core.

That look crosses his face especially if I tease him for a moment and walk away. Riling him up is like playing with fire.

Every so often he would mutter under his breath when she became too much but she caught his clipped voice clearly on more than one occasion.

He talks about me being repressed but I see the twitch in his hands at times. He did say he was going to punish me but didn't act upon it. I do commend his self-control.

Even more so that she was waiting for him to finally snap. Michelle knew she wasn't normal but being around him set her with a type of chaotic energy, a mixture of defiance and nervousness that washed, starting at your toes and crawling up like the kudzu vines that invaded her country home.

I wasn't this nervous when I was a virgin. He's known me for over seven years!

Warmth spread over her face as her lips parted in a smile. She let out a laugh, silliness overcoming her. Her mother would say Michelle was 'head over heels' for her friend and lover.

Then again, I did lose my virginity to someone dressed up as the Phantom at my senior masquerade prom while I was dressed up as a glowing fairy. All while being tipsy and not getting his name. Luckily either he never remembered me or he kept it to himself cause the drama that would have caused!

Her marching uniform was with the drama department for tonight. She's glad they had her size, but it was cut to her form. Clinging to her form. Made to hug and highlight her feminine build in ways she usually does not. A smile overtook her face as she dialed the number in her phone.

"Hello, love." Osirion's voice drifted in her ear, content. "How are you today?"

"I'm good, sweetie." She stretched. "Enjoying the early morning in my new room. You?"

"Just relaxing." He sighed. "It's nice to just rest and not have somewhere to be right now."

"Where's your roommate?"

"Darius is out getting breakfast for the both of us." Osi laughed. "He lost our bet and has to go to the diner way Downtown."

"Oh, you're alone then." She laughed. "That must be nice."

"It is."

The two settled into a comfortable silence. Michelle breaks it with a laugh.

"What are you up to?" Suspicion laced his voice.

"So accusing. I was just thinking about my sweet man." Michelle pretended to be offended.

He didn't get into college being stupid.

"I was just thinking about you too." His tone lowered. "So many things about you, as always."

"Really now?" She smiled through the phone. "Will you tell me what you were thinking about?"

She heard his laughter over the phone, much darker than his normal cadence. She swore she could feel his gaze on her and she held back a groan.

Oh God I'm such a sap. Romantic but still sappy.

"Holding you." His voice brought her back to the present. "Caressing you in my arms, kissing all along your cute face. Watching you laugh."

"That's so sweet." She cooed, a happy smile on her face.

"I wasn't finished." He growled at her. She heard his breathing becoming heavier with time.

"Oh, then go on." She chuckled at his irritation.

I shouldn't egg him on, but I can't help it sometimes.

"I dream of bending you, of pushing you to the point of breaking but never quite doing so." The statement made her eyebrows rise, mind starting to swirl with curiosity.

"How?"

He let out a breathy sigh. Her ears picked up the distant squishing sounds in the background, soft and consistent enough for her to blush with the realization. "With a bright rope...white or red to contrast your skin. Making you into a beautiful shibari portrait in a sturdy chair...I just won't cut your hair."

She didn't know what the word translated into, but she could see a beautiful pattern made of gold rope against her skin. "That's poetic actually...to break someone upon their throne. Dark, but poetic nonetheless."

"Oh yes..." She could tell he liked that suggestion. His breath hitched, long moans filling her ears as her face became more heated. A strong throb called her attention underneath her skimpy shorts, wetness growing as he let go. "I will put you back together...just how I desire...to take you in my arms and drag you to rapture."

Even masturbating he can be poetic...that's frightening. How long has this been playing in his head?

"That is beautiful." Michelle was impressed.

His moans went up an octave as he drew out one long string of sound. She could see him on the bed, eyes closed as thick white ropes are shooting in the air landing on his body in decorative patterns. She pressed her thighs together, gasping as trickles of moisture soak through her clothes.

Did I just...I didn't even touch myself! He certainly didn't help my predicament.

"Thank you." He chuckled, catching his breath. "Now I can be good again, at least for the moment."

"That's good cause you owe me some stress relief." She looked at the time. "I should get up and get ready for the last rehearsal today. I'll see you at the performance tonight."

"Until tonight love." He made kisses over the phone. "Have a good day."

"You too." Her eyes lit up.

He does give me some good ideas to write about though.

"Michelle." Greg was standing in the shadows, the band waiting for their que to go onto the grass. "Why are we doing this again?"

"Cause we're keeping our word." She poked at his bare stomach. The upperclassman was fit, oiled, and a beautiful olive tone to match his loose, dark hair. "The good thing is, it's less than five minutes!"

"I'm going first." He stared at her. His face was already flustered and red. "I need a drink after this."

"A lot of folks are going to need a drink looking at you." She laughed. "You're making the band thirsty."

He smacked his head with a hand before adjusting his stance. A loud clap got their attention as the band shuffled into marching formation. "We're on."

The drum majors went first, with Greg leading the group as they marched into position. Michelle had her back to the audience when she got into place but could hear the instant commotion.

"Whooo!"

"Oh my God, Greg has that under his clothes?"

"I see some legs!"

"Get this wet wet Greg!"

Michelle almost lost her composure. She could see him out the corner of her eye, a hand placed to his forehead.

The amount of thirst he was getting from the audience was insane.

We know the audience is mostly women, but I feel sorry for him. It's so intense!

Everyone stood at attention, instruments at their sides waiting for orders. She could see the shake in his arms as he clapped.

"Band, horns up!" The three majors held their arms out, ready and waiting. Greg took a deep breath in before motioning downwards, starting the band. The notes filled the air as Michelle and Diane took the task of conducting. He stepped away from the band, starting the group off.

He started off and the place erupted. Partially in realization of what song was being played, and for the fact that an oiled, muscular man was winding and grinding in the air in nothing but some jeans and a large buckle to draw attention to his midsection.

The air is vibrating with the amount of thirst over here. This is going to be something...

They had seen each other's routines, so Michelle knew exactly what he was doing as the crowd screamed. Greg can be seen as sexy but not as sexual.... he exuded an air of 'too niceness' or 'big brother energy'. Watching him gyrate his hips to a panting crowd was definitely something she didn't see happening this semester. She couldn't think about it too long since her section was quickly coming up.

This shouldn't be too bad...

Michelle discarded her cover up on the grass nearby, walking to address the crowd. She saw Osirion right in the middle, giving her a wave from his seat. At least he was happy.

"Shake that ass!"

"Wait, **she's** been hiding that body!"

"This is why I fuck with tomboys, the best of both worlds!"

Michelle could only imagine her beloved's expression as she sashayed her hips to and fro. Her arms rubbed across her face, trailing down her chest, wrapping around her waist, before drawing attention to her hips and thighs. To be honest she probably looked really good gyrating with her body glitter dazzling in the evening light but her face was surely red and visible to everyone, maybe even turning a shade of purple.

At least it's over quickly.

She went back to her position conducting the band as the third of the trio took the crowd's attention. She knew Diane was about to faint during her routine as she finished the song. All three majors ended the song with a flourish as the band bowed before marching away. The three drum majors took a bow before retreating backstage.

"That was fantastic!" Some of the drama department came up to the majors after their changed out of their uniforms.

"The three of you commanded the crowd! It was beautiful!"

"It was embarrassing!" Greg turned red once more. "There's a bunch of women waiting for me outside!"

"I can't even imagine what went through their minds." Diane groaned. "This is never happening again!"

"Seriously!" Michelle joined in. "Did you hear some of the things they said?"

"I mean, it's a college environment." Someone in the drama department shrugged. "Some of us can walk you three back to your dorms..."

"I'm going to get a rum and coke downtown." Greg shook his head. "I might as well start the summer off by getting laid."

"Well, you won't have any problems with that from now on." Michelle laughed. "I might join you with the crew. We're supposed to go out anyway."

"We should walk together." Diane rung her hands. "I'm sure both of my boyfriends are already picking out a seat for me."

"Two?" Michelle questioned.

"Yep!" The sweet woman smiled. "I'm about that poly life."

The group ducked out from backstage, trying to avoid as many people as possible. Downtown was already going to be crowded with the leftover students celebrating the start of the summer.

"Hey Big Sis!" Michelle heard Toshiro's voice as he wrapped her in a crushing hug. "You looked adorable out there! Didn't she, ani-ki?"

Osirion flipped his younger brother off before giving her a hug. "You looked amazing, honestly. He's been teasing me ever since your performance."

"Not my fault you were about to ruin your pants just staring." Toshiro laughed.

"Toshiro!" He chased after his younger brother as they walked on the sidewalk.

I was about to ask did he like the performance, but I don't have to now!

"He's just being a little brother." She eventually caught Osi by the shoulder, giving his red face a rub. "You smell good."

"Glad you like it." He gave her a smile, hints of sandalwood and jasmine hitting her nose. "It's not like he can talk."

"Hey." Toshiro walked to her other side. "I am a straight man! I can enjoy some hips every now and then."

"Don't lie like that. Every now and then?" Michelle laughed. "Be serious for a moment."

"I can go in on you too." He huffed. "Little miss masochist."

"Excuse me?" She adjusted her frames. "I have no idea what you are talking about."

"Deny all you want." He smirked, holding the door open. "You're my brother's type. I can only imagine what you two get up to..."

"You're hilarious, Toshi." She cackled in his face. "I am an innocent woman with a sweet gentleman."

"I can't say anything about you." The group found a seat in the corner, lights flashing to the beat of the music as the

DJ spun his magic on the dance floor. "However, I've lived with your 'sweet gentleman' enough to know that's a lie."

"Little brother." Osirion floored him with a stare. "Do you want me to expose you?"

"I'm going to get some drinks." He changed up suddenly. "Just tell me what you want, and I'll go and get it."

Michelle relaxed in the cushions, finally done with the semester. She waved at Angel and Raven from a distance, inviting them over. "I take it that you liked my performance?"

"Liked isn't the right word, but I enjoyed it." He kissed her cheek, lips going to her ear. "I can show you how much later tonight."

"Such big talk for a little man." She chuckled at his expression. "Maybe I should hold you to it."

She saw that expression on his face, a darkness taking over his eyes with a smile. The two women took their seats nearby, each giving the couple their own greeting.

"You did so good out there!" Angel wrapped her in an embrace, giving Michelle a peck on the cheek. "You and Diane were amazing!"

"Very sensual." Raven arched an eyebrow at Osirion. "I'm surprised you're so composed."

"Well, it was just a performance." He smiled. Michelle felt his hand tickle against her jeans. She cut him a peek, but he didn't respond. "Why would I be upset?"

"Here are the drinks." Toshiro placed the glasses on the table. "Angel, nice of you to join us. Who is this?"

"I'm Raven." The Goth woman shook his hand, giving him a hard glare. "I'm Angel's girlfriend."

"I see." Toshiro tensed but his smile didn't slip off his face. "It's nice to meet you. I'm—

"Toshiro, right." She cut him off. "Osirion's nosy baby brother. Angel has mentioned you a few times. ."

Michelle felt the tension thicken in the air. She looked at her roommate, who had her head hanging to the floor. Osi's creeping hand stilled on her thigh.

Oh, something is going on here.

"Yes." Toshiro gave her a tense reply. "I'm the younger brother."

"Not that impressed." She gave him a cruel laugh. "Thought you would be taller..."

"Raven." Angel stopped the argument. "Comportarse."

"You should take your own advice sometimes." Raven bristled but sighed. "I'll go and get a drink. Do you want anything, Angel?"

"Something sweet." She was flustered. "And pretty strong if you're not going to behave tonight."

Raven kissed her on the lips before pulling away to the bar. Her dark eyes didn't leave Toshiro once during the exchange.

"Toshiro..." Osi started but was cut off.

"I'm going to dance." He finished his drink in one go. "I'll be back in a few."

"I can't believe her!" Angel groaned.

"What's going on here?" Michelle questioned.

"She slept with my brother." Osi's cold tone cut the other woman. "Apparently your lover knows as well?"

"Oh, shut up." Angel snapped. "We are two consenting adults...and I wasn't with Raven at the time. She's just being a jerk."

"Angel." Michelle gave her a motherly tone. "This is so messy."

"I'm sorry." She winched. "It's complicated."

"Complicated..." Osirion bristled at the woman but didn't move from his seat. "Sure, it is."

"Don't start with me." Angel rocked her head at him. "It took you six years to get the woman **you** wanted."

"If you two don't stop." Michelle glared at them both. "I will tie you both down and give you a good Southern whooping right here."

"Ma'am, you didn't have to say that!" Angel laughed, turning red. "I just got back with Raven, evil temptress!"

They both know how I meant that! Still, that could sound like fun, maybe?

Osirion had closed his eyes, emitting an amused chuckle. His face was turning a nice shade of red as he looked away.

"You're thinking about it, aren't you?" Michelle chuckled at him. "You cannot catch a break tonight, huh?"

"Apparently not." He mumbled. "Angel, my brother likes you. He would like to date you. Leave him alone before you break his heart, please."

Angel stared at him, face softening at his tone. "Alright. I'll let him down gently. It's too bad...he's a cute one but not the right one for me."

"See?" Michelle smiled, curling up to his side. "Was that so hard to do?"

"Yes." Raven returned with a drink, which Angel took in a few big gulps. "I'm going to dance. Ladies?"

"I'll catch you both in a little bit." Michelle waved the two off as they got out the chair. "We'll be here to watch the purses. Go and let loose...summer has started!"

Angel gave her a sly look. "Okay...have fun you two."

"What are you up to?" Osirion kissed her forehead.

"Cuddles." Michelle nestled into his side more. "I can't like cuddles now?"

"Of course." He laughed.

Time to put my plan into action.

The two relaxed as the music played, making small talk here and there. The dance floor was filled with all kinds of sweaty, partially drunk, and very horny students leaving all their cares behind. She closed her eyes with a smile, a small hand creeping up his thigh.

"Hmm."

"Yes?" She gave him a light scratch through his pants.

"Do you want something?"

"That's a loaded question." She laughed. Her hand went higher, landing on his stomach. "A better one is what do I not want?"

"Why don't you tell me, or are you scared?" He flashed her a smile.

Her eyes looked around. Nobody was paying them any attention. "Better yet why don't I show you?"

She knelt down under the table, releasing him with a pull of his zipper. She saw him swell before wrapping her lips around his shaft, nose touching his soft hairs. His stomach muscles twitched under her palm as he trapped his fingers in her loose hair, massaging at the scalp.

I can't believe I'm doing this! Thank God everyone else is too occupied to post this online.

Her tongue swirled across his head and down to the base, bobbing her head up and down. A bit of suction added and he flooded her mouth fast and hot as he let out a long groan. He gently led her back up on the seat by her hair, letting her see his sweaty face.

"We're leaving." His voice was low as he dabbed the corner of her mouth with a napkin. He still had the mind to fold himself back into his pants and adjust his clothing, standing up on shaky legs.

"You're shaking." She pointed out with a smile.

"Why is he so wobbly?" Angel sat back down in her seat; eyebrow raised. "Did he actually drink something this time?"

"I have no idea." Michelle shrugged at her friend.

He looked over at her before heaving Michelle on his shoulder. "Good night, Angel. We'll see you in the morning."

"Wait...you can't just take her like a sack of potatoes!" At least Angel handed Michelle her small purse as he started to walk away.

I never thought I'd get potato-ed in my life.

"Watch me." He walked out the club and into the night, and not one soul dared to stop him.

He walked all the way from Downtown to his dorm as calmly as she'd ever seen a man walk. He even hummed a little tune as she bounced to and fro trying to keep her heels from falling off her toes.

"Hey Osi…" She chuckled. "You're very calm."

"Why wouldn't I be?" His strides were purposeful. "It's a wonderful summer night. Clear skies. Nice breeze. Quiet."

"I'm glad you're steadier on your feet now." She couldn't resist poking fun at him.

"Yes I am." His pleasant tone only made her more nervous.

Not even a smart remark. Is this good or bad?

"We're going to your room?" He turned the corner as she looked around.

"Yes we are. My place is closer." He was still chipper. "Besides, what I need is in my drawers."

"What do you mean by that?" He took out his student card to open the building. The entire dorm was an eerie quiet just occasionally broken by a few muffled sounds.

"My love, my supplies are in my room." He balanced her on his shoulder as he unlocked his main door. A few strides and he opened his bedroom door wide before slamming it shut.

His workouts paid off to carry me like that. Very nice indeed.

"Oof!" She made a little noise as he stood her back up again. His room was simple: a wide bed, a sturdy desk, an end table, another door leading somewhere else, and some miscellaneous items that he owned. Besides the shrine in the corner, it was a standard college dorm.

"Now, I have you all to myself." He kissed her lips slowly, using his tongue to part her mouth open. His hands roamed down her back as she closed her eyes. He took his time, coaxing a breathless moan out of her mouth when they parted. "Walk over to the desk, put your palms on top of it, and bend over."

She bit her lip but obeyed, placing her glasses to the side as she bent low.

"Has anyone ever spanked you before?" His hand circled her hips, working off her pants. "As an adult, that is."

"No." She stepped out of her pants, heels sinking into the soft carpet.

"No?" He couldn't keep the surprise out of his voice. "Not even your ex-lover?"

"Oh God, no!" She shook her head, making him laugh. "We didn't do a lot of things couples would do."

"I'm not surprised." He stood behind her, hands rubbing at her soft, frilly lavender panties. "You're telling me I'll be the first to bend you over and light up this pretty little ass?"

She huffed. "Yes, if you get on with it. I'm a bit worried..."

"Don't be worried." He traveled up her back, massaging her muscles. "I might be driving but you'll control the flow of traffic."

"I remember." She gave him a soft smile.

"Red, yellow, green." He stepped back slightly. "Like the traffic lights. If you want me to stop, say red, yellow is to slow down, and green is to go ahead."

"You can let go. Trust me." She relaxed. "I'm ready. Green."

He gave her rear another slow rub, hands going over smooth skin. The room was silent for a moment before his hand came down onto her left with a loud slap.

She gasped as he made contact. The sting was sharp but light, the pain ebbing away into a pleasant warmth on her flesh. Michelle felt her sex starting to moisten as the bursts of pain turned into arousal.

This is new. I need...more?

"Are you alright, Love?" Osirion stopped at six, tracing small circles into her cheeks.

"More." She cleared her throat. "Can I have more...harder?"

"Harder?" He traced the seam of her panties, pressing his thumb between her wet lips. He traced from her throbbing clit to her opening and further up, spreading her arousal.

"Yeah." Her legs strained to keep her upright. "I want you to punish me."

He let out a ragged groan at her request. His hands massaged her body harder, fingers digging into her warming body. Her breathy moans ignited a certain tendency that he had buried deep away until now. "Count."

"Until?" Michelle heard the light sound of a zipper, followed by the rustle of clothing.

"Until I stop." The first smack was given hard to her right, her body swaying with the force. The pain was much sharper surrounding her entire right cheek...but the pleasure afterwards was so much greater.

"One."

Smack.

She panted, eyes closed shut. "Two."

Smack. Smack. Smack.

"Three, four, five." He grabbed her hips and ground his erection right into her opening. Only two articles of wet cloth prevented him from fully sheathing into her. He rolled into her several times as she grabbed at the desk, heated waves crashing over her body.

Smack.

"Six..." Her clit was throbbing with each hit, aching painfully into her annoying undergarments.

Smack.

He ground into her once more as her legs wobbled. She felt him drag his tip across her wet folds, paying special attention to her bundle of nerves. Her ass felt like it was on fire, but it was too good to slow down. "Seven..."

"You're making a mess all over me." He pulled down her panties and exposed her to the warm air. His briefs were stained with a large wet spot making them see through. "A big, wet mess."

"Ah..." Her face was burning red out of arousal and embarrassment. "It's **your** fault."

Why do I like this so much?!

He leaned forward, putting her flush against him. "Damn right, and I'll make sure you won't forget it."

Smack. Smack. Smack. Smack. Smack.

He dealt out those few in rapid succession, not giving her time to fully absorb the impact until the last one.

Michelle let out a long cry as her walls constricted around the air. The building tension in her body snapped, releasing a gush of fluids onto him, her thighs, and the carpet below. He leaned forward to catch her before her legs gave out.

Fuck. He literally whooped my ass and I came like a wanton whore? Something is wrong with me...

"...Michelle." He whispered, breaking her internal conflict. "Are you alright?"

"I'm alright." She took a moment to catch her breath. "I...didn't expect that."

He kissed her on the shoulder, rubbing her thighs in slow strokes. "I'm here. It's alright. Just rest for a minute."

She knew he could feel her arousal and embarrassment coming off in waves. She buried her head between her arms, trying not to look at him. "I can't even believe that."

He chuckled at her, pulling his throbbing erection away. He gently turned her in his arms until she faced him, looking eye to eye. "There's nothing wrong with being a masochist."

She saw him go into his drawer, pulling out a simple clear band. Osirion removed both of their undergarments, throwing them to the wind before rolling back his shaft and...banding himself?

"What are you doing?" His dick jutted out between them, as large and thick as she's ever seen him.

"I learned something from you." His face was chipper as he hoisted her on the edge of the desk.

"What is that?"

He entered her with one deep stroke, kissing her lips as they both groaned. His hands ran down her sides to position along her waist. "You'll see."

She wrapped her legs around him, hands going to steady on his shoulders. He snapped his length into her, deep and purposeful again and again. The ache behind her complemented the full pressure in the front as her moans filled the room. He picked up speed, fucking her harder against the desk as she felt her right thigh tense up once more. His kisses were tender along her face and neck, pausing to nibble and suck here and there.

"I-I-I" Her nails dug into his arms as she felt his muscles working her over.

He looked at her, eyes lidded with pleasure. She pushed back his sweaty hair as he leaned into her ear. "Come for me, darling."

She squeezed around him with a scream, muscles spasming with her orgasm. He slowed down his thrusts, holding her tight and marking her neck with lips and teeth. "My good, little brat. You're so wet squeezing me all around. So good..."

He slowly stroked her through her orgasm, picking up force as she ebbed away from it. She looked in bliss and disbelief as he showed no hint of slowing down. "Osi...what did you do?"

The smile that broke across his face made her clench. "Remember your little trick after the gala?"

"Trick?" She closed her eyes. The rhythmic thumping of the desk against the wall helped to bring her back somewhat. "What did I...oh."

"Yes, **that**." He picked up speed again as the coil in her stomach tightened. "I was so close, and you stopped it. Remember?"

Realization washed over her as he was thrusting at the perfect angle. "You haven't came yet."

"No." He gently kissed her face. "I'll come when I'm done with you, and not a moment after."

He placed her back on the desk, pulling her until her legs rested on his shoulders. He shifted the angle to thrust deeper as her leg tensed again.

Points for creativity...but this is...

Her thoughts scrambled as another orgasm ripped through her body, her releasing fluids trickling down his legs.

"Three down. How many more to go?" He scooped her off the desk and laid her onto his smooth sheets, length still buried inside.

"You can't be serious." She stretched across the covers. "Satin?"

"Satin. I knew you would enjoy them." He slowly pulled out of her, smacking her sensitive lips with his overly swollen dick. "Now, where do you want me to come?"

"Uh..." She stared as he traced around her mound using his tip like a paint brush.

"Inside?" He thrust deeply as they both moaned before pulling out. He traced along her belly button to her thighs. "Outside? A little of both?"

"You know better." She groaned. "As much as we both want it..."

She rolled her hips at him as they both gasped. As blissed out as she was, she still had a shred of common sense...at least this time.

"I won't test your birth control yet..." He laughed. He dragged his head past her opening, giving her tight ring of muscle below a deep prod. "You're too tight for now."

He would be too much in here.

"Your finger would be too big." She managed to talk. "I don't want to think about your erection going in there."

He came back to nudging her clit up and down. "That will be another adventure for another day."

Oh my. She swallowed hard in response.

"Such a delicate flower." He leaned forward, hair brushing against her skin. He kissed along her chest, swirling his tongue around her pebbled nipple now and then. She felt two fingers enter, rubbing inside. "I'll have to open you up again."

"Ugh..." Her head lolled to the side as his fingers pressed into that particular area within. A set of fingers rubbing her G-spot while his thumb rolled across her clit worked her fast and heavy into her fourth orgasm of the night. She didn't have the energy to sit up and look at him. "You can't go on forever."

"Why not?" He leaned back on his legs and pushed the top of his hair away from his face. He rubbed her sprawled out thighs with his strong hands and hissed at her. "I'm only getting started."

His right lashed out against her swollen lips with a steady smack. She jolted against the bed as her walls clenched around empty air.

How long can he actually go on?

Each wet slap sent flicks of pleasure to her oversensitive body as her legs shook against his sides. All she could do was take the sensations he gave as she came apart once more.

Am I going to have to stop him?

"What...do you get out of torturing yourself?" She gathered the strength to rise forward, her nails digging into his thighs.

He cracked a smile at her she's never seen, hissing like a snake. "I get to torture you. This is what you wanted...to be punished."

"You're evil." She moaned as he grabbed a handful of hair and forced her to stare at the ceiling.

"Then stop me." Osi licked a wet swipe up her neck. His hands enveloped her breasts as she threw her head back. "Just say the word and I'll stop."

Her hands dug into his shoulder as he kneaded her chest. His teeth scraped against her neck in a silent plea before biting down. Michelle was aching and twitching but she held her tongue from saying the magic words.

"Nothing to say?" His breath was ragged against her ear as he laughed. His hands wandered her body, touching all the sensitive spots he could find. Her eyes rolled back as she rode out the waves of pleasure twisting her around in a hormone laced whirlpool.

"You're...dedicated." She looked at his aggressive erection nudging against her body. He couldn't hide the traces of suffering in his eyes but the semi-manic glee illuminated his face. She groaned. "But that has to hurt right?"

"You're right." His hands dug into her hips as he pulled her closer. He was drenched in sweat but smiling. "Sit up and look at me."

"Making me spend energy I don't have." She mumbled under her breath. "You shouldn't be so short."

"Don't be lazy." He smacked his head against her swollen lips. "It'll be worth it, I promise."

Michelle managed to get on her elbows and gasped. He looked wicked as his hand rolled up and down his length. He bit his lip as his hands grasped the band, freeing himself at last. He only needed a few strokes before he tensed up, pointing his head directly...

"Ah!" His first load splashed on top of her swollen sex, dragging his dick up to paint across her stomach and chest next.

"Such...a pretty...picture." He groaned out as waves of white landed next on her exposed thighs, flooding her lower half with his semen before collapsing next to her in a satisfied heap.

"Oh..." She touched the cooling fluids on her body, feeling the stickiness in between her thighs. "Tempting fate, aren't we?"

He laughed. "If I had filled your pussy up and ate you like my favorite dessert that would be tempting fate."

She chuckled as her face flushed. "Such a filthy mouth on a perverted gentleman."

"Says the one that soaked me from being spanked."

"The sadist over here is the one to talk." She kissed him. "Torturing yourself to torture me is dedication to the craft."

"I'm glad you enjoyed my suffering." He got up and walked into the bathroom. She could hear the sound of water filling the tub followed by the scent of vanilla and sugar. He returned with a hot towel, taking his time to wipe away his generous donation sticking to her body.

"Immensely." He gently picked her up. The bath filled as he carried her into the bathroom, taking the time to pull up her hair into a pineapple with a thick, stretchy band.

"Satin sheets, long band, scented bath. You came prepared."

"Only the best for my love." He eased her into the hot water before climbing in himself. "I even have a silk scarf and fluffy robe for you afterwards. You're not getting your panties back though."

"You want to keep my ruined underwear?" She sighed as he gently washed her.

"I do." He kissed her shoulder, getting her to stand so he could soap her down with loofah in hand. "Something to remember your first real punishment, love."

"You're a freak, you know that?" She stared as he hissed at her again. "A freaky snake."

"Glad you know." He tapped her necklace. "But I'm your snake."

"That's true." She laughed. "Don't ever say that in front of church folks though."

Or maybe he should. I can't imagine their reaction to something like that.

He was gentle, making sure to wash and rinse the suds off of her supple skin. She looked into his eyes and saw nothing but love and devotion all directed at her. It was a simple act, but her heart swelled with the love and care reserved all for her and nobody else.

"Let me." She squeezed some soap on a sponge, taking care to sud him down. He smiled, content to let her return the favor, finishing with gently washing his short hair. He helped her out the tub, wrapping her body with a fluffy towel before they dried themselves off.

"This might be my favorite part." He poured some lotion in his hands before starting on her shoulders. He massaged the cocoa butter in her skin, kissing as he went along her body. She tried not to look him in the eyes, enjoying his hands molding her flesh too much. "I know you want me..."

She chuckled at his sing-song voice. "I'm already going to walk funny tomorrow."

He finished his ministrations along her arms, dragging his erection along her thighs on his way there. "Does it hurt anywhere?"

"Oh no." She kissed his cheek. "I'm perfectly fine but you are unhinged sir. You almost scared me."

"Almost?" He carried her back into his room before seating her in the chair. His hands changed the sheets and placed a new set on the bed.

"I'm not scared of the dark, you know." Michelle made herself comfortable while he worked. "I'm a preacher's daughter."

"Now you are." He couldn't help the laughter that spilled out.

"You're my fiancé so hush." She chucked a pillow at him. "Don't make me get my Dad on you. He'll beat you up meanie."

He rolled his eyes before laying her out on the bed. He draped the cover over their bodies as the two snuggled close. "All I have to do is describe tonight and he'll pass out from shock."

"You wouldn't, Osi." She nipped his neck with her lips, face touching his thick serpent necklace.

"If he's disrespectful to me I will." His arms wrapped around her. "If he's nicer than I won't have to scare him."

"I'm sure he'll warm up to you soon." She yawned as they settled in for the night.

That's a damn lie. They both knew it in their hearts, but it was always good to hope.

The End...

Acknowledgements

I have to send many big thanks to so many people that made this book possible.

The readers that both love and hate this book, and the ones that will come to read. Y'all are the reason this book can exist, and all the things that come with it!

My editor that went through and helped this book become the polished gem that it is now. You rock!

My artists that created all the extras for this book! Especially **Joanne Kwan**, **Nixmely**, and **Florence Peregrina Jorge** for making the words on the page come to life visually. They did wonderful jobs and definitely commission them if you need some character work done!

Joanne: IG & Threads @jrkingart

Nixmely: X @nixmely

Florence: IG & Threads @oleelawdigiart

My TikTok hommies **Jada** and **Author Kittin Pawell** for reading and giving crucial feedback on the early stages of this story. They suffered through all the plot holes, weird text, and odd formatting for this story to grow up into something better.

Meet the Author

This author loves to day-dream and then try to write those dreams down into book form to make a living in the real world. As an adult she uses her philosophy background to write themes of social justice, feminism, and other themes in her work.

Aside from her novels, her poetry publications include Contemplations of the Faithful, Fall Fancy, and "Barter" in the Poetry Leaves 2020 Anthology. When she's not writing you can find her gardening, practicing archery, spending time with her daughter, and supporting indie artists.

You can find her online at: https://linktr.ee/J_Clark

Summer
Semester

WEEK ONE

*T*his is a sneak peek into the sequel novella, *Summer Semester*. Although mostly structured, things are liable to change for the final story.

As the Spring gives away to a hot Southern summer, Michelle and company go through the work to attempt to heal from their traumas, have a bit of fun, and not implode their social lives in a few short months. Good luck to them.

"My name is Michelle Winderson and I'm here because I can fuck but kissing makes me school girl nervous." She figured why waste time here in the cream-colored office when they can just get straight to the point.

"Okay!" The therapist jotted down some notes on her electronic pad. "Well nice to meet you, Michelle. I'm Dr. Clare and your sister Yvette referred you to me, right?"

"She did." Michelle chuckled. "I might have come on too strong."

"I mean your opener is strong but you're a writer, right?" Dr. Clare tapped on the screen with her stylus. "Let's open up your paperwork. Zaria Michelle Winderson, the youngest of Pastor Tony's children. I stream his services online. Anyway, you're in college pursing a Creative Writing major."

"That's correct." Michelle smiled.

"Really basic info." She tapped on the screen. "So, you're here because you have intimacy issues? Can you go into detail about that?"

"Well, it's pretty straight. Having sex with someone is alright but when I think about kissing, touching..." Michelle groaned, face flustered. "Things outside of sex make me nervous."

"Like butterflies in the stomach nervous?"

"More like falling off a cliff and into fire nervous."

"Oh." Dr. Clare tried to hide her grimace. She partially succeeded. "That sounds like condemnation more than nervousness."

"It feels like that." Michelle shrugged. "A splash of guilt, a good dose of judgment, with a teaspoon of anxiety and doubt. I hope I explained it well enough."

"I think you did a good job." Now she's moved on from tapping the screen to full out writing on it. "Just to be sure you know I'm a secular therapist Miss Winderson."

"I actually prefer that honestly." Michelle gave a tense smile. "I've had lots of church therapy in my life. Trying something new is exciting."

"I have some background questions." Dr. Clare looked as she was in thought. "How many people have you had sex with?"

"Two."

"You don't have to lie to me, Michelle. I'm not going to tell anyone anything that you say in your sessions."

"That's good to know." Michelle blinked. "The answer is still two."

"Okay. How many people have you dated then?"

"Does high school count?" Michelle frowned.

"Did you have intimacy issues in high school?" Dr. Clare asked. "If so then yes."

"Then that would be six in my life."

"So, you've dated six and had intercourse with two." Dr. Clare gave her a peculiar look. "How many have you had non-sexual intimacy with? Kissed? Touched? Cuddled?"

"One." Michelle paused for a moment with a frown. "Well two. I'm not the one to make the first move...so two without feeling like I need to peel off my skin."

"Now we're getting somewhere." Dr. Clare wrote down some more notes. "You don't initiate intimacy with your significant others. Were your parents intimate with each other growing up?"

"My parents?" Michelle was taken aback by the question. "...honestly, I don't remember. I didn't see them kiss or hold hands. They have three children together so I would assume."

"Having children together doesn't mean you are intimate with someone." She wrote down some more notes. "Sex **can** be an intimate act obviously. It can also be a duty that one does in marriage. A way to shut someone up. It's the reason why you're here right now."

"I mean..." Michelle trailed off before resuming. "They weren't the lovey-dovey couple. They were kind and polite but not passionate. I think we as kids kissed them more than they kissed as a couple."

"There is a pattern maybe." Dr. Clare looked at Michelle. "Your parents didn't show intimacy with each other, and now you don't show intimacy with your partners. So the two you've had sex with are also the two you can be intimate with?"

"No..." Michelle coughed into her hand. "I did touch and kiss my ex-boyfriend but never had intercourse with him. I tried to have a sexual relationship with him, but it didn't work out."

"Oh?" Dr. Clare let the question ring in her statement. "This adds more layers to the equation...how did you lose your virginity if you don't mind me asking."

Michelle looked off to the side, an odd expression worn on her features. "High school prom."

"So your high school boyfriend?"

"No, I didn't have a senior year boyfriend." Michelle groaned. "It was a masquerade themed prom. I slept with the Phantom after drinking some spiked punch at the school."

"Do you know who the Phantom was?" Dr. Clare wrote down even more notes.

"Nope." Michelle shook her head. "I didn't unmask him, and nobody ever came out afterwards to me so...it was the Phantom."

"I see." Dr. Clare spoke slowly, digesting the information. "Who is the second?"

"My fiancé." Michelle smiled. "He's a sweetie, very affectionate, and talented with his hands. I like kissing him but...I can't shake those feelings of guilt and judgment."

"Now I'm seeing a clearer picture." She smiled. "Congratulations on your engagement. I bet your family is very happy. Can I assume that your intimacy issues are causing problems with your husband to be?"

"Yeah. I want to be cuddlier, and I know he's very affectionate with touch." She laughed. "My Dad wants our relationship to fail so we won't get married. Not sure about my siblings...I'll have to tell them when I stay at home for a minute."

"Your family doesn't approve?" Dr. Clare gave her a sad look. "Why not?"

"Long story short…my Dad pulled a gun out on my fiancé when we were around 15, got into a few fights with his father, stuck me in Purity Camp when I was 17, and now at 22 we're engaged and going to the same college!" Michelle gave a sweet smile. "So like maybe three sessions and we should be good?"

Dr. Clare put down her tablet and stared at Michelle. A good minute of silence went by before the professional spoke. "Is this a joke?"

"Not at all." Michelle shook her head.

"You're absolutely serious." Dr. Clare let out a long sigh. "Sis, let me hold your hand when I say three sessions will not even begin to scratch the surface of all of this."

"…I know." Michelle closed her eyes. "It's so much! At least let's work on the intimacy part…the other stuff is for later."

"Alright. We can set up meetings for the summer." Dr. Clare grabbed her pad. "I'll be giving you 'homework' so once a week should be a good pace."

"Homework?" Michelle groaned. "Like assignments and such?"

"Oh yeah. We're going to dig deep over here." Dr. Clare laughed. "Yvette should have warned you I will push you out of your comfort zone. You have to face your problems eventually. I get the honor of helping you through the process."

"Well…" Michelle let out a breath. "Why not? This can only help."

"Alright. I think I can come up with some homework for this week..."

"Before that." Michelle interrupted. "Let me tell you about Purity Camp because it's start of my issues..."

Michelle didn't appreciate the absolute look of horror on the therapist's face as she described the ordeal that was put onto her soul at a young age. She didn't spare many adjectives when talking about the ruler against her knuckles until they bled, the soulless remembrance of purity, or even the utter terror implanted by the notion of being defiled by someone who wouldn't care for her and leave her out in the lurch.

This is going to be a fun experience.

Michelle walked steady in her heels as they clicked against the sidewalk. Normally not impressive but she was walking after being spanked, rough housed, and brutally fucked by her loving and wicked artist boyfriend. Said boyfriend was walking alongside her as she fished out the golden key to her new residence.

"Shhh...people are still asleep." Michelle reminded Osirion, pointing to the kitchen clock as they entered the residence. It was 6 am on a Saturday morning on the first day of Summer. The residence was silent. She turned towards the right and opened her bedroom door, nudging him inside.

"Nice room." He looked around the spacious room. To start it was hers alone with a queen sized bed, closet space, a large desk with her writing supplies including a type-writer, a bookshelf, a small recliner, and miscellaneous items. He flopped face first on the covers. "This feels good."

"Going back to sleep already?" Michelle was shuffling through her closet, pulling out some fresh clothes.

"Getting only three hours of sleep will make you tired." He groaned. "I spent all my energy on you last night."

"You don't have to remind me." She laughed. "My limping walk and aching body does that enough. I'm going to change."

He waved her off as she exited her room and went into the shared bathroom. The whole space was quiet as she flipped the switch on.

"I told you we would get caught!" A woman's voice called Michelle's attention to the bath curtain.

"Umm...you in here Queen?" She called the name of her roommate. The curtain was very high but she could see someone's head move.

"Michelle is your roommate?" A man's voice broke into laughter. "This is hilarious!"

"Darius?" The curtain was pulled back, exposing the two much to Queen's embarrassment. Her roommate stood only a few inches under Darius that towered over six-foot-three. The couple made Michelle aware of her five-foot-three inches.

"Why are you two in the dark?" Michelle laughed as they climbed out the shower.

"I was taking a shower..." Queen pointed a thumb to him. "But he woke up and next thing I'm in the dark."

"Trust me, Michelle." Darius laughed. "She just got the ability to talk again, my beautiful stallion."

"I need you two to get out." She pointed towards the exit. "I need to have a relaxing soak before getting breakfast."

"Oh, are you alright?" Michelle hobbled over to the bath, rinsing out the tub before drawing up the warm water. Queen looked at her with a sheepish look.

Darius burst out laughing. "He finally put you in a blender! Is Osirion in your room? I'm going to tell him about himself."

"Why did you say it like that?" Michelle flushed, pouring some bath salts. "What you mean finally?"

He just doubled his laughter. "You know what I mean!"

"Well, at least you enjoyed yourself." Queen was so positive in critical times. "We're just gonna leave now."

There goes his noisy roommate.

Michelle stripped off yesterday's clothes before sinking going into the steamy water. She winced as the hot water touched her tender skin but let out a sigh as she submerged herself.

This feels so good.

She closed her eyes, the muffled sounds of Darius saying something reaching her ears.

"He's going to wake up the entire house if he keeps it up." Michelle wiggled her toes in the soapy water. She gently sponged herself in the water, gently going over her sore spots.

"Here, love." Osirion walked through the bathroom door, holding out her ringing phone. "This is for you."

"Oh!" Michelle sat up, shaking up her wet hand. "Thank you, sweetie."

He walked over to the mirror, removing his outer shirt. Raised red scratches decorated his back and probably part of his front. He roamed around, probably for first aid supplies.

"Hello, Mom." Michelle stepped out the tub and started to dry off with a towel. "What's going on?"

"I'm just calling to talk." The older woman laughed. "I didn't think you would be up so early!"

"Oh, I just relaxing after some exercise." Michelle wrapped the towel around her and got out the alcohol and some cotton pads.

Better than telling your Mom you were showing after getting...pounded. Why are sexual terms so violent?

"Look at you taking charge on your health!" She paused. "I saw the picture of the Gala in the newspaper. It was a good shot."

"Yeah, it was an interesting night." She dabbed at his scratches.

"I'm glad you got to go as well. I'm sure your father was happy to see you."

"He was for like three seconds." Michelle laughed.

"I would pay to see his face when Osirion walked next to you." She sighed. "I'm sure he'll call and give you a run down on what he thinks soon enough."

Yay, just what I need.

"Oh and Michelle, can you put Osirion on the phone as well? I know he's over there with you."

"What are you talking about?" Michelle feigned ignorance. "Mom, it's early! He's asleep in his room."

"You would never get up this early on your own. Unlike your father I live in reality and I know you well." She laughed. "Put it on speaker."

Michelle paused in tending to his wounds to push the button.

"Hi Osirion!" Her voice made him jump. "I already know you're there so don't try to hide."

He paused, clearly called out. Michelle urged him with a nod of her head, resuming tending to him. "Hello...what should I call you? Is your last name still the same?"

"Ms. DelVolture, but you can call me Miss Tisha since we're on such good terms." Tisha chuckled. "I think we should sit down and have a little meeting?"

"A meeting?"

"Yes! I'm actually near your campus right now. Had some work related travel and all that." She hummed. "Is that breakfast spot on the corner of Main and Central still open?"

"The Breakfast Hot Spot? It's still open."

"Perfect." Tisha spoke. "You two meet me there in thirty minutes, my treat! See you both very soon!"

Michelle sighed as Tisha ended the call.

He turned to Michelle slowly, eyes showing traces of fear. "We haven't sat down with your mother alone. Is this going to be the second part of the interrogation?"

"Not as bad as your dinner at the Gala." She gave him a sympathetic look. "If it makes you feel any better, I'm going to catch hell with your mother. I know she's waiting to talk to me alone this time around."

"Of course she's been biding her time." She spoke words of comfort over his paling face. "It won't be that bad."

"Let's get ready." He sighed. "Better to get this over with now."

The Breakfast Hot Spot was bustling with people, tables filled with the left over families of spring graduates looking to eat before leaving the college area once again. Michelle pointed Tisha out in the back seated at a small table and the couple went to sit with the older woman.

"Good morning, Michelle." Tisha kissed her daughter's cheek before giving Osirion a polite bow. "Good morning Osirion."

"Good morning, Miss Tisha." He returned her bow before pulling out Michelle's seat for her to sit. He only took his seat after pushing her close to the table.

"Such a gentleman." Tisha smiled. "I love to see that."

"Of course." Osi smiled. "Michelle deserves the best, right? I can't deny her that."

"See?" Michelle smiled at them. "How's everything, Mom?"

"It's good." Tisha looked over the menu. "My place in Midtown is under 3k a month so that's a bonus. These prices are getting out of hand for apartments."

"Yeah they can get expensive." Michelle nodded her head in agreement. "Can I get the veggie omelet with feta? Oh and add some home fries and two slices of bacon."

"Before I forget, I'll be heading back to New Orleans around the end of the summer." Tisha tensed but continued. "Your grandmother lives in the Quarter alone and she had a small health scare. I would love for you to come and visit with me, like a family trip."

"That sounds awesome." Michelle smiled. "What about Yvette and Michah?"

"They're coming." Tisha smiled. "I'll have my three babies with me this year. Now Osirion?"

"Yes?" He gave Tisha a smile before turning to the waiter. "I'll have a French toast with strawberries, toast, and maple sausage."

"Did you plan on asking for Michelle's hand in marriage before dating her or after?" Tisha stared at him. "That's not the usual order."

"Ah." He tilted his head to her. "I've always loved Michelle for years. Is it a problem that I didn't wait?"

"Not a problem but it did raise my eyebrows." She admitted. "Then again, you both have known each for years. I think it's sweet."

"So how are you going to tie this thing together?" Tisha motioned with her hands. "Marriage. Like are you having the ceremony here or will we have to fly over to Japan?"

"I'm not sure." Osi admitted sheepishly. "I would have to look up what could happen to my citizenship if we married here. Does she automatically become a citizen? Would I lose citizenship? Japan doesn't allow for dual citizenship though."

"Interesting." Tisha sipped at her water. "I know a few lawyers so I can ask around for you."

"I would appreciate it." He smiled. "My parents are not sure since we don't have anyone in our immediate family that married a foreigner."

"You'll be the first in the family to do so, then?" Tisha paused in contemplation. The waiter brought out the food with a smile before she continued. "I have no problem with your parents, but I've never met your grandparents. Your cousins. Your extended family."

"Not yet." He poked through a sausage with his fork. "We should get our families better acquainted."

"We should. Are they going to respect my daughter if she travels with you? What will your grandparents think when you walk in with a Black woman as your wife?"

"Your mother is very different than the woman I once met." Osi was walking at a leisurely pace so Michelle could keep up.

"As she said, divorce changes people." Michelle sighed. "They split as soon as I graduated high school. She basically left with nothing but some cash in an envelope, from my Dad of course."

"She didn't get anything in the divorce?"

"My Dad got the best lawyers for his case, and it's not automatic in Georgia surprisingly." She fanned herself as the heat started to roll in. "He wanted to hurry and she didn't have the funds to draw it out, so they compromised."

"Oh." He stopped, motioning to his back. "Hop on. I'll carry you."

"Feeling bad for me?"

"No, it's hard for me to walk this slowly." He laughed while she smacked his shoulder. "Ow. You scratched me like a cat."

"Well, when we both have sex like cats what do you expect?"

"I wasn't that violent." He shivered, balancing her with his arms. "Cats are on another level."

The silence was comfortable as he walked along the sidewalk, her head resting on top of his own.

"What kind of family business was my Mom talking about?" Michelle decided to rip the band-aid off quickly.

She felt him tense up but his stride didn't falter. "That's personal."

"Too personal for me?"

"It's just..." He sighed. "We came here for a reason and we don't want it to get out. We want to keep some stuff to ourselves."

What can be that serious that he won't even tell me?

"Is her knowing a bad thing?" Michelle frowned. "You don't have serial killers in your family, do you?"

"No! Why is that your first guess?" He laughed before going quiet. "It's unnerving that she could get that information. I'll have to make a call later today..."

Interesting...everyone has their secrets, I suppose. Makes a girl think.

"Let's round up the crew and see what everyone has planned for the day." Michelle decided to let it go for the time being. "They should be up by now right?"

"I'd drink to that!" Raven cackled as she downed another beer. It was rare to see the Goth woman so cheery but the other three women appreciated whatever got her in a jovial mood.

"She's about to drop some gems on us." Michelle sipped her drink delicately. All four women were piled in the living room flipping through the channels on the floor.

"Is Raven drunk?" Queen chuckled. "I wouldn't peg her as the type to get wasted."

"She's not." Angel snuggled up next to the Goth woman. "She's in a good mood, thanks to me."

"I am! Angel, you always put me in a good mood but I just don't show it sometimes." Raven gave Angel a kiss on the face, leaving a purple lip print.

"Drunk Raven is a hoot." Michelle laughed. "What y'all been up to so far?"

"Taking an online class." Queen sighed. "It's a discussion style class in a forum. Lots of posting. Other than that just work and lounging around."

"Peaceful." Angel shrugged. "I'll be going back home in the middle of July until late August. Before that I'm just having a good time. Thinking about starting a side hustle. Spending quality time with my lady. Having a good summer."

"I am going to live!" Raven tipped over laughing. "To be specific I am going to enjoy myself, go swimming, not get a tan...just have a good summer with you ladies."

"That's so sweet." Michelle cooed. "Just a bit of writing, relaxing, helping out with some church things I said I would do...some self care."

"Hey, it's that new movie about the billionaire seducing some random college girl." Queen tilted her head at one of the more romantic scenes. "It's already went to streaming? It **just** came out a month ago."

"Streaming is the new way of life." Angel shrugged. "Is the way he's groping at her supposed to be hot to straight women?"

"He's so clumsy with it." Michelle critiqued. "Too much force in the grab, not enough squish in his hands. Looks like it hurts."

"It probably does." Queen blinked. "He's getting off on it but she looks uncomfortable but trying to make it work."

"What a fitting metaphor." Raven swallowed some beer. "She's uncomfortable but trying to make it work. That's why women with men orgasm the least."

"What?" All three of the ladies looked at Raven.

"Oh it's real." The Goth pulled up some research on her phone. "Sad really. Women are patient enough to learn what women like but the same can't be said for the males."

"Straight women are at the very bottom." Michelle cringed. "Almost half don't orgasm with their partner."

"Embarrassing." Queen shook her head. "Too bad I'm not attracted to women."

"Glad I don't have to worry about that." Angel laughed. "Yeah that doesn't look comfortable at all."

"Now he's telling her about his sex drenched past." Queen lowered her pitch. "I used to be a sex-stallion but now you've changed me and I will tell you how good I am now being by making sure you know how bad my past was."

"The billionaire romance formula!" Michelle laughed. "It's there for a reason."

"At least this isn't a 'I'm-having-the-billionaire's-baby' type of story." Angel rolled her eyes. "I read F/F and M/F romances."

"Which ones are written better?" Michelle blinked.

"The F/F ones but I'm biased." Angel snuggled closer to Raven. "I'm getting hungry."

"Where are those guys anyway?" Raven looked around. "You know who I'm talking about."

"They're having a boys night." Queen whined as her stomach let out a growl. "I'm hungry too."

"They should bring us food." Raven stated. "At least then they'll be useful since they aren't giving out orgasms."

Michelle chuckled. "I'm hungry too."

Queen dialed up her boo on her phone. "Hi Darius! How are you guys? Yeah we're doing good. Remember you owe me one? We're hungry...and we're not able to drive right now."

"Lay it on thick." Angel cheered. "I want some wings if that's possible."

"Wings sound so good." Michelle hummed. "Lemon pepper wings especially."

"Uh huh." Queen looked around. "Y'all could sleep in our living room but it's too cramped. The student rec center could be open...sleeping bags? Like an adult sleep-over?"

"I haven't done a sleepover since I was a teen." Raven tried to think. "Preteen actually."

"If you deliver the food then okay." Queen listed some items for him to order. "You wrote that down, right? Okay. We'll see you guys in thirty minutes or so."

"So, as I was saying..." Raven cackled while the ladies laughed. The usual male suspects of Darius, Osirion, and Toshiro had joined the quartet, and they were all sprawled on the floor of the large entertainment room. She stared at the three men before continuing. "Straight women have the least orgasms, and I think it's a crime."

"Excuse me?" Darius frowned, grabbing a wing. "What are you trying to say?"

"Men are horrible at sex." Raven ate some of her food. "So bad that almost half of the women are not satisfied by the collective male effort."

"Who brought this topic to the discussion?" Osirion arched an eyebrow.

"Raven. She's a bit tipsy right now." Michelle rubbed his arm. "The sake you brought is really good, by the way."

"The alcohol is delicious." Raven agreed for a moment. "Still the lack of orgasms is truly frightening. You straight women have my condolences."

"I never got that kind of complaint." Darius frowned. "From any of my partners, past or present."

"Queen, are you getting the orgasms from Darius?" Raven turned to the taller woman. "This is a safe space. We will hold him down and stab him with glass bottles if he tries to get violent."

"What the hell?" Toshiro gaped. "What are doing here tonight? This was supposed to be a harmless sleepover."

"We are drinking good quality alcohol." Angel muttered. "Right now, it's harmless."

"Yes, Raven. I am getting excellent orgasms." Queen giggled. "I can't believe this topic came up in conversation."

"I guess I'm curious." Raven turned to Michelle. "Same question, Preacher Girl."

"God, Raven, yes!" Michelle fanned her heated face. "I've very satisfied, thank you very much."

"Excuse me for never being with a man then!" Raven held up her hands in defense. "It just doesn't look pleasurable compared to the things we do, right Angel?"

"It feels different, baby." Angel patted her head. "My first time was absolute trash though. Not pleasurable at all. Quick, messy, and I was still frustrated at the end of it so you're not totally wrong."

"Your first time as a woman is horrible." Queen shivered. "It's so sad especially if he doesn't know what he's doing, but that's not worse than the old guys that want to creep on you before your even eighteen."

"Don't make me sick." Michelle gagged. "My Dad's girlfriend is Toshiro's age but he's in his fifties!"

"I know what his favorite music chord is..." Queen laughed.

"Y'all stop." Michelle cringed. "I help with the music ministry back home too. It's so hard not to play it for him, but he wouldn't know what I'm talking about."

"Michelle, I'm sorry." Queen gave her a sympathy hug. "That's embarrassing cause you know one day someone is going to say it to him."

"I know." Michelle sighed. "I just hope I'm there to explain what went down when it happens."

Osi looked at her, eyes gleaming with curiosity. "What about your first time Michelle?"

"Excuse me?" She feigned ignorance.

"Wasn't her first time with you?" Raven squinted. "Unless it wasn't..."

"How did you know?" Michelle glared at him.

"I didn't." Osi smiled. "But since you said something now I know. I'll tell you if you tell me."

"Ooh some drama in paradise." Angel scooted closer. "I wanna hear the stories! I gotta know!"

"Y'all so messy." Michelle rolled her eyes. "Also I can guess your first time Osi. Was it Beth?"

"Oh no!" He laughed. "Thank Kami but no."

Is he serious? No!? I mean I need to work though my virginity mystery anyway, but she wasn't his first?!

"Oh now I'm curious." Michelle shifted on her pillow. "I need story time too cause this is a mystery!"

"Ladies first." Osi smiled. "I'll try not to get too jealous as you're telling the story."

"It's a weird story!" Michelle cleared her throat. "First it was senior prom. Second, someone spiked the drinks and got half the school drunk. Third, it was a masquerade theme. I had sex with the Phantom of the Opera."

"He was disfigured like the Phantom?" Raven tilted her head.

"No honey." Angel patted the Goth's head. "She slept with someone dressed like the Phantom."

"I'm sure you know who it was under the mask." Queen smiled. "Was he handsome?"

"I don't know." Michelle sipped some water. "I never figured out who was under the mask. We didn't take off our costumes."

"Oh wow." Queen laughed. "Role play at such an age! It's always the creative ones with the good stories."

Floor please swallow me whole now.

"Was it pleasurable though?" Raven pipped up. "That's the real question. Did you have an orgasm?"

"Actually yes." Michelle cleared her throat. "Not from the thrusting but he was nice enough to...finish me off. Plus he used protection so double win!"

Osi had an odd look on his face. "What was your costume?"

"Oh I was a gold fairy!" Michelle smiled. "A nice mid length dress, with a sparkle mask over my glasses. The wings I made myself so in the dark they would glow...

"...a blue-green color." Osi finished her sentence. "Right?"

"Did you happen to see me that night?"

"Hehehe...." Toshiro started to chuckle. It started off light and airy until he tipped over from the force of his jolting body. The chuckle evolved into laughter as he held his sides on the floor. His hands slammed against the carpet as he continued to laugh. His face blossomed into a cherry red as he railed against logic to laugh without breathing. The others started at him with concern while the slight melanin in Osirion's face seemed to bleach from his skin as he stared with an unreadable expression.

"Is he going to die from laughter?" Raven frowned. "They didn't say anything funny."

"Toshiro." Michelle gave him a cross look before turning to the older brother. "Why is he laughing so hard?"

Osirion didn't say a word. He pulled out his phone and started to scroll. It took him a minute, but he tapped on a photo and showed it to Michelle.

" "
"..."

Michelle stared at the screen for a full minute, taking in every detail in the picture. It was like going back in time with a new set of eyes as all the gears in her head were spinning at once. She didn't have anything to say. She just held up the picture to the eyes of everyone else.

"Hey, it's the Phantom!" Raven smiled.

"Well, now you know who took your virginity." Darius laughed. "You were a virgin too though...so you two just did a V—card swap?"

"I be damned." Angel chuckled. "It's a small world after all."

"I don't get it." Raven squinted. "Was there more than one Phantom?"

"Raven." Queen clapped her hands. "If. Johnny. Has. Four. Apples..."

"I knew it!" Toshiro had finally finished to do a small victory dance. "I just had a feeling when you told me!"

"Oh my God, Raven." Darius gave her a concerned look. "Don't you ever drink in your life again. Just no alcohol until you die."

"Honey." Angel gently tilted Raven's head with her hand. "Michelle and Osirion had sex at their prom and were too drunk to remember. They finally found out."

"...oh shit." Raven finally caught up with the group. "That's too funny!"

Everyone let out a collective groan at the Goth woman. Michelle flopped on her back, hands hiding her face from everyone. Her body started to jolt a little, but no noise could be heard.

"Oh no! She's crying!" Queen instantly tried to comfort her. "It's okay Michelle! You two can laugh about it now!"

"She is laughing." Darius pried her hands away. "She's alright!"

Michelle had her face scrunched up as the sound finally poured from her mouth. Osi let out a soft chuckle but soon joined her on the floor in a bout of laughter. They both hugged each other as they laughed their mystery away.

At last I finally solved the mystery...

Michelle walked into the large studio on campus carrying a large paper bag. The scent of succulent food wafted to her nose but she stayed strong instead of tearing into the hot lunch. Inside the mostly empty building Osirion was seated at an easel, hands speckled with paint as always. She instantly frowned once she saw his horrendous posture.

"Sit straight." Her voice made him jump. "I swear I'm going to get you one of those posture pillows for your back."

"I just started." He was quick to defend himself against her glare. Osi did straighten up however. "Is that lunch?"

"It is." She brought over a small table and sat down next to him. "Since you hate the food Downtown I decided to cook for you."

"You did?" His face lit up in interest. "What's inside?"

"Stewed tomatoes, okra, and corn; some collard greens, and fried catfish fillets." She laughed as he perked up over the last item. "I know you love catfish."

"I do." He shamelessly drooled as she set out the small containers and cutlery. "You didn't have to do this."

"I know." She speared her fish, drizzling lemon on top of the seasoned crust. "But I wanted to so enjoy the fruits of my labor. Plus I finally got a full kitchen on campus and some cookware."

"Arigatou." *(Thank you.)* He gave her a full smile before eating his food. "This is so delicious."

"I'm glad you like it." She smiled before passing him a cup of sweet tea. The two ate in a peaceful silence as the wind carried the smell of drying acrylics away from the couple.

"So I started going to therapy..." Michelle tried to casually bring it up during a lull in conversation. She looked out the corner of her eyes to see his reaction.

His brows raised as he chewed a bit of his second fillet. "That's interesting. What brought this on?"

"Well I guessed it was about time to untangle some of my issues." She tried to keep her voice light. "I told you about Purity Camp...and some other stuff."

Anger overtook his features before he could catch himself. She saw him turn his face away from her sight. "I remember. I'm proud of you for facing that."

"I even got some homework." She brushed her hand against his own. His fist loosened up under her touch. "No sex for a week."

"Excuse me?" His head snapped back to her. "For a week? It's the summer..."

"It's just a week!" She chuckled at his shocked expression. "I can still feel you inside of me, sweetheart! It's to focus on the other ways we can connect with each other."

"Ah." He gave her a smile. "Since it's only a week I'll be alright. Is this meal part of your homework?"

"No." She shook her head. "I know you. Once you get to work on a project you lose track of time! I'm trying to keep you alive."

"Oh." He laughs with a little bit of embarrassment. "I'm not that bad."

"How long have you been in this room?"

"Since..." He tapped his screen and cringes. He gave her one of his lady killer smiles. "Since six this morning..."

"It's noon." She gave him a blank stare. "It's been six hours. Did you have breakfast at least?"

"Coffee, marinated salmon over rice, and miso soup." He stuck his tongue out at her. "A healthy breakfast I may add."

"Get up and walk around." She ordered him as she finished her food. "Now."

"Yes ma'am." He gave her his version of a Southern accent but did what she asked. He almost stumbled as his legs were stuck so long seated, but he didn't fall down.

"If you took proper breaks, you wouldn't be stumbling." She smirked.

"Should I get on my hands and knees next?" He quipped back but blushed when she started to give it some thought.

"Not this time, sweetheart." She smiled. "This room doesn't have carpet, and I wouldn't want to hurt your knees."

"How considerate." He smiled while bending down.

"Now, I'm going to go and do some writing." Michelle gave him a small kiss on the cheek. "I'll be back in a few hours so you can get some work done. You won't be spending this evening in here, right?"

"Who told on me?" He rolled his eyes.

"Toshi." She tapped his nose. "You were in here until ten at night?"

"Ah, well..." He looked away from her face. "I lost track of time."

"I'll be back soon, sweetie." Michelle laughed before she walked away.